Danger UXB

Cast

Brian Ash	Anthony Andrews
Susan Mount	Judy Geeson
Dr David Gillespie	Iain Cuthbertson
Aunt Dodo	Moyra Fraser
Mrs Baker	Marjie Lawrence
Norma Baker	Deborah Watling
Reg Preston	Alfie Bass
Angie	Lousia Rix
Nicky	Geraldine Gardner
Chris Craik	Nick Tate

Officers of 97 Company Royal Engineers (Bomb Disposal)

Major Luckhurst	Peter Cartwright
Captain Francis	Kenneth Farrington
Lt Ivor Rodgers	Jeremy Sinden
Lt Alan Pringle	Osmund Bullock
Lt Hamish Leckie	Royston Tickner
2nd Lt Ken Machin	Steven Grives
2nd Lt Tim Carter-Brown	David Shaughnessy
2nd Lt Gresham	Nick Brimble

Men of 347 Section

Sergeant James	Maurice Roëves
Corporal Horrocks	Ken Kitson
Sapper Wilkins	George Innes
Sapper Salt	Kenneth Cranham
Sapper Mulley	Gordon Kane
Sapper Powell	Robert Pugh
Sapper Copping	Robert Longden
Sapper Baines	David Auker
Sapper Binns	Bryan Burdon
Sapper Scott	John Bowler
John Brinkley	Martin Neil

DANGER UXB

by Michael Booker

PENGUIN BOOKS

Penguin Books Ltd, Harmondsworth,
Middlesex, England
Penguin Books, 625 Madison Avenue,
New York, New York 10022, U.S.A.
Penguin Books Australia Ltd, Ringwood,
Victoria, Australia
Penguin Books Canada Limited, 2801 John Street,
Markham, Ontario, Canada L3R 1B4
Penguin Books (N.Z.) Ltd, 182–190 Wairau Road,
Auckland 10, New Zealand

First published simultaneously in Great Britain by
Macmillan London Ltd and Pan Books Ltd 1979
First published in the United States of America by
Penguin Books 1981

Printed in the United States of America by
Offset Paperback Mfrs., Inc., Dallas, Pennsylvania

This story is based on the television series 'Danger UXB', produced for Euston Films Limited by John Hawkesworth and devised by John Hawkesworth and John Whitney from stories by Major A. B. Hartley, MBE, RE.

Chapter 1

It took a lot to irritate Brian Ash. Normally the most easy-going of men, he was now irritated. Definitely. Bordering on the bolshie, in fact. And with some cause. It was a glaring day, the early September sun was unusually hot, and for nearly three hours he had been cooped up in his noisy little MG sports car battling eastwards from Reading to London and had not been helped by the absence of any clue as to where he was at any given time, even whether he was on the right road with not one single place name to be seen. This was 1940. The invading Germans were expected from hour to hour, and in the theory of confusing them Britain had been wiped geographically clean. The familiar white arms with their raised black lettering pointing direction and distance to the next town or village had vanished, and when you got there you were none the wiser. The time-worn sign over Tilehurst Post Office now read '—Post Office'. Every single place name across the entire country had been painted out, covered up or taken down. Even local delivery vans had not escaped and proudly announced their phone number as '—4281'.

Leaving Reading, Brian had put the sun across his right shoulder and kept on going. London after all was big enough. He was bound to hit it sooner or later. He knew London about as well as an Eskimo knows Cape Town, and he was looking for the south-east suburbs and a particular road in Catford; all without signposts, but with the dubious aid of at least one air battle overhead. His irritation was understandable. He had stopped many times and asked the way to Catford, but the population was well trained and most of them, suspecting any stranger of being a German parachutist in disguise, pleaded ignorance. A blessed few looked at his khaki uniform, with the single pip of a 2nd Lieutenant on the shoulders, and helped him on his way.

At least he knew now that he was in Catford. Cruising along, peering at painted-over road names which only made them that much more difficult to read, he could feel himself getting more impatient. So near, yet so far. Then suddenly, off to the right of the main road, there it was: Tundale Road. With a quiet smile of joy he made the turn and was soon pulling up behind an army truck. As he switched off the engine, a surge of triumph replaced the irritation. He sat a moment in the car and looked about him. Semi-detached houses – new – neat gardens, the last roses adding splashes of reds and yellows. Commuter country: the men going off every morning to their city offices, catching the 6.20 back. Orderly little lives. Or had been, up to a few short months ago.

He was parked outside a big red-brick building that in peace time (and before the kids had been evacuated to safety) had been a school. Now, in the gateway to the asphalt playground stood a Royal Engineers sapper, watching Brian intently, trying to decide whether to dock out the cigarette he held hidden in his half-closed fist. Brian climbed from the car, reached into the back for his kitbag and battered suitcase, and hauled them to the pavement. The sapper watched unmoving, his weary face screwed up in concentration as the newcomer lifted the car bonnet and took out the rotor arm – in response to Government advice – to deny enemy troops the use of the vehicle.

There was something about this young man, now moving towards him, that the sapper did not quite understand. True, he was in khaki. True, he had a pip on each shoulder. But the battledress was like his own, the ill-fitting, off-the-shelf sort issued to Other Ranks. The boots too were definitely not *Officers, for the Use of* . . . ! And yet there were those pips. As a precaution the sapper quietly docked the cigarette and slipped it into his pocket, straightening himself up a shade.

'Is this 97 Company?' Brian asked him.

Sapper Wilkins considered the question from his six-foot-something, then spoke with a distinct London accent. 'Can I see your paybook, please, sir?' It was the loose term given by all servicemen to the slim, bound book that identified them – recorded their postings, inoculations, everything that happened to them, bar getting killed.

Brian, suddenly tired after the journey, tried again. 'Is this 97 Company?'

'Sorry, sir – paybook, please. Orders.'

'Look – if this is 97 Company, my name's Lieutenant Ash and here are my joining instructions.' Growing irritable again, Brian unbuttoned the top pocket of his battledress blouse and produced the buff document.

'The only reason I'm on guard now, sir, is because last time I forgot the identity bit and got meself done by the Sergeant Major.'

'Oh very well . . .' More fumbling in the pocket, and the little brown booklet was brought to light. Wilkins opened it, scanned it carefully. Brian went on, 'It's still got to be changed – I've only just been commissioned.'

'I see, sir. Hang on a minute, would you?'

Wilkins turned and walked off into the school. The big, rather gloomy building echoed to different sounds nowadays: heavy boots on wooden flooring, the sharp clack of typewriters, the occasional bellow from some irate NCO, a snatch of vulgar song. Just inside the main doorway an office had been made into a guardroom, and Wilkins hurried inside. A small group of off-duty sappers were stretched out fully clothed on army cots, reading, writing letters, or just gazing at the high ceiling. Smoke hung heavy in the air. Corporal Horrocks, a solid slab of a man from Sheffield, looked up from the table at which he was sitting.

Wilkins motioned him to the window. 'Take a look at that bloke down by the gate, Corporal. He says he's an officer.'

Horrocks looked. 'Well . . . he's got pips.'

'Yeh, but look at his boots. And this . . .'

Wilkins handed over Brian's paybook. The rest of the guard looked on idly and awaited results. Horrocks noted that the book identified a Private Ash, no mention of a 2nd Lieutenant Ash. He looked out of the window again, and saw that Ash had picked up his gear and was crossing the asphalt towards the building.

'He's not dressed as a nun – that's something!' It was a heavy little joke. Rumours abounded of Germans parachuting into the country dressed as nuns, with tommy guns secreted in the ample folds of their habits.

Wilkins pressed on. 'Suspicious though, in't it. Could do ourselves a bit of good here.'

'Could drop us-selves in t'clack too, lad.' The Corporal thought a little more, made up his mind. 'All right – I'll take him along to the Sergeant Major.' He moved to the door, and found Ash in the corridor scowling about him.

'Would you come with me, please, sir.'

'Look, Corporal – all I want to know is, am I at 97 Tunnelling Company, Royal Engineers?'

'If you'd just come along with me, sir. No need to bring your kit – it'll be safe enough.'

Brian gave up. He followed the implacable Corporal down the corridor, leaving Wilkins to return to the gateway with the glowing feeling of a job well done. Doors lined the narrow corridor; as they approached one marked 'Headmaster', it opened and an officer with a friendly, quiet face came out. Brian just had time to notice the greying hair, the major's crown on the shoulders and the slight but definite limp before he stopped alongside Horrocks as they both saluted.

The Major nodded, then stopped too as he saw the new face. 'Hello – who are you?'

'Ash, sir. Trying to join 97 Company.'

The Major smiled slightly at the faint note of annoyance in the young man's voice. 'Well, you've come to the right place.'

Corporal Horrocks felt duty bound to explain. 'Sir, this man was acting in a suspicious manner. Here's his paybook, sir.'

As the Major glanced at it, Brian began explaining. 'I was given a direct commission, that's why—'

The Major cut in. 'Ah yes, of course. Well done, Corporal – you did the right thing. Come along in, Ash.'

Horrocks, left stranded, retired down the corridor even more baffled than usual by the ways of officers.

The room was large, and very much as the headmaster had left it when the school had been evacuated. A large and well-polished desk, certainly not army issue, behind which the Major seated himself in the comfortable, high-backed swivel chair. Lines of bookshelves, blue carpet. The windows, like all those in the building, were criss-crossed with gummed tape as a precaution against splintering from bomb blast. Brian stood in front of the desk, at attention.

The Major looked up at him, his eyes probing. Then 'Oh – at ease. Er – do sit down.'

'Thank you, sir.'

'My name's Luckhurst, by the way, I'm the Officer Commanding this unit. You have your joining instructions, I take it?'

Brian handed the document across the desk. Major Luckhurst picked up his horn-rimmed spectacles and read. 'I see,' was his only comment. He turned the handle of a field telephone. 'Oh – Sergeant Rose – have we had anything about a Mr Ash joining us? . . . No. Right. Thanks.'

Brian was beginning to feel desperate. 'If you'd care to telephone, sir – my old unit . . .'

'No telephones at all. They've all been blitzed. Everything's got into such an awful muddle, what with this wretched bombing.'

Silence fell as Major Luckhurst read the document again, twice. Then, 'Anyway, glad you found us. It can't have been easy, with no signposts or street names.'

'Particularly as they sent me to Reading.'

The Major smiled. 'Oh dear.' He gestured towards the field telephone. 'As you will have gathered, communications are rather patchy just at the moment. We left Reading three weeks ago, when the bombing started in earnest.' Again, he looked steadily across at Brian. *How old? Early twenties? No more, certainly. Fresh faced, obviously untested by life. That would come. A touch earnest, but signs of a sense of humour about the eyes; good, he'd need that.*

'So – tell me about yourself.'

Brian swallowed. 'I've just completed my ten weeks basic

training, sir – at the Hampshires' depot. Then on Friday I was sent for, given an immediate commission in the Royal Engineers, and told to report here, sir.'

'Yes – things are apt to move quickly these days. What were you doing before you were called up?'

'I'd just taken Part One of my AMICE at Guildford Tech.'

'Guildford. A pleasant town. You live there?'

'Yes, sir.'

'I had an uncle who lived that way – we used to play a bit of golf. You a golfer?'

'No.'

'Not married?'

'No, sir.'

'Good.' The word was almost breathed, rather than spoken out loud. 'What about your parents?'

'They're in India, actually. My father's a doctor out there.'

The Major leaned back and locked his hands behind his head. 'Were the Engineers your first choice?'

'I'd put down for the Tank Corps, actually.'

'That's the army, for you. If you'd said you were a crack rifle shot they'd have put you in the heavy artillery. Me, I taught science before – and here I am, back at school.' He smiled, rubbed his eyes. 'At least you know a bit about mechanics . . .'

'Not much about tunnelling, I'm afraid.'

'Oh, that doesn't matter. We're bomb disposal now, of course.' It was tossed off, matter-of-fact. But the Major saw the shock on Brian's face, and realized the awful truth. 'Didn't they tell you?'

It had come as a bad jolt. 'Don't people have to volunteer for that, sir?'

'I don't think so. Nobody asked *us*, for sure. When this flap started a few weeks ago they simply told us we'd got a new job, and that was that.'

'But . . . I don't know the first thing about bombs.'

The smile that came across the desk back at him was pleasant but not very reassuring. 'Nor did we – but we're learning fast. You see, there was no need for bomb disposal before, because there weren't any bombs. Everyone expected them all to go off bang when they were dropped, anyway, so no one bothered in particular. It's all jolly interesting, as a matter of fact – you're a bright lad, you'll soon pick it up.'

'When do I go on the course, sir?'

Major Luckhurst looked blankly at him. '*Course?* In bomb disposal? There is no course.'

'Oh.'

'But don't worry.' The tone was brisker again. 'You report to Captain Francis, the second-in-command. He's also the Training Officer – he'll fix you up.' The Major stood up. 'Good, then – nice to have you with us, Ash.'

Brian stood up. 'Thank you, sir.'

'To be honest, we are having a bit of a rough time just now, but ... er ... don't believe all the stories you hear. You know – it's like at school ... rumours, and all that.'

Brian managed a small smile. 'I'll try to remember, sir. There is one thing, though ... about uniform. I didn't have time ...'

'Ah ... yes ... Have a word with Corporal Mould. He's in charge of the Mess – runs a damn good one too, all things considered ... we don't enquire too closely where he gets most of his supplies. He'll fix you up with a uniform, too.' He looked at his watch, and his face became serious. 'I'll see you later – I've got a Court of Enquiry starting in a couple of minutes.'

Feeling shattered, Brian went in search of Captain Francis. 'Sorry, sir,' the Lance Corporal clerk in the 2-i/c's office told him, 'the Captain's at a Court of Enquiry. I'll tell him you were looking for him, though.'

'Thanks. Can you tell me where I'll find Corporal Mould?'

'He'll be in the Officers' Mess, sir. Up the stairs, turn left, second door on the right.'

Obviously it had once been the staff common room. Large easy chairs grouped haphazard at one end, dining tables at the other. Off it was a small office, used by Corporal Mould to keep his accounts and his stocks of cigarettes and liquor. It also contained a selection of dress uniforms, neatly valeted and hung.

Brian had been glad the Mess was empty, and found some

comfort in Corporal Mould. A man of generous girth, the Corporal had a deference found in butlers of long standing. He treated 'his officers' – always using the butleresque possessive – with a courtly respect that would not have varied had he been commiserating with one of them on being cashiered, or congratulating him on a VC.

Expertly chalking a sleeve for shortening by one of the Company drivers who had been a tailor in civvy street, Corporal Mould explained as circumspectly as he could his supply of uniforms. 'You see, sir, when one of my officers – er – departs, I look after the effects as you might say. And mostly their families have no use for the uniform and such like . . . so I arrange to send them the cash instead.'

He produced a Sam Browne belt, and with great care fitted it on Brian. 'This is a real nice piece of leather, this, sir – been well looked after.' He tut-tutted gently. 'Mr Atkinson – that's his Enquiry going on now – he didn't last long, poor man. You might say, sir, he wasn't quite the man for the job.'

Brian could have wished that the Corporal, well-meaning though he was, had not explained. To be kitted out from this khaki memorial to his predecessor did not add to his already depleted confidence.

A peaked cap was found that fitted him well, and Corporal Mould stepped back to judge the result. Brian gathered his courage and asked him the burning question. 'Many – er – many casualties lately?'

'Yes, sir – the more's the pity. There – you look just the thing, if I may say so, sir. To the manner born. Tea will be ready in about an hour, sir. If you'd care to sit in the Mess meanwhile, read perhaps . . . ?'

'No thanks – I'll take a walk around, I think. Get my bearings.'

In truth Brian was glad of the chance to get even a little used to the soft barathea, the tailored jacket, the peaked cap. His Other Ranks battledress would still serve for work. He was not alone for long. He had hardly left the Mess when he came face to face with a small, ginger-haired full Lieutenant.

'Ah,' said the stranger. 'Is your name Ash, by any chance?'

'Yes. Brian Ash.'

They shook hands. 'Good. Glad I met you. They told me you were here. I'm Alan Pringle, the Company Intelligence Officer. You're a most welcome sight, believe me. Look – are you occupied at the moment?'

'Just wasting an hour before tea, that's all.' Brian rather liked Alan, with his friendly manner and no-nonsense approach.

'Good, good, good. If you'd like to come along, I'll give you a first introduction to enemy bombs.'

Brian smiled at that pedantic 'enemy'; *they'd hardly be our own bombs, after all.*

They went quickly into a classroom. On one wall outlines of bombs had been painted one within the other; an actual bomb stood in front of the blackboard; mysterious bits of machinery were spread on a bench. Brian suddenly realized he no longer felt tired. An hour before he had been lost in the London streets, hot and irritable; things had developed so fast since then that he had no time to feel tired.

Alan stood against the outline drawings. 'Well now – bombs. They – we're talking about the high-explosive variety of course – come in four sizes. Fifty kilogram . . . 250 kilos – they're the most common – the 500 kilo, the 1000 kilo, known not very surprisingly as the Hermann . . . and this great brute, the Satan, weighing over a ton.' By now Alan was almost on tiptoe as his hand followed the drawn outline. 'Main filling, TNT or amatol.'

They walked over to the upright bomb. 'And here is the only 250 in captivity. Don't worry – it's tamed.'

Brian touched the rough metal. 'Was this a dud?'

'We don't get many duds. You see, during the Spanish civil war the Germans came to realize that bombs which didn't explode immediately caused far more trouble than those that did. Especially if they were close to railways or hospitals, somewhere they couldn't be simply detonated. London is now getting the benefit of that experience. We get daily reports from the ARP people; and this morning's brought the total up to nearly four thousand unexploded bombs – UXBs, we call them, by the way – in the London area alone. And three hundred of those are Category-A – and that means they're in such vital spots that we've got to defuse them or get blown up in the attempt.'

'Three hundred!'

'Yes. And about fifty of us left at the last count.'

There was a slight pause whilst Brian tried to think of something to say, but nothing seemed suitable. Instead Alan launched briskly into bewildering, rapid-fire explanation of gaines and picrics and tremblers and all the rest of the known technicalities of the bomb business; he made it only too clear that there might be further lethal technicalities they had not yet come across. They moved down the bench, examining fuses of various types, Alan explaining how they were made safe and withdrawn from the bomb casings. After forty-five minutes Brian's head was reeling. Alan saw his look and smiled.

'You can liken it all to Russian roulette, I suppose. But don't worry – you won't get a section until you've watched other people at it for a week or two. Well, that's enough for now, I think. Get along to the Mess for some tea. I'll see you there – got a spot of work to finish in the office.'

Three minutes later Brian had shyly entered the Officers' Mess; he was trying to hide himself in a corner, deep in that week's *Picture Post*, overhearing snatches of the conversation coming across the room to him from two officers standing by the fireplace. They were Lieutenant Leckie, First War ribbons on his tunic, grey-haired, and Lieutenant Rodgers, a smooth twenty-five-year-old section commander.

The talk was disturbing. 'Definitely this new Type-17 fuse, Sergeant Voles saw it himself . . . Old Dickie went at it with a hammer and chisel, that's what started the clock going again – that's the court's verdict, anyway . . .'

Dickie, Brian presumed, was the Mr Atkinson mentioned by Corporal Mould. The older man spoke now, in a deep Scots accent. 'Will they never learn . . . Treat bombs like women, with gentleness and respect – that's what they told us in the last show . . .'

Corporal Mould came in, bearing a tray of crockery which

he began to set out on the tables. The silent entry disturbed the two officers, who in turning saw Brian for the first time. The younger one came up to him.

'Hello, old chap. Sorry, didn't see you.' He held out his hand when Brian stood up and introduced himself.

'Ash,' repeated the young man. 'Good name for this job – *ashes to ashes*, and all that. Sorry, an appalling joke in the worst taste, but you'll get used to me. I'm Ivor Rodgers, Admin Officer around here – and this is our ancient warrior Hamish Leckie.'

The older man shook Ash's hand. 'Glad to meet ye. And welcome.'

The talk became more general, and soon Alan Pringle joined them. Over tea, and later a few drinks, Brian relaxed a little. New men drifted in, drawn and weary from a day facing the stark possibility that every move could be their last. There was a comradeship about them that comes only to an élite group who live in common danger, and it impressed him deeply. Inevitably the talk was of bombs and of the enquiry into Dickie Atkinson's death. By early evening Brian felt bold enough to contribute occasionally to the conversation.

'They said he used a hammer to it,' he told one man. 'I'll remember that.'

Hamish Leckie overheard, and joined them. 'Aye, do, laddie. I heard it before you were born, and I'm likely to be here after you've gone if you start using a hammer and chisel.'

'I wonder if it was booby-trapped, like Sergeant Voles reckoned,' mused Rodgers.

Brian turned to the red-haired Alan Pringle. 'How can you tell if a bomb has a booby trap on it, Alan?'

The answer came with a shrug. 'You can't – not until afterwards.'

Ivor Rodgers made one of his jokes. 'Then you find yourself telling St Peter all about it. You a good runner, Ash?'

'I did a bit at school.'

'Good – 'cause you'll need to do the hundred yards in about a millionth of a second flat, in this job.' Rodgers waited for the laughter to fall and then came in again with expert timing. 'I'll tell you this much – when the invasion comes, the first Jerry BD bloke I see, I'm going to take him off to one of my bombs and tell him, "You made the boody thing, you de-fuse it" . . . see if *he* knows if it's booby-trapped.'

He strolled off to talk to someone else, and Brian noted that a certain bravado had crept into Ivor's behaviour. Was it the effect of a couple of Scotches, or was he showing off? Brian had a nasty feeling that two weeks from now – if he survived that long – he'd be a class one alcoholic.

Suddenly an officer looked up. 'Hello, Fanny,' Leckie greeted him. 'Get you a drink?'

'No thank you – I still have work to do.' He looked at Brian with a disdainful air. 'Are you the new man?'

'Yes, sir.' Brian saw that the rest of the group had drifted away. Before he could continue, the Captain went on, 'Don't call me sir, except in the office. I'm not a field officer.'

'Sorry.' Brian did not like Captain Francis, the second-in-command of the Company. Obviously a regular, dry as dust, a bit stuck-up, probably bitter about something and taking it out on everyone else. But he pressed on, 'Major Luckhurst said to see you about training . . .'

'If you think I've got time to lay on special training just for you, you're mistaken. You'll just have to go round the sections and pick it up . . . show a bit of initiative.'

'Yes – of course.'

'And Mr Ash, there is one other thing – and this applies to everyone – ' the rider was pitched louder for the room's benefit, and accompanied a sweep of those narrow eyes ' – we carry our respirators and steel helmets with us at all times.' His own respirator was carefully slung over his left shoulder, the broad sling of its case threaded through the chin strap of his helmet so that they rested one above the other.

Without a further word Captain Francis walked off and out of the Mess, leaving Brian stranded. Leckie, Ivor Rodgers and Alan Pringle rejoined him. 'Don't worry about him,' Leckie reassured him. 'He's the sort that gets the army a bad name.'

Brian grinned. 'I noticed you all disappeared.'

'Sort of initiation test,' beamed Ivor. 'Face him, and you can face anything. Windy little twit – shit scared of bombs.'

'Which is a pity – no chance of blowing him up,' observed Leckie.

Corporal Mould eased past them with big, black-painted rectangles of four-ply. 'Excuse me, gentlemen. It draws close to blackout time.' Mould fitted the wood up to each window in turn, and drew the heavy curtains.

'Yes, by God – so it is,' said Alan Pringle, checking his watch. To Brian he went on, 'We'd best get you down to your billet, hadn't we. Give you time to settle in a bit before coming back for dinner.'

Dusk had nearly faded into the night by the time they had picked up Brian's kit from the guardroom, loaded it up into the car and moved off.

'Not far,' Alan told him. 'Only about five minutes to walk, actually. Turn left at the top, here.'

Brian, unused to blackout driving in strange roads, went very carefully. It was rather like driving into a void. No street lights, black metal masks over the headlamps with three hooded slits to make them almost useless. Eventually they pulled up outside a little house in a quiet street of little houses, its windows criss-crossed with gummed paper strips against blast. Alan rang the bell whilst Brian unloaded the car.

The hall light of the house was switched off, and the front door was opened by a large woman with greying hair. She fidgeted with her hands as she spoke, and the words tumbled out with hardly a breath.

'Oh, Mr Pringle . . . I was upset at the news. I've put his things together so you can take them. I was so upset I sat down and cried my eyes out. I just couldn't stop. So young . . . still only a boy really. It seems so wrong.'

'Yes,' replied Alan, wishing she'd stop. 'It was very sad.'

'I expect you're used to it, but . . . well, I remember the first war – I had a brother killed in 1918, the eldest – but it didn't seem so bad because it was out there, in France. I mean, this being right on our own doorstep, not literally, but quite near. Norma said she heard the bang on her way back from work. I'll just slip up and get his case.'

Alan got a word in. 'We wondered, actually, Mrs Baker, if you could be very kind and take in another officer.'

She was surprised. 'Take in another one . . . ? I wonder if we should, I really do, Mr Pringle. I mean, I hope this house hasn't got a jinx on it.'

'No, I'm sure it hasn't.'

'No – silly of me, that, wasn't it. Very well then.'

Alan called Brian, waiting by the car. Introductions were made, and they went into the house. As they started up the steep narrow stairs, Brian caught sight of a girl in the kitchen doorway, a drying-up cloth dangling from her hands. She was, perhaps, twenty, black shoulder-length hair, big eyes, and a shape that was accentuated by a tight-fitting, brilliant red sweater. Their eyes met for a second; she smiled quickly and openly at him, then he continued climbing.

Mrs Baker was in full flow. 'Bad again last night, wasn't it? They say there was four hundred killed in a shelter – Wandsworth, they said.' For Brian's benefit she threw in as they reached the landing, 'The bathroom's at the end, there.' Turning into a double room, she forged ahead and carefully closed the blackout curtains. 'I can't sleep. It's my nerves, they're all used up. Not like my husband. He works in the City – they've been bombed out twice, too – he's as chirpy as ever. I don't know how he does it, I really don't.'

She switched on the light to reveal a pleasant room, twin beds, second-hand furniture, lino beneath the slightly worn carpet.

'You're very kind, Mrs Baker,' Brian felt constrained to say. 'This looks very comfortable.'

She bent to the gas fire. 'The gas is on again, that's one thing to be thankful for. It's been off since Monday. Do you know, that blessed doctor of mine won't give me a thing for my nerves, only earplugs. I said to him he could keep them – if one's got my name on it, I want to hear it coming, I told him.' Her eye caught a suitcase by the wardrobe. Brian had seen it two seconds before: it carried the initials R.A. It seemed he was being haunted by Dickie Atkinson.

Mrs Baker only made it worse by saying, 'Oh . . . er . . .' as she picked it up. Alan quickly took it. Brian pretended not to notice and busied himself looking around the room.

'Will you be having the same batman coming?' she asked him.

Alan answered for him. 'I don't think so, Mrs Baker. The previous man is being invalided out, I believe. We must see about that for you, Brian.'

Just then the sirens began to wail up and down in a tone that could pierce any background noise. Brian's stomach did a double flip, but he managed to hide it.

'There they are,' Mrs Baker remarked gloomily. 'On time, as usual. Mr Ash, we usually go down to the Anderson shelter in the garden now. You're welcome to join us. Dick, my last gentleman, preferred to stay up here, though.'

'I think I'll do the same, thanks very much.'

'Just remember, then – if it gets too bad, come down and join us. You're very welcome.'

'Right, then, Brian?' inquired Alan. 'We'll go back and get some food, shall we.'

They walked back to Company HQ through a dark, moonless night which now – like every night at this time – was *quiet before the storm.* Very few people were about. They would be settling down, half underground in the earth-covered, corrugated iron shelters in their back gardens named after the Home Secretary who had introduced them; completely underground in the dank Tube stations; or merely in their sitting rooms, at least until things hotted up. Buses were still running, an occasional car crept through the almost solid blackness. They met an air raid warden, one of that army of civilian volunteers unmarked yet by uniform. Only an armband with the letters ARP, for Air Raid Precautions, and a steel helmet with a white W for Warden distinguished him. He would patrol through the night; whatever the Germans threw down on his patch he would be there to bring first news of 'incidents' and give first aid to any victims.

Suddenly his voice rent the quiet air. '*Put that light out!*' He had spotted a chink of light through some imperfectly drawn blackout curtains. Again came the cry, then he moved on, apparently appeased.

'I wouldn't have his job,' muttered Alan. 'Out all night in the thick of it.'

After dinner, a drink and talk in the Mess, it was nearly eleven by the time Brian made his way back to his billet. The raid was well under way now, and he hoped he looked braver than he felt in his first experience of the blitz. Bombers droned above, the distinctive double throb of their engines full of menace. He watched searchlights probe the dark sky. Suddenly a plane was picked out; other beams swung on to it but the pilot had no difficulty escaping back into darkness. There seemed to be fewer planes about than he had imagined there would be; tonight's raid was concentrated to the north, across the river, he guessed; an ominous red glow of fires came from that direction.

Thankfully he reached the shelter of the Bakers' house. No lights were visible, and there was no sign of movement as he let himself in and went upstairs. But there was light coming from the room facing him as he reached the landing. The door was slightly open, and he found himself looking straight at Norma, lying reading in bed.

'Hello,' she said, smiling. 'You must be Brian.'

'Yes.' He did not quite know whether to stay and chat, or flee.

'Quiet tonight, isn't it?' Still that smile.

'Not too bad. Perhaps I'll get a good night's sleep, after all.'

He decided on flight, and used the banality as an exit line. Secretly he would have preferred to follow Mr and Mrs Baker to their Anderson shelter, but the thought of joining complete strangers in the intimacy of sleep put him off. Instead he undressed and climbed into one of the beds in his own room. For a long time he lay awake, listening to the bark of anti-aircraft guns – it was not a continuous barrage; he could pick out the individual shots, sometimes one from some distance off would be followed immediately by a shot from a gun that could not have been more than half a mile away and which made him jump every time it fired. He heard the crumps of bombs exploding, mostly in the distance. And always that double throbbing from above.

He was just dropping off to sleep when a noise like an enormous sheet being ripped by his ear made him duck instinctively beneath the blankets. After a second's terrible silence he heard the roar of an explosion. Then a second, a third and a fourth in rapid succession, each further away. By the time the last one had burst, the house was shaking from the first. He had been told about this in the Mess just that evening; although a raid might be concentrated on the docks, the East End or the smart West End, the Jerries did drop odd sticks anywhere around London – either out of nerves, an evil sense of humour or a desire to keep everyone on their toes. For a long time afterwards Brian lay shaking, his heart thumping. In time, he hoped, he would get used to it as most Londoners had by now, and as Norma along the corridor most certainly had. He just hoped it would not take too long a time.

It was a somewhat dark-eyed Brian who breakfasted in the Mess the next day. He was starting on the toast and marmalade that followed an enormous plate of bacon and eggs when Major Luckhurst passed the table on the way out.

'Good morning, Ash. Drop in and see me when you've finished, would you?'

Brian watched the limping figure retreating. 'Wonder what that's all about?' he asked Leckie, deep in the *Daily Telegraph*.

'Shouldn't worry, laddie. Probably just to assign you to a Section.'

That was a reassuring thought. Everyone had said he would have a week or two, going out with Sections to get the hang of that job. In the absence of a proper course, it was the best he could hope for.

Major Luckhurst took his glasses off as Brian came into his office in answer to his call of 'Come in.' Brian, dressed, he hoped correctly, in his old battledress, saluted and became aware of a tall, slightly balding Sergeant standing to one side. The Major invited Brian to sit down.

'I had a call from the Directorate last night, Ash. We're under pressure to get results. The civil authorities are making a lot of noise – quite rightly, I suppose. But the outcome is – I want you to take over 347 Section immediately.'

Not for the first time in the last few hours, Brian was shaken. So much for the promised, gentle easing into the job. 'You mean – now, sir?'

Luckhurst smiled slightly. 'A bit sudden, I appreciate that, but I can't afford to have one whole Section off the books. Don't worry – Sergeant James here knows all about the work. He's your Section Sergeant – I'm sure he'll show you the ropes.'

The Sergeant spoke for the first time in the crisp, business-like way of all Regulars. 'Of course, sir.'

'That's all, Brian. I don't doubt you'll like to have a talk with the Sergeant. Good luck to you.'

He hoped he had not sounded too abrupt. Left alone, he let out a sigh, and slowly shook his head. Brian Ash looked so damned young! He hated sending these raw young men out before they had had a chance to sort out one end of a bomb from the other, but what else could he do?

Out in the corridor Sergeant James was gently taking charge, his twelve years' experience of the army coming to the fore. 'You'll wish to meet the Section straightaway, I dare say, sir.'

Brian was grateful to him for at least pointing him in the right direction. 'Yes, of course.'

'If you can give me half an hour, I'll see that the lads are on top line, sir.'

He talked for another ten minutes, about the men who were now under his command, where their billet was, the recent history of 347. He wound up with 'Like the Major said, sir – don't worry. We're in this together, if I may say so – we'll see you through.' It was not altogether a charitable thought; Sergeant James had more than once narrowly missed being blown up on active service in France and at Dunkirk, and he had no great wish to be blown up on his home ground.

They went their ways, Brian seeking out Alan Pringle, but

his instructor of last night was already out with his own Section. Brian wandered into the classroom, and spent the next twenty minutes desperately trying to remember what Alan had told him the previous night, picking up the fuses on display, turning them over in his hands but remembering hardly a word.

Then he steeled himself and went off to the Section billet. A few weeks before, he had been a student at Guildford. A few days ago he had been a private in the Hampshires. A few minutes ago he had been expecting to act as an observer, being taught the way of unexploded bombs. And now, commissioned in the Royal Engineers, he would be called upon at any minute to actually go out and do the bloody job.

Life in the Bomb Disposal Squad, he reflected as he drove his fluttering stomach towards the men he now commanded, was certainly proving to be an unpredictable experience.

Chapter 2

Three-four-seven Section was billeted in a two-storey, semi-detached house in a quiet side road in the vicinity of the school. At first glance it looked like all its companions. Then you noticed there were no lace curtains, the front door was always open; at times there was a great deal of bustle about it. You had to look hard for the discreet little sign bearing the unit's number and name. Only the army trucks, often parked outside, really gave the game away.

Sergeant James quickly got the men moving and was soon in the main barrack room – in happier times the larger bedroom – upstairs. Eight palliasses were stretched out on the bare floor, each with a man's kit displayed in regulation style. He walked round the room, glancing at the kits and the man standing in front of each palliasse. Silence prevailed. At the last man he said, 'Right. Not bad – not good, but not bad. Stand easy.' The men relaxed.

'What's he like, Sarge?' asked one of them.

'The new officer? Looks all right to me.'

'Not a loud-mouth, is he? Can't stand them.' The opinion came from the far end of the room.

'Seems quiet enough. Young, too. Commissioned only a week back.' The Sergeant was keeping an eye out of the window, watching for Brian.

'Wonder if he knows he's taking over from Lieutenant Atkinson? I liked him.'

A Welsh voice joined in. 'No accounting for some tastes. They haven't lost any time with him, have they?'

'Know why they jump these blokes up from private to Second Lieutenant and give 'em a section right off? No Officer Training, nothing? Because they think – why waste time and money training 'em when they'll be dead inside two months? That's why.'

Sergeant James jumped on that one. 'That's your considered opinion, is it? How very interesting. If you must know, I reckon this one'll probably last a good few of them out. He's the quiet, thoughtful type. Met them before – and remember, in my time I've had more officers than you lot put together have had NAAFI girls. If he doesn't get blown up, he'll finish up with a medal. I'd lay odds.'

'What are you offering, Sarge? Five-to-one?'

'I'm not a betting man. More useful things to do with my money.' The arrival of the little MG attracted his eye. 'Stand to your beds – here he is.'

He went downstairs to meet Brian, and soon their footsteps were heard coming up the stairs. Then Sergeant James was filling the doorway. He shouted, 'Room! Room – 'shun!' The house trembled from the shock of eight pairs of boots slamming down on the flooring, and the Sergeant was saluting as Brian came in.

'Number 347 Section ready for your inspection, sir.'

Brian returned the salute. 'Thank you, Sergeant.' And for the first time in his brief army career he was on the handing-out end of an inspection. Sergeant James fell in beside him as he moved to the first man.

'3082273 Corporal Horrocks, sir,' the big Yorkshireman announced, hoping Brian would not recognize him from the paybook episode of the previous day. 'Washing at the wash, one pair of boots at the bootmaker's shop, otherwise kit present and correct, sir.'

Brian gave him a small smile. 'We've met before, haven't we?' he said, and noticed the Corporal swallow hard. 'What did you do before the war, Corporal?'

'I was on t'Corporation, sir . . . recreation grounds, cemeteries and that.'

'Rather appropriate.' Brian moved down the line. Ted Copping, serious of face, a carpenter from Leicestershire; Tiny Powell, a milkman from South Wales, all dark hair and dark looks; Salt, a craggy, lined man, ex-Manchester gas works; Wilkins, the Londoner who had first challenged Brian the day before; Mulley, a pale Scots lad from Dundee. Brian had a word with them all, and was quite beginning to enjoy himself when a despatch rider roared up outside and came clattering up to the stairs.

He hesitated in the doorway. Sergeant James stepped into the breech once again.

'Yes, laddie?'

'Looking for Mr Ash, Sergeant.'

Brian came forward. 'Yes?'

'Message, sir.' Brian signed for it, looked at the buff envelope. Everyone in the room knew what it would say. Everyone, that is, except Brian. He read it. '*IO to OC* 347 *Section. Proceed at once to UXB No.* 38 *Woodbine Grove, SE*20. *Category A.*'

He showed the message to Sergeant James, who gave it a practised glance. 'Permission to dismiss the parade, sir?'

Brian nodded. The Sergeant was already halfway to the door as he ordered, 'Corporal, take over.'

Brian followed him down into the office. A map of south London nearly filled one wall and dominated the two desks. Sergeant James searched for the address. 'Woodbine Grove –

I know that. Here it is, sir – about two miles. Category-A – that means *disarm on site.*'

'I know.' Brian did not sound very happy about it.

'Shall you want me on the recce, sir?'

'If that's all right . . .'

'Quite the usual thing, sir.' The Sergeant bellowed up the stairs. 'Corporal Horrocks!'

Horrocks clattered into the office, was rapidly put in the picture, given instructions on rendezvous point, and as quickly left. The Sergeant turn to Brian. 'Ready, sir?'

'Er . . . what do I need? To take with me?'

'Nothing, sir. It's all in the trucks.'

'Is there a pamphlet or an instruction book? On defusing bombs, I mean.'

'Not that I've seen, sir. Don't worry, sir – we'll run through the procedures first.'

Twenty minutes later, from the pillion of a motorbike driven by Sergeant James, he saw the barrier across the street of small, rather dingy terraced houses that was Woodbine Grove. Propped against the barrier, in the middle of the road, was a large piece of boarding on which was chalked in uneven lettering:

DANGER – UNEXPLODED BOMB

Brian's legs were like jelly as he clambered off the bike and walked with Sergeant James up to the barrier. A police sergeant, tin hat at rakish angle, saluted, and a small crowd looked admiringly at Brian.

Sergeant James took control inconspicuously, without seeming officious. Brian was grateful for his understanding. 'Time of incident?' he asked the policeman.

'Approximately 03.10 this morning. Pretty big one, judging from the Warden's report . . . shook the house.'

Sergeant James, making notes, was sceptical – he'd heard it all before. 'We'll see about that. Right – where is it?'

The three of them stepped over the barrier, and fifty yards down the street turned into a narrow alleyway between two gardens. Just down the alley a fence had been broken down to reveal a long, narrow garden at the back of the house. The policeman led the way through the break and indicated the torn-up grass and flower bed.

'This looks like the point of entry.'

Sergeant James said nothing, but walked over the patch of lawn, looking for something. Soon he stooped, picked up a twisted bit of metal, examined it.

'Here's a part of the tail fin, sir. Two-fifty kilo. Why did they give it Category-A, Sarge?'

The policeman nodded towards a small brick building, little more than shed-sized, in the bottom corner of the garden. 'There's the electricity sub-station . . . and there's main power lines and sewers along the line of the pathway. Twelve feet down, I'm told.'

Sergeant James considered the situation briefly. 'Right,' he said. Like all long-serving NCOs, he was prone to preface most utterances with that word. 'Right – we'll let you know when it's clear. Just keep everyone well away – we don't want any sightseers.'

The policeman went off, to be met by Corporal Horrocks assembling the three sections of a metal probe.

'Good man – got here fast,' Sergeant James greeted him. 'That's the entry point, I reckon.' Horrocks gently put the probe into the ground, and even more gently jiggled it around.

'Yes, Sarge – here it is, I'd say.'

Sergeant James took the probe, confirmed the metallic touch of the bomb, then put the rod to his ear.

'Fair enough,' he pronounced. 'Get digging.'

Horrocks went out to the street, and Brian asked Sergeant James, 'What were you listening for?'

'Ticking. Sometimes the probe picks it up.'

'And there was none?'

The Sergeant smiled at him. 'No. You may just be lucky, sir.'

For the next quarter of an hour Brian could only stand aside and marvel at the cool teamwork of the Section. Horrocks came back at the head of the whole section laden with spades, buckets, picks, sandbags, all the necessary gear. Digging started and the grass was strewn with cast-off battleblouses as the sun warmed up to the promise of another hot day.

Sergeant James marked a line on the grass between the bomb and the electricity sub-station. 'Right – we'll have a line of sandbags down here. Chest high.'

They watched as the men carefully lifted the turf and neatly piled it up. After the first spadefuls, Powell announced, 'Bit of clay on top, boyo – then there'll be chalk and flint, most like. Nine or ten feet, I'll bet.'

'Might be worse,' said Salt.

'The fence'll do for shoring up,' said Copping, and began to gather the slats. Mulley came back from reeling a field telephone line towards the trench shelter at the bottom of the long garden, and now stood ready to take his turn at digging.

After a few minutes Sergeant James came up to Brian. 'If you'd move down to the safety point now, please, sir ... in the shelter.'

'I'd rather watch, thanks.'

'There's field glasses down there, sir.' The Sergeant's tone was firm. Brian took the hint.

The shelter was just a trench with a corrugated iron roof, earth piled up over it. Not the sort of place to spend a whole night. Wilkins was busy at one end, brewing tea. Now there was nothing for Brian to do but wait. This would be worst of all. Wilkins tried his best and chatted about anything but the bombing: the weather, Winston Churchill, the army, families, the lack of adequate seating in the shelter. Brian answered automatically. Most of the time he was peering over the top of the shelter towards the site of the bomb. Half of him wanted them to reach the thing quickly, the other half hoped fervently they would never reach it.

A mug of tea materialized before his eyes. 'Oh – thanks.' Brian stopped watching and sipped. 'This your usual job, Wilkins?'

'I'm the unit driver, sir. But on the job, I'm safety point man – 'ere to tell the tale if the others . . . er . . .'

'Cop it?'

'In a manner of speaking – yes, sir.' Wilkins had not liked to put the possibility into so many words.

'That ever happened?'

'Not with this section, sir, no. Last week 349 copped it – three of 'em and the Corporal. They reckon someone hit the bomb a bit hard with his pick.'

Brian was silent, conscious only of the dragging time and the growing dryness in his throat, despite the tea. Wilkins seemed to have run out of small talk. After a while Brian asked, 'Does it usually take long . . . to get to the bomb?'

'All depends. Last one was a real pig – took a couple of days.'

Still the work went on. They were getting deeper now, nearly up to their shoulders as they stood in the dig. Copping, the peace-time carpenter, was sawing the fence slats for shoring; Powell and Horrocks were digging; the others were wheeling the earth up a plank and tipping it into a growing pile a few feet away. Sergeant James was stood close, supervising. A snatch of song came up from down the hole.

'*I don't want to set the world on fi . . . re,*

I just want to start a flame in your heart . . .'

Wilkins grinned. 'That's Taffy Powell, sir. Right Welshman, he is – still be singing if they was chopping his head off, he would.'

The long wait dragged on. Brian was sweating now, and not from the heat. He picked at the callouses at the bottom of each finger, tried to remember what Alan Pringle had said to him the night before, tried to picture the various fuses that might be awaiting him, tried not to think of the consequences of carelessness.

There was sudden activity out at the digging: sappers coming out of the hole, Sergeant James going down. Brian moved to climb out of the shelter.

'Not yet, sir,' Wilkins said to him quietly. 'They've probably reached it, that's all. Having a look before they expose it completely. They'll say when it's your turn.'

Brian settled down again, half ashamed that he had revealed

his anxiety. The next half hour seemed like half a day. Then, at last, the men came back, Sergeant James leading them. Brian went out to meet them.

'It's exposed, sir,' Sergeant James told him evenly. 'Like I thought, a 250 kilogram. Only one fuse . . . Type-Fifteen.'

That range a bell. There were two fuses known so far – and Type-Fifteen was by far the easier to handle. That much he did remember. Sergeant James saw the relief on his face, and smiled. 'Your overalls are at the site, sir.'

They moved towards the hole, and Brian was very conscious of the sappers on their way to the shelter watching him carefully. Then he was gazing down at his first UXB. The shaft was neat, shored up against collapse, the bomb resting at a slight angle on an earth platform that had been cut around it. The fuse was clearly visible half way up to the case. Sergeant James was doing his best to pump confidence into him.

'It looks straightforward, sir. There shouldn't be any complications.'

'Fine. Thanks.' Brian was giving his hands quick little shakes as they hung at his sides, trying to get the tension out of them.

The Sergeant handed him a holdall. 'Here's your kit, sir. Crabtree discharger, universal key, hammer and chisel, rags and sacking, torch, string. You know about the discharger, do you?'

Brian was climbing into the overalls. Now the action had come, he was beginning to feel a little better. Not much, but better than he had felt in that trench.

'Thanks, Sergeant.'

'Give the Crabtree a good three minutes – that's the secret. Right, sir – if you go down, gently, I'll follow.'

'No you won't. You'll get the hell out of it back to the safety point. That's the rule, isn't it?'

Sergeant James looked at him for a second. He had been right. There was more in this youngster than met the eye at first meeting. 'If you're sure, sir.'

He waited for the Sergeant to reach the trench, then after a deep, deep breath he took up the holdall and, carefully avoiding the shoring planks sticking out untidily around the shaft, slowly and very, very carefully went down the ladder. 'Tread softly around a bomb' – that's what they had told him; and no one had ever trodden as softly as he was treading now. Then he was face to face with the thing, crouching beside it, touching it. He wiped the sweat of fear from his eyes, breathed deep to calm himself; then, suddenly, wanted to pee, very badly indeed. That was the other thing they had told him – always pee first. He had thought they were joking. Plainly they had been serious.

As carefully as he had come down, he climbed the ladder again and made for the nearest tree, conscious of being watched from down in the trench at the bottom of the garden. Then back down. And miraculously it all came back to him, just about everything Alan Pringle had told him.

The Type-Fifteen, he could hear Alan saying, *is the most common type we find. All known German fuses are electric. This fuse is like a little electric battery – there's a device on a telescopic arm that pumps juice through one or other of two spring-loaded plunger terminals as the bomb leaves the plane, and once it is thus armed the least knock or vibration will set the whole thing off. The reason why a UXB doesn't explode when it hits the ground is that it takes eight seconds before the condensers are fully charged. So, if you drop it below a thousand feet up it'll go deep into the ground without exploding – all ready for suckers like us. And the reason it doesn't go off bang when you touch it is because luckily a bloke called Crabtree invented his discharger. You clip it only to the fuse boss, and wind. That depresses the plungers and causes a short. After three minutes the juice is discharged and the fuse is fairly harmless.*

Great. Simple. Nothing to it – in theory. But there was the little matter of accidents, of booby traps, of this particular bomb being the first with some new little contrivance. Brian took the Crabtree from the holdall and with shaking hands eased the clamp over the bomb. The damn thing fell off. Another try, the sweat falling into his eyes, the thought of the sensitive trembler uppermost in his mind. But this time, success. He tightened it up and it clipped into the fuse boss. Brian raised his eyes heavenwards and sighed a deep sigh of relief. Maybe the worst was over now.

All that remained were the three minutes whilst the condensers discharged their current. What had Alan said about the next move? Oh yes . . . unscrew the locking ring, tie a long string to the top, retire a safe distance and pull. Job done. The fuse will slip out. No more sweat. Even then, care is necessary. Normally when the trembler switch functions there is a small flash sufficient to detonate the primary charge of penthrite wax – what they called the gaine. That in turn sets off the little cylindrical pellets called picrics at the bottom of the fuse, which in turn explode the bomb itself. If the picrics go up with the fuse in your hand, you might as well have set the whole bomb off as far as your immediate future was concerned.

Time was up. His watch showed the three minutes had gone by. Was it nerves or imagination, or was it getting bloody hot down this shaft? He glanced up and saw a cloudless sky, the top of a tree, its autumn leaves not stirring. No wind, then. The heat he felt was probably a bit of both. Wiping his hands down the seams of his trousers, he reached for the universal key – a steel bar about a foot long, down which could be slid two adjustable lugs to fit into the locking ring. In the slowest of slow motions he fitted the key, then tried to turn it. The ring stayed put. More pressure: still no movement. He began to put his whole weight on to the lever, pushing down on it in little jerks, sweating from exertion. It was no use. The bloody ring was stuck fast. *What now? Call for Sergeant James? No – why the hell should he?* In desperation he reached for the hammer and chisel, and before he knew what he was doing, gave the ring an almighty thwack.

Only then, with the sound of hammer on chisel still ringing, did he remember what old Hamish Leckie had said to him: 'I'm likely to be here after you've gone if you start using a hammer and chisel.' A shudder went through him. But on the other hand, nothing had happened after that first go – so maybe he'd be OK. More gingerly now, he tapped away again.

Engrossed, he did not sense Sergeant James appear over the lip of the shaft above him.

'Sir . . .' The tone was urgent.

At that moment the ring began to give. Brian looked up. 'It's all right – it's coming now.'

'We heard the hammering in the trench.'

Brian was unscrewing the ring by hand now. A huge excitement was beginning to surge through him. He'd as good as done it, and could have whooped with joy.

A warning voice came from up on the surface. 'Don't withdraw the fuse, sir – it may be booby trapped. Tie the string round, and come up.'

'Yes, I know.' At that moment the ring came away – and brought with it the whole fuse, complete with deadly gaine. It fell into Brian's lap. He sat looking down at it. 'Oh Christ . . .'

Sergeant James had ducked back when he saw the fuse coming. Now he peered once again down into the shaft. 'Come up, sir. Unscrew the gaine first – and treat it very gently.'

But Brian, numbed for the moment, did not wait. He climbed up the ladder, the complete fuse in his hand. Standing in the sunshine again, he asked, 'What do I do now . . . ?'

Sergeant James was patience itself. 'Unscrew the gaine like I said, sir. Always do that right away.' Having said it, he wisely stepped back a few paces and watched, tensed, whilst Brian did as he was bidden.

'That's right, isn't it?'

'Yes sir – well done, sir.' The Sergeant took the fuse and tapped the side. There was a small crack as the detonator cap went off. Brian swallowed hard.

'If the gaine had still been attached . . .'

'There wouldn't be much of us left now, sir,' the Sergeant completed for him.

'I was just bloody lucky, wasn't I?'

The Sergeant smiled at him. 'Better lucky than dead, sir. Souvenir?' He handed the now harmless fuse to Brian, and blew a long blast on a whistle. The section came out of the trench and busied themselves with erecting block and tackle to recover the bomb for destruction in the remote safety of Hackney Marshes. Brian didn't take much notice of them – he had retreated to a corner of the garden, and was being heartily sick.

The verdict that night as the Section lay on their palliasses in the dark, the night's blitz banging around them, was that they had a lucky Lieutenant on their hands, and that could not be a bad thing. Three officers killed before their eyes in the last two months was not good for morale; perhaps things would change for them, now.

'I reckon the Sergeant's right – he'll get a gong, this one,' Mulley said.

'If this bombing goes on much longer, he'll be like the rest of us – killed in his bed,' Copping moaned. Nothing was ever right for Copping. On this night he did have a point; the Jerries seemed to have a personal grudge against this part of London. As the house shook yet again in the shockwave of a bomb too close for comfort, Copping went on, 'All very well for Churchill going on like he does. All he's doing is provoking Hitler – and look what it's got him. The whole place burning about his ears.'

Corporal Horrocks couldn't resist a little baiting. 'I thought that was God's will, Coppy . . .'

The Leicestershireman took it. 'So it is. You may laugh, but London's a wicked and adulterous city. You should hear our parson goin' on about it at home.'

Wilkins joined in. 'Never mind – God'll protect Leicester for you.'

'What about Sheffield, Wilkie? If this bombing spreads, I reckon Sheffield'll be on t'list – all them steel works.' Corporal Horrocks was showing genuine concern for his home city.

'And Manchester.' Salt's Lancastrian tones were sharper than Horrocks' Yorkshire. 'Still, at least I've got the missus and kids out of it – safe in Cheshire, they are.'

'All right for some of you,' said Wilkins. 'My old mum and me kid sister are in the middle of this lot – down near the docks, they are.'

MANUAL OF BOMB DISPOSAL

(PROVISIONAL)

1941

CHAPTER I

GENERAL ORGANIZATION

CONTENTS

[Security B 499—1]

German Bombs

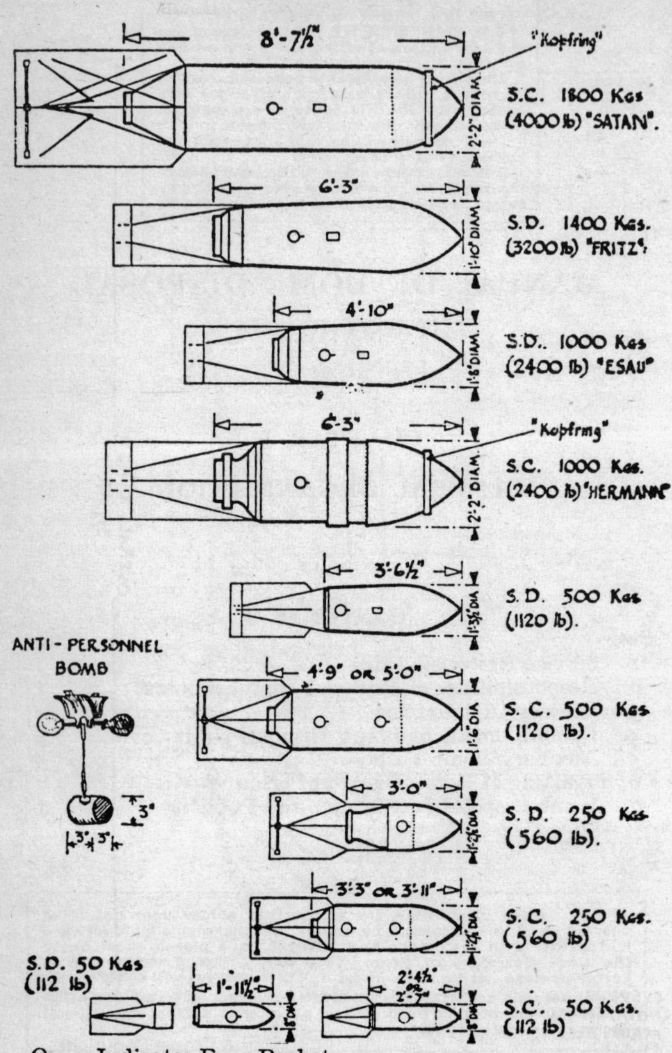

Q Indicates Fuze Pocket.
S.C. Indicates Spreng Cylindrish, *i.e.*, H.E. Thin Walled.
S.D. Indicates Spreng Dickenwand, *i.e.*, H.E. Thick Walled.

PLATE IV

GERMAN 50 KG. HIGH EXPLOSIVE BOMB

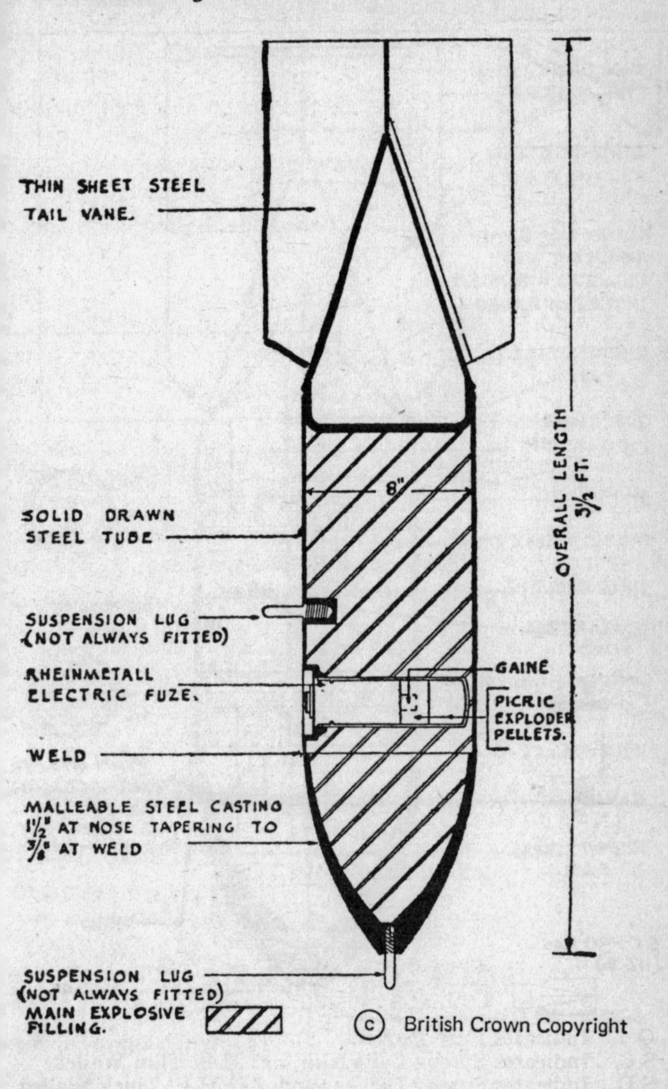

PLATE V

German 250 Kg. High Explosive Bomb

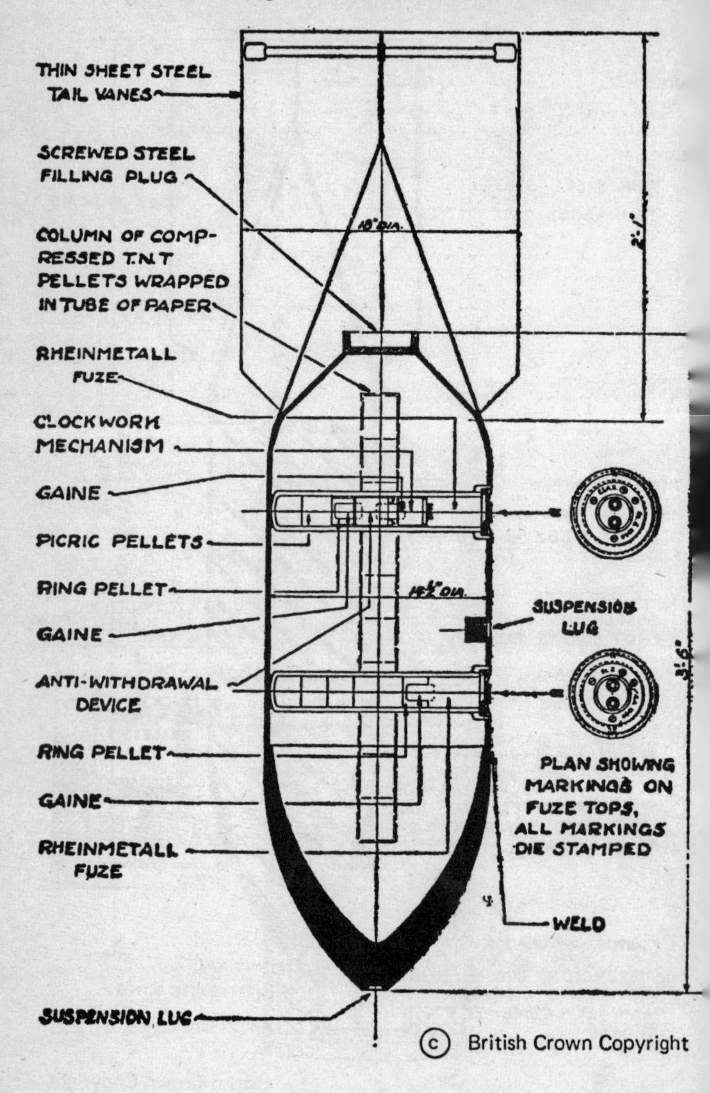

DIAGRAM OF ANTI-WITHDRAWAL DEVICE FITTED TO No. (17) CLOCKWORK FUZE

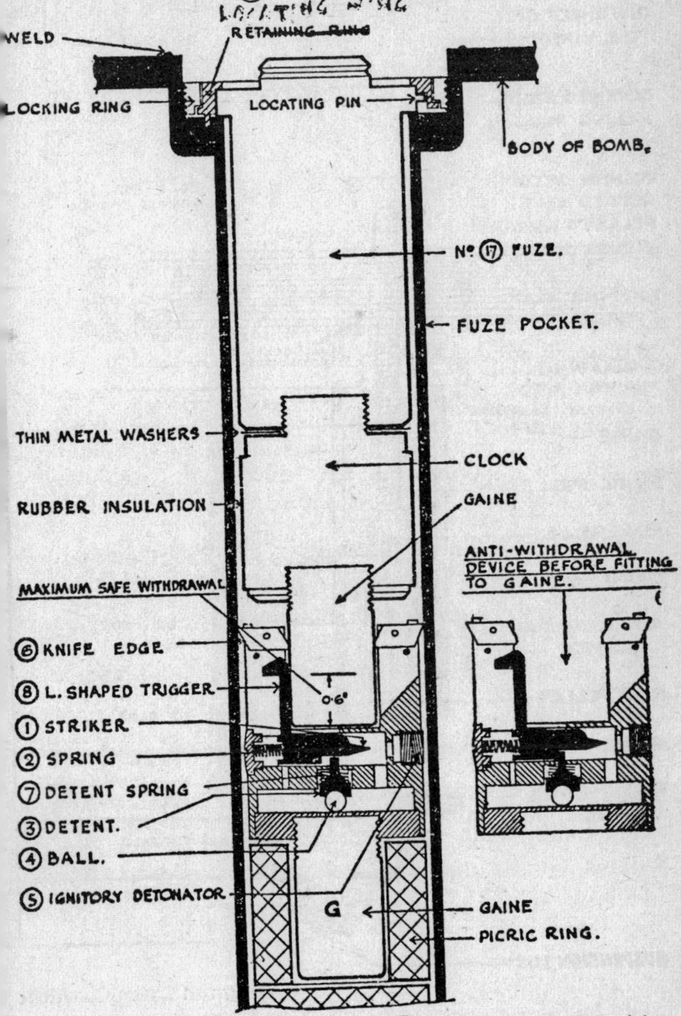

LOCATING RING
RETAINING RING
WELD
LOCKING RING
LOCATING PIN
BODY OF BOMB.
No (17) FUZE.
FUZE POCKET.
THIN METAL WASHERS
CLOCK
RUBBER INSULATION
GAINE
ANTI-WITHDRAWAL DEVICE BEFORE FITTING TO GAINE.
MAXIMUM SAFE WITHDRAWAL
0·6"
(6) KNIFE EDGE
(8) L. SHAPED TRIGGER
(1) STRIKER
(2) SPRING
(7) DETENT SPRING
(3) DETENT.
(4) BALL.
(5) IGNITORY DETONATOR
G
GAINE
PICRIC RING.

Amdt. 2
Oct., 1942

DIAGRAM OF FUZE EXTRACTOR DESIGN NO. II

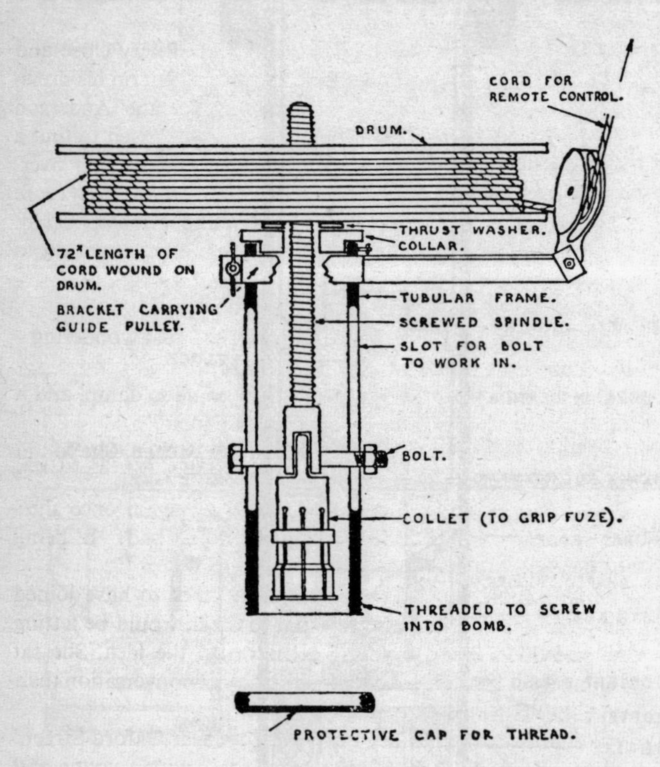

A silence of sympathy fell on the room. There seemed little else to say, after that.

It was a sleepless night for Brian Ash, too. Not only the bombing was keeping him awake, but he kept going over in his mind every move he had made down that shaft during the morning, and shuddering when he realized how stupid he had been to use that hammer and chisel. He wouldn't do that again in a hurry.

About two in the morning a bomb landed very close and Brian decided *to hell with bravery*. He got up, put on his dressing gown and went downstairs making for the Anderson shelter. At the bottom of the stairs he was surprised to find a mattress with bedclothes on it which he had to step over. Wondering which way to go for the garden, he was even more surprised when the kitchen door opened and Norma appeared. Her dressing gown, tied tightly about her, drew attention to her figure.

'Hello,' she smiled.

'Hotting up a bit,' he replied. 'I was – er – just wondering – if we shouldn't join them – in the Anderson.'

She pulled a face. 'Down there? God no – too damp, and it smells. It really does. Like to join me in a cuppa?'

'Well . . . all right.' He joined her in the kitchen. She found an extra cup, poured for him.

'Mum turns the gas off – and I turn it on again once she's in the shelter. I only come down when it gets bad.' 'It' being the bombing.

Brian would, in all honesty, have preferred to have joined her mum and dad, but also felt that to do so would be letting the side down when a young girl scorned the idea. She sat smiling up at him. He asked, more by way of conversation than anything, 'Where do you work?'

'Telephonist in an office up West. Just near Oxford Street.'

'Oh.' The techniques of making idle talk with a young and undoubtedly attractive girl in her night clothes whilst being bombed to kingdom come were rather outside his social experience. A bomber could be heard coming in lower than the rest. Very quickly there came that sheet-tearing sound once again, and the roar of the explosion, the house shuddering, the kitchen light flickering on-off-on. He winced, but she sat still, an excitement growing in her dark eyes.

'Close,' he remarked, superfluously.

'Smashing, isn't it.' She got up and carried her cup to the sink, close to where he was leaning against the cooker. 'It makes me go all goosey.'

'Me too.' But not in quite the same way.

She moved close to him. 'Does it? I wondered if it did. Thrilling, isn't it. I'm . . . I'm glad you came down, Brian . . .' And quite gently, she kissed him, watching his face as she did so.

Brian was too surprised to react. She leaned back from him and whispered, 'The last boy was nice – he really was. Pity about him. Come on . . . don't worry. Mum and Dad won't be up from the shelter until the All Clear – that won't be for hours yet.' She kissed him again, more urgently, her tongue pushing its way into his mouth, her body close against his.

Brian struggled free. As he did so she quickly untied her dressing gown. Beneath it she wore nothing.

'What's up?' she asked. 'Why not?'

'Not tonight, Norma, thanks. I've had a hell of a day . . .' It was only partly true. She had one hell of a body, but he was not sure that bomb-excited girls were really quite his meat. And there was that old saying about not fouling your own doorstep to say nothing of yet again treading, as it were, in Dickie Atkinson's footsteps. In the kitchen doorway on the way back up to his room, he turned. She was still standing with her dressing gown open, but her face had a plea in it now. He said, 'Sorry. Thanks for the tea, anyway.'

She shrugged.

It was a bad-tempered Norma who settled down again on her mattress, and a slightly perspiring Brian who got back into his own bed.

Chapter 3

Under Brian Ash, 347 Section settled down well. They moaned and complained, as all soldiers will, but at least as their new OC survived first one week, then a second, a third and a fourth, spirits rose and respect for him grew. Even Sergeant James began to have confidence in him. Brian grew in stature daily until there was less and less doubt as to whose Section it was.

The bombing continued, night after night, from first dark to dawn, never a night missed. And each morning the list of UXBs lengthened. For every bomb dealt with, ten might be added until the Disposal Units over the whole London area were overwhelmed. Some incidents could be dealt with in a few hours, others would mean two or three days of digging; it all depended on how the bomb had fallen. Each bomb, too, had to be treated with all the care of one's first. There was no room for over-confidence. Even so, faces disappeared from the Mess; they bade a cheery 'See you' after breakfast but you did not see them again. A Court of Enquiry would be held, and in due and often short course a new man – likely as not commissioned only days beforehand – would arrive to be kitted out from Corporal Mould's melancholy wardrobe.

It was life on the ends of your nerves, and by the middle of his fourth week Brian was beginning to feel it. There was, to start the ball rolling, the incident of the burnt toast at breakfast. The Moss electric toaster chose a bad moment to go berserk, so that just as Brian was mournfully extracting two very burned pieces of toast, Captain Francis the 2-i/c was passing his table. Minutes later Corporal Mould came discreetly up to Brian.

'Excuse me, sir,' he said quietly and deferentially. 'Captain Francis's compliments, and would you report to him in his office as soon as convenient.'

The odious Captain's office was like its occupant, neat and fussy. Charters and maps covered the walls, coloured pins on them advertising the fussy military bureaucrat and the smallness of mind that goes with the breed. The Captain was at his most disdainful; and proceeded to read Brian the riot act about the sins of burning toast . . . Did he not know there was a war on . . . men risking their lives to bring the raw materials of that toast across the Atlantic . . . a glaring example of sheer waste . . . would he kindly go back and eat the burned toast at once . . . he must be reminded again, there was a war on.

Brian managed to contain himself. Only the fact of a letter to be posted but left on his table took him back into the Mess. Corporal Mould was clearing the table.

'If you were about to enquire as to the whereabouts of the toast, sir . . . the caretaker's dog is partial to titbits.' Brian could not help smiling through his anger. Mould went on, 'I am sorry the machine let you down, sir. And if I may, I will cook your toast for your personally in the future.'

'Good man. Thank you, Corporal.' It had all been the kind of farrago that normally Brian would have dismissed with a shrug and forgotten. But he was still seething when he went into the Company office where the Admin Sergeant collared him.

'Glad you're here, sir – I was just going to get this off to you.' He handed Brian a message form. It listed three UXBs for attention, and for once they were all Category-C which meant there was no urgency. It made a pleasing change.

'OK – I'll get the Section out straightaway.' Driving down to their billet, the irksome memory of Captain Francis was already beginning to lose its sting. Now, he had other things to think about; there was, all said and done, a war on.

Twenty minutes later, luxuriating in the Section office over the lack of urgency, Brian was hearing the good news that he at last had a batman.

'Yes, sir,' Sergeant James was saying. 'Mulley, sir. He volunteered.'

The slightest of pauses before that 'volunteered' made Brian smile. His own days in the ranks were too recent to fall for that one. 'Did he, now?'

'Oh yes, sir.'

'Does he know about Norma?'

'One or two of the lads filled in the details, sir.'

'I imagine she's quite an incentive for volunteering for the job.'

'I have reason to believe it was the use of the bicycle that tipped the scales, sir.' Humourless as ever.

'Well, I'm sure he'll be very good. Not that there'll be that much for him to do. Mulley . . . he's the pale-faced Scots lad, isn't he?'

'That's correct, sir.'

'I'll have a word with him later. Right – let's get some work done, eh?' He read down the message form he had brought with him. 'One on a bomb site – and they say lightning never strikes twice – one in a park, one on a golf course. Let's do that first, shall we – make sure the members don't miss their weekend round.'

He was just getting up from behind the desk when Alan Pringle came striding in. Sergeant James snapped to attention.

'Hello, Alan – what are you doing here?'

The Company's Intelligence Officer was brisk, plainly not on a social call. 'Got a job for you lads.'

'We've got three already.'

Alan was peering at the wall map, his finger hunting for a location. 'This one's urgent. It came over the phone direct from the ARP people. There are some offices still burning after last night . . . ah, here we are, close to the railway . . . and the fire blokes say they can't get on because there's a bomb wedged high up behind some coping.'

Brian joined him and saw where Alan's finger had settled. 'That's a likely tale, isn't it? Probably a hot water geyser or something.'

'They say not.'

Brian looked sharply at him. 'You aren't joking . . .' One look at the serious Pringle showed he was not. Sergeant James saw the look. 'I'll get loaded up, sir,' he said, and left.

Alan said, 'Come on, Brian, I'll take you. I've got the pick-up.'

'Oh – you're coming too, are you?'

'I've brought the new fuse extractor to show you how it works.'

On the way to the incident, Brian found himself becoming both annoyed and tense. Annoyed that what had promised to be a comparatively easy day was obviously going to be a bloody difficult one, and tense because of that very difficulty. Not that he was ever completely relaxed at this stage. Butterflies in the stomach, yes; a touch of healthy apprehension, certainly, just enough to stop him getting cocky and careless. But this was his first bomb all over again. With every justification he thought of himself now, in his fourth week, as a seasoned bomb disposer, more than halfway through the average expectancy in the job.

The fears were justified. It was not a hot water geyser balanced forty feet up on the jagged wall of the badly damaged building. They were in a railway shunting yard, and the office building on fire was close enough for the heat to make it dangerous up there by the bomb. Brian, Alan and the fire chief stood a healthy distance from it, inspecting it in turn through binoculars. They could see the thing clearly, even pick out the fuse which at least had not settled inaccessibly.

'Yes . . .' said Brian, pensively. 'Right, Alan – where's that box of tricks of yours?'

Alan Pringle opened the lid of a large box at his feet and Brian had his first sight of a No. 1 Fuse Extractor already known not too affectionately as Freddie. He had a confused impression of clamps, a cylinder, a lot of knobs, before Alan brought out the Roneo'd instructions.

Alan was reading them. 'Trouble is, it says the bomb must be on level ground so that the pull from the jack is in line with the axis of the use assembly.' They both looked up at the bomb, but neither spoke. 'Otherwise, once the sparklets of carbon dioxide are pierced and the gas begins to work the jack and so forth to get the fuse out, you've got two minutes to clear out to safety. That can't be bad.'

The humour of the situation was lost on him.

Brian asked, 'Have you actually used this thing?'

'Er . . . no. But I've seen a demo.'

'Jesus Christ.' Alan knew Brian well enough to be surprised at the oath, and looked sharply at him. 'Bit of a dead loss for this job, isn't it.'

' 'Fraid so,' agreed Alan.

Brian turned to the fire officer. 'Could you get your turntable ladder so the top is near that bomb?'

The fire officer was not over-enthusiastic. 'Yes, I suppose so. But I don't like it.'

'I'm not keen either,' Brian snapped, and his tone brought another puzzled look from Alan. 'Have a go, would you?'

They stood and watched the ladder being manoeuvred, saying nothing to each other. Sergeant James came up to them with Brian's bag of kit.

'Just got here, sir. It looks a nasty one.'

'Yes. Got the Crabtree in the kit?'

'Yes.'

They began to walk slowly towards the ladder, now nearly settled in position.

'I'll give you a hand,' said Alan.

'Oh no, chum. One man, one bomb.'

Alan nodded. Brian was quite right. It was his bomb, no one else's.

Alan and Sergeant James turned back to the safety point, and the firemen were sent packing. Brian, clutching the toolbag, his stomach churning, began the long climb.

A hundred yards away, the rest of the unit, with the firemen, watched intently.

'He's a lunatic,' breathed Wilkins.

'Mr Ash knows what he's doing,' growled Corporal Horrocks.

'I only hope so,' breathed Powell.

They watched as Brian climbed slowly, uncertainly. The ladder swayed unnervingly, the smoke from the nearby fire swirled about him, the crackle of the flames loud in his ears. He reached the top, trying not to look down, and concentrated on the bomb. He leaned out and managed to clean the fuse with his gentle fingers: a Type-15, first bit of good-ish news all day. But the bombcase was hot with the fire and his fingers were burnt already. Coughing in the smoke, sweating in the heat, he hooked the kitbag to the top of the ladder and carefully twisted himself to get one foot on the walltop, watching the bomb like a hawk. *If it slipped now . . .* Some rubble tumbled down from beneath his foot, and he froze, but the bomb held. He reached for the kitbag with his free arm and somehow got the Crabtree out, began to fit it over the bomb. *If only the casing wasn't so hot . . .* He looked down and back, saw Alan standing halfway to the safety point, and made signs.

Alan cottoned on, and after a few minutes' shouting a fire hose was turned on. Brian could see it begin to writhe down there on the ground as the water filled it. 'Come on, you stupid sod,' he muttered, and broke off choking as he caught a lungful of smoke. The next he knew, as he came out of the coughing spasm, he was being damn nearly knocked off his perch as a cold jet of water hit him. This time he shouted out loud, 'Oh, for Christ's sake, watch it, can't you.' Alan quickly adjusted the aim, and soon a fine spray was falling on the bomb – and, unavoidably, on Brian.

After a minute or two, Brian waved, and the hose died. To the heat from the fire was now added the cold and wet from the water. Life was never straightforward. After an eternity the Crabtree was on, however, and the plunger depressed. *Two minutes to wait, plus one for luck.* Then time for the trick bit with the universal key. Five minutes later, angry almost beyond measure at a locking ring that refused to budge, Brian got out the hammer and chisel. This was something he had sworn never to do again, but the bomb was getting hot again, and his fingers were scorched. Under pressure of the hammer blows, it moved slightly and sent a small shower of rubble to the ground.

A shout from below. 'You all right?'

Brian shouted back. 'The ring's jammed. The fuse should be dud by now – the Crabtree's been on a hell of a time.'

'Come down.' Brian did not move. 'What are you going to do?'

He shouted at Alan, 'Get out of it. Go on. Scram. Move it, can't you?'

Alan retreated towards the safety point. Brian watched and he seemed to take an age. Finally he was there. With a final effort, Brian shifted his position slightly so that he could get a purchase. Then he put a boot on the bomb, and shoved. He knew it was wrong, that it would probably be the last thing he ever did. But it was all he was capable of doing. Even then the thing did not shift. He pressed and heaved, all his strength in the one leg. He was vaguely aware, at the edge of his vision, that two figures had emerged from the safety point and were watching him, very possibly in sheer horror. All he wanted was to get this bomb off this wall. One final effort, and at last it slid, oh so slowly, off its perch and fell in a shower of bricks and rubble. Brian closed his eyes tight and hung on to the ladder. Nothing. No bang. No heavenly choirs. Slowly he looked down again, and there was the bomb nestling close to the ladder turntable. There, too, were Alan and Sergeant James running towards him.

He almost fell down the ladder in his haste, shouting to the others to get back. They paid no attention. When they arrived, they all looked down at the bomb.

Alan, almost too calm, broke the silence. 'We could have hauled it down, you know. Still . . . let's try the key again. OK, Sergeant – away you go.'

Reluctantly, Sergeant James returned to safety. Brian, sweating from the heat and shivering from his dousing at the same time, panting from exertion, watched as Alan deliberately fitted an extension to the universal key and using the extra leverage, managed to loosen the locking ring.

'Thanks, Alan. Now push off whilst I defuse the bastard.'

'I've got the new extractor, here.'

'Oh no . . .'

'Fanny Francis said it was to be used.'

'Bugger Fanny.' Alan Pringle was a great chap, but apt to be a shade pedantic. The 2-i/c had ordered: end of story. *Birds of a feather.*

'Orders, Brian.'

Brian was too weary to battle on. 'All right.'

Alan became absorbed in the extractor, the business of setting it up, getting the faintly bizarre mechanism just right, being maddeningly precise about it. Even the collapse of a blazing wall a little too close for comfort did not disturb him.

'Now then . . . *put the saddle over the bomb first* . . . so. The cylinder fits into this hole. Then what?' He checked the instructions. 'Oh yes. Screw down this knob . . . *make sure the extractor rod is exactly in line with the eyebolt in the fuse* discharger . . .'

The impatience showed in Brian's voice. 'It's been discharged once already.'

'*Couple the extractor rod to the fuse discharger.*' Alan obviously had not even heard Brian.

'Look, Alan – does all this take very long? Because I reckon this bomb's been very patient, all things considered.'

'*Adjust the rod till it's just bearing against the distance gauge.* Is it? Good. *Put in an ordinary sparklet* – funny, when you think a gadget for making soda water is just as useful for this, ain't it – *push the tit to pierce it* . . . so . . . and Bob's your uncle. That's the best part of the whole business – you've got up to two minutes to get clear whilst the arm takes up the play and begins to withdrawn the fuse. Right – let's go.'

At last they walked off across the desolate shunting yard, stubbing their toes occasionally against a sleeper or a rail, the crackling of the burning office block the only sound. Each lit a cigarette. 'What's it called again?' Brian asked.

'The extractor? Fuse Extractor Number One – Freddie for short. Going to add considerably to our peace and quiet, I reckon.'

'All contributions gratefully received,' Brian mumbled.

They were quite near the safety point when the bomb exploded. They threw themselves down, and were showered with earth and rubble. They looked at one another, got up and carried on without speaking.

After that, the golf course bomb had all the excitement of cucumber sandwiches in a nunnery.

*

The day's work done and the toad-in-the-hole eaten, Sapper Mulley mounted his new badge of office, the Section bicycle, and went off to the Bakers' house. 'Time spent in reconnaissance,' he said darkly, quoting the army manual, 'is seldom wasted.'

The girl who opened the door was the type that weary bomb disposers dream of. 'Is this where Lieutenant Ash billets, miss?'

'Yep.' Dark and lively eyes, slim, a figure a man could really get to grips with.

'I'm his new batman.' Mulley, quiet, shy, sober despite being Scots, was bowled over. New vistas stretched before him.

'Oh good. Come on in and I'll show you his room and that. I'm Norma Baker.' She need not have told him; the lads at the Section had not been wrong.

'My name's Mulley. Gordon Mulley.'

She was closing the door. 'Gordon – that's a nice name. I've never known a Gordon before.'

After he had seen the room, she said, 'I've just made a pot of tea. Come down and join me. Mum's gone to her sister for a few days' rest, and Dad's mucking around in the garden, so we won't be disturbed.'

She poured the tea and sat down. 'Don't mind if I get on with this, do you?' She was sewing a collar on to a blouse. 'Been in the army long, have you?'

'Six months.'

'Quite an old soldier. What did you do before?'

Mulley, still on edge, could hardly take his eyes off her. 'In civvy street? Och well, ma' family's from Dundee . . . and there are nine o' us and ma' dad drinks most o' the cash so I've been working since I was seven . . . paper round before school, and that. Then I went on the docks, but I didn't much care for it. Last couple o' years I've been in a bicycle shop.' He was conscious of the words pouring out, and felt foolish for it.

'Were you? You can mend mine, then. The chain's gone.' She, in contrast, was bright, relaxed, friendly.

'Sure I will. I like mechanical things.'

There was an awkward pause. Mulley had a feeling he was supposed to say something, but could think of nothing. She came to the rescue. 'I think you're ever so brave.'

'Being on the bombs? Och no . . . we just do the digging. It's the officer who gets the thick end. I wouldn't have his job, taking out the fuses.'

'He's ever so nice, isn't he? Always the gentleman. Never presumes!' She examined the sewn-on collar. 'Right – let's see what it looks like.' To Mulley's horror she stood up and slipped her sweater over her head. The sight of her well-filled bra did a lot to his pulse rate. She laughed. 'You'll get a squint staring like that.'

'There's quite something to stare at.' As the words came out he realized his boldness. 'Oh Lord, I'm sorry. I'm not . . .'

She laughed again. 'You're awful, you are, Gordon. And stop blushing. I don't mind – honest. Here – do me up, there's a love.'

She twisted round. As he was fumbling with the hooks and eyes, she said, 'Do you ever get any time off?'

'Saturdays – if we're lucky.'

'How about you and me going to the flicks, then?'

He was glad it was she who had asked. 'Yeah . . .'

'Eddie Cantor's on at the Rialto.'

'If it's still there by Saturday.'

'Don't be such a gloomy-guts.'

She was buttoned up and looking into a mirror. 'I'd best be getting back,' he said. 'Before it's dark. Thanks for the tea.'

Cycling off back down the quiet road in the gathering dusk, Mulley thought, 'Bloody hell, she's a raver, no mistake.' Watching him from her front door, Norma thought, 'There's a challenge, if ever I saw one . . .'

Next morning, Brian met Major Luckhurst in a corridor of Company Headquarters.

'Ash – glad I've seen you. Got a minute?'

He led the way to his office. Closing the door, he said, 'Sit down.' Then, limping round behind the desk and seating himself, 'How are you after yesterday's – er – exploit?'

'A bit scorched, and my fingers are still rather sore – otherwise all in one piece, thank you, sir.'

'Good.' The Major was looking hard at him. Yesterday afternoon, Alan Pringle had been in to see him and had brought disturbing news from the shunting yard incident. 'Good.'

Brian was faintly disturbed by the look. 'I'm – I'm sorry we lost the new extractor. The bomb just . . . just blew up.'

'So I heard!' Major Luckhurst struck a match, put it to his heavy pipe, and spoke between pulls. 'I haven't been disposing of bombs for very long, Brian . . . none of us have . . . a bit longer than you, though . . . A pithy and accurate way of summing it all up, I find, is . . . *Never trust a bomb*.' He shook out the match and put it in the typewriter ribbon tin that served as ashtray.

'Yes . . . sometimes they do seem to have a will of their own.'

'If you've learned that, you've learned something. I've had a pretty senior fire brigade officer on the phone, singing your praises. Personally I say you should be given six of the best on your backside for being a blithering idiot. I was sorry to hear that an officer under my command could make such a fool of himself.'

Brian felt himself bridling. 'The fire people were in trouble, sir. My orders were to help them out – and I was given to understand it was urgent.'

'That bomb had no official priority. It had not even been reported in writing.' Luckhurst's tone was that of a reasoning parent rather than a reprimanding OC.

'No, sir, but the fire people said—'

'To hell with what the fire people said. Your behaviour was foolhardy and reckless in the extreme. We are not in this business to become heroes, neither do we take unnecessary risks – there are enough of them about, as it is. If that bomb had gone off, which it might have done at any moment, all that would have happened was the destruction of an already useless building. No one was in danger. And to kick a fused bomb off a ledge forty feet up . . .' Words failed him.

'The discharger had been depressed the correct number of times, sir, and anyway I reckoned the heat from the fire would have emptied the condensers.'

'Don't try to blind me with science, Brian – I've been teaching it for twenty years. It was an act of the greatest possible stupidity to endanger your own life.' There was a pause, then the Major's tone was softer. 'I'm sending you on a weekend's leave.'

'I'm quite all right, sir. Really.'

'Brian – it's an order. You're on leave as from tonight – and I don't want to see you back in this office until breakfast on Monday. Get away – relax – unwind – get some sleep. God knows you look as if you could do with it.'

Sleep . . . unwind . . . Aunt Do-Do's cottage tucked away in Surrey . . . peace and quiet . . . The mere thought knocked the fight out of Brian. All he could say was, 'Thank you, sir.'

Walking down to Captain Francis's office to tell him to fix Brian's leave pass, Major Luckhurst pondered upon how right Alan Pringle had been. The look on Brian's face at the end of their talk had shown that.

Brian drove down to his aunt in Surrey in the autumn dusk, having first spent an hour poring over road maps, charting and noting his route door to door, trying to avoid a repetition of that first mind-bending journey up from Reading. He had no time to telephone. But he knew he would be made welcome, fussed over, cosseted a little, and the thought was comforting. Thinking back over the Major's lecture as he drove he could see that he had deserved every word. What on earth had possessed him on that fire ladder in the shunting yard – he would never know. A shudder ran through him as he remembered. Of all the stupid things, to actually kick that bomb off that wall . . . Discretion, caution, every first principle, forgotten. All he had known was that he *had* to get the bomb off that wall, and quickly, no matter how. The strain of the last few weeks must really be telling. All sorts of other minor little things came back to him, things over the last ten days that usually he would have taken no notice of but which had irritated him almost to screaming point. Yes, Major Luckhurst had been right. He did need a break, and a full night's sleep. If only Aunt Do-Do's blasted mini battalion of dogs didn't spend the whole weekend yapping at him, maybe he'd feel better after it.

With their OC on leave, 347 Section was stood down for forty-eight hours, in a state of limbo, unable to get away but not actively working. On the other hand, if an emergency rose they could be sent off to it, Brian's place being taken by another officer who would spend his time rushing between his own Section's bomb and 347's. Even so, with their second bomb of the day safely blown to smithereens, the unit's three-tonner had a holiday air about it as it drove back from Hackney Marshes accompanied by the ribald songs soldiers sing as they crowd the tailboard to the amusement of passers-by.

On Saturday morning Sergeant James allocated them jobs about the billet, but from lunchtime they were free. Most of the lads spent the time stretched out on their palliasses (one day, one glorious day, actual real beds would leap off the requisition forms and into their room), some sleeping and others reading books ranging from the adventures of artistic ladies in Paris to, in one much-commented upon instance, J. B. Priestley's *The Good Companions*. Others wrote letters or moodily read old ones from home. Corporal Horrocks was out in the crisp autumn sunshine digging over the garden. Powell and Copping caught up on washing that should have been done weeks ago. Over the communal basin, Powell said, 'What's up with Salty? Been mooning about like a love-sick druid all day.'

'He had a letter from his missis, didn't he.'

'Not a "dear John", for heaven's sake? She hasn't run off with another bloke?'

'No, no – nothing like that.' The mere idea offended Copping. 'You know she's taken herself and the kids out of Manchester? Well, she's getting fed up living out in the country, wants to go back.'

Powell lifted his dark Welsh eyes to the ceiling. 'Some people are never satisfied, are they now, Coppy-boy. I'd be out of Cardiff like a shot, let me tell you.'

'Salty reckons Manchester's going to be bombed any time now. That's the point.'

'He could be right.'

'That's what's worrying him.'

'Wants the family to keep out of the way, like?'

'And she can be stubborn, so he says.'

'He feels these things, does Salty. Underneath, he's real soft.'

Copping considered. 'Yes – you're right. Given to the ways of the flesh perhaps, but not all bad in spite of that.'

They took their pairs of socks and underwear out to join the washing already festooning the line stretched between two trees in the garden. Taffy Powell was thoughtful. He called across to Corporal Horrocks, still digging and showing every sign of enjoying it.

'Reckon they'll ever bomb Cardiff, Corp?'

'Yon buggers'll bomb everywhere before we're done, mark my words.'

'Mmmm,' mused Powell, and said no more.

After tea, the unwritten 'in bed or out of barracks' rule came into operation. Mostly it was out of barracks as pub time came round and girl friends sloshed on the scent and prepared – most of them hopefully – for the worst. Young Mulley, extra-closely shaved and well spruced, put up with a deal of advice and ribbing about his date with Norma. He dismissed it all with a shy, 'Och, away,' but secretly took it all in. Hitherto his knowledge of women had been confined to unsatisfactory fumblings and gropings which had always met a point where the Scottish lasses of Dundee had said a firmly Calvanistic 'That's enough.' As he walked out of the billet he had a gut-trembling feeling that the chance was before him to put theory into action.

The wiry Wilkins went out too, among the last to go. All day he had been brooding, not joining in the chat and jokes, lost in thought. The nightly air raid sirens were wailing when at last he crept into an unused room in the house and tip-toed to the small tiled fireplace. From up the chimney he withdrew a tin box, grunted with satisfaction as he checked the contents and stuffed them into his battledress pocket. Only then did he leave and catch a bus heading eastwards. Forty-five minutes later he was standing at the corner of his home street of two-storey terraced houses, black from generations of smoke, crowding in on one another – open the front door and step straight into the 'best' room, kitchen beyond. The streets all around were the same, and showed many ugly gaps. The corner shop where he used to buy his fags and *Daily Mirror* had been flattened, so had the pub opposite. Houses where he used to knock and haul out his schoolmates for games of street soccer were no longer there. The barrage guns were barking at the double throbs of the bombers overhead as he set off in the pitch blackness down his own street, half fearful of what he would find. It was a chilly night with a hint of frost, not improved by the ever-present damp from the broad Thames not more than half a mile away. He glanced upwards and above the rooftops there was a dull red glow, faint as yet, but growing stronger as the fire took hold. The crump of bombs from its general direction added themselves to the AA guns; and as he watched, another glow began to show near it. Walking with eyes skywards he did not see the shadowy figure looming out of the dark. He had not expected to meet anyone – the whole place had a ghost town feeling. Oaths were exchanged, and apologies, then came recognition. He had bumped into a near-neighbour, now doing duty as an air raid warden. It was from him he heard about his mother's house: flattened, four nights before, by a bomb in the back yard. Luckily only a small one, luckily not a direct hit, otherwise . . . The man shook his head. Only then did Wilkins notice the many boarded-up windows along the street.

Sickened, he set off for the Rest Centre where he would find his mum and sister. If Wilkins had ever felt shame in his life, it was now; shame at himself for being such a self-contained bugger, shame that, living as he was only a handful of miles away from them, he had not kept an eye on what remained of his family. The Rest Centre was an old warehouse, huge and

Dickensian with its flickering candles lighting bundles of homeless humanity bedded down on the cold stone floor as best they might for another long night with no promise of hope come the dawn. He walked down the long rows of men, women and children who should have been safely evacuated but whose parents had refused to be parted from them. There was little talk. An occasional WVS lady, bristling with efficiency, passed him with bundles of blankets. The blitz rumbled and boomed away outside. A child whimpered, half asleep. Empty eyes watched him. A game of rummy was being played around a candle. It was as if the world had slipped back two hundred years.

Then he saw them. The gloom could not hide how pretty she had been. His sister was only just twenty and looked nearer forty. She was tired, dark rings around her eyes; the long fair hair that was her pride – unbrushed and unwashed for days; a new hollowness in her round cheeks. Wilkins was shocked.

'Hello, Cis,' he said, quietly.

Her eyes brightened, she smiled. It must have been the first time she had done that in a long time. 'Jim . . . for Christ's sake . . . where've you sprung from?'

'How's things? Mum all right?' He nodded down at the dishevelled bundle curled up alongside her, sleeping deeply and noisily.

'Not bad, considering.' She leaned over to shake the older woman.

'No – don't wake her.' The last thing Jim Wilkins wanted was his mother awake. He had been relieved that she was asleep. It would only mean her having a go at him again, creating a scene, and he didn't want that, especially in front of all these people.

'She's pissed again, matter o' fact. Can't blame her, really.'

He put out a tentative finger at the baby in Cis's arms. 'The nipper's all right, by the looks of him.'

'He's too young to know, isn't he?' She rocked slightly and the baby gurgled. 'Good to see you again, Jim. Keeping right enough, are you?'

'Can't grumble, I – I met Ted Philp. He told me about the house.'

'Bad night, that was, Jim. The Cohens at the bottom corner got it the same time. Direct hit, theirs was. Two days before they was dug out – all seven of them gone.'

'Nice lot they were, too.' He indicated the old fibre suitcase and the two bundles beside her. 'That all you managed to save?'

'Yes.'

'What are you doing, then, Cis?'

'Living here. What else can we do?'

He looked all about him. 'Jesus.' He took the scene in, then on an impulse undid his battledress pocket. 'We've got to get you out of this, haven't we?'

'Yeh, great – but how?'

'Here – get yourselves down to Uncle Eddy's at Bristol. You'll be OK there.' He pulled out a fat bundle of pound notes and, carefully concealing them from prying eyes, slipped them to Cis. An hour or two before they had been hidden up a chimney in his billet.

Her eyes nearly popped out. 'Here – how did you come by all this?'

'Put it away, quick.' She slipped it down her dress as he went on, 'Never mind how I got it. Matter of fact, I was on me way to see a bloke – bit of business, you know – and I suddenly thought I'd stop off and see how you was getting on. Lucky I had it on me.'

She smiled. Jim had always had 'a bit of business' on the go. Ever since she could remember her big brother had been making a bit extra. She'd never enquired how, just taken it for granted. Most of the men down this way did the same. It seemed the army had not changed a lifetime's habit.

'Promise, now. First thing tomorrow – down to Bristol, all of you.'

Her eyes filled with tears. 'Ta, Jim – I don't know what to say . . .'

'Don't, then.' He stood up. 'I'd best be off to see this bloke.'

Desperately she tried to keep him. 'Here – I got a photo of Sid this morning. God knows how the postman found us. Look.' From her crammed handbag she produced a picture of her husband, Tank Corps beret on the back of his head, shorts well creased, the Pyramids as a backdrop.

Wilkins looked at it. 'Yeh – good. Got it cushy out there, lucky bugger.'

'I wouldn't say that, Jim.'

'At least he's warm and he's not being blitzed every night. And he's got all them belly dancers. Anyway, got to get moving. You be on the first train in the morning, eh, love? And pour a bucket of water over Mum and give her a kiss from me. Send us a postcard, mind. See you.'

And he was gone, disappearing into the gloom, out of their lives again, to pop up briefly once more some time, no one could say when: that was Jim Wilkins. His sister's eyes were still wet when an hour later she tried to settle herself to sleep.

It was close to midnight by the time Wilkins had seen his pal and got back to the billet, having had to walk the last four miles and dodge for shelter a couple of times as bombs ripped down uncomfortably close. He was last in only by a short head. Mulley was still undressing in the unlit room as he crept in.

'That you, Wilkie?' whispered the Scots voice.

'Yeh. How'd it go, mate?' They both knew to what he was referring.

'Fine, ta. Great.'

'Lucky sod.'

Mulley had not been strictly accurate. Proceedings had opened with great promise in the pictures, he and Norma with hands on one another's thighs. Then came a drink and fish and chips when the pub closed. She held him tightly around his waist as they walked back to her house through the blitz, and at the front door he had kissed her. It was no ordinary kiss either, it was of an urgency he had never met before. As they broke, she whispered, 'Come in for a while, Gordon.' It was then that he got cold feet. He wanted to, by God he wanted to, but when it came he backed down, muttered something about being on duty early in the morning, and fled. Now, in bed, he was cursing himself as he lay hot and throbbing with the memory. He wanted Norma Baker as he had wanted no other girl. Tomorrow, though – that would be the day. He had a perfect excuse for going round. As his batman, he just had to check on Lieutenant Ash's gear for when he came off leave. That was it; he'd time it so there was a raid on and she'd be worked up and excited. It'd be a gift. *Then*, at last . . .

So, after a do-nothing Sunday that dragged into eternity, Mulley went into battle once again. The guns were banging away nicely when he arrived at the Baker's house and rang the bell. Norma opened the door, and he gulped hard at the sight of her, but she gave him her usual flashing smile. Five minutes later, having had a purely formal and distinctly fevered check around Brian's room, he was downstairs again. A dim light was on in the sitting room, the door half open.

'Are you there, Norma?' he asked.

'Sure. Come on in.' As he did so, a mischievous grin spread across her face. 'Not running off tonight, then?'

He blushed. 'Er . . . no.'

'Good. Sit down.' She patted the sofa and he sat close to her. She close her eyes tight, and smiled. 'Oh, listen to those guns, will you . . .'

Wondering vaguely how you managed a woman on a sofa – none of the books handed round in school when the master wasn't looking had covered the eventuality – he put his arm around her and kissed her. She opened her eyes and, still smiling, said, 'Take that jacket off, then.'

He undid his battleblouse and threw it aside. Suddenly he was acutely conscious that army braces and thick khaki shirt without collar were not the most svelte of gear; but before he could become too bothered about it she was kissing him again, deeply and urgently. Their tongues met, and his hand was moving up her body to her breasts. A moment later, still kissing him, she leaned back a little. He took the hint and eased up the hem of her sweater. She drew in her chest, and he was fumbling inside the bra, feeling with his fingers for her nipples.

'Oh, Gordon, love,' she breathed. 'Come on – now.'

She broke away, and drew the red sweater over her head. At the same time he stood up and slipped his braces over his shoulder. He was just undoing the top trouser buttons when a face in the hall mirror, seen through the open door, caught his eye. He froze. Lieutenant Ash was standing out there, watching everything. Mulley looked down at Norma, who was reaching back to unhook her bra. She slid it off, looking up at him, her back to the door. Jesus wept, he had never even imagined tits like hers. Full, and proud, and the sexiest nipples. 'Come on, then – they won't bite,' she murmured.

He looked again beyond her at the mirror. Thank God, the Lieutenant had gone. Upstairs, presumably. There'd be bloody murder in the morning, now. 'Sorry, Norma – I've just remembered – got a job to do . . .'

'Oh bloody hell, Gordon – never mind that. Come *on*.'

He was still buttoning up his battleblouse as he slammed the front door behind him and belted up the street.

Brian had a warm welcome back to the Mess for breakfast the next day. Alan Pringle, sitting with a stranger, waved him vigorously to join him. 'How was the blessed peace of Surrey, then?' he asked.

'To tell you the truth, I'm damned if I know. I slept most of the time – all of it apart from the odd meal, if I was strictly honest.'

'Good.' He was conscious of Alan examining him minutely. 'You certainly look better. No more rash moves, I trust, eh?' They exchanged smiles. The memory of the bomb on the railway yard wall was still potent. Alan nodded towards the newcomer. 'Let me introduce you. Ken Machin. Only just this minute arrived. He's down to work with you for a few days – learning the ropes, the usual thing. Oh – and he'll be sharing your billet; no problem, I take it?'

'No, of course not.'

Second-Lieutenant Ken Machin was young, eager and full of himself. Good looking in a matinee-idol sort of way, thin

Ronald Colman moustache, face tanned from an open-air life, eyes darting everywhere. Brian was not at all sure he took to him. 'Well, at least this is a bit more like it,' Machin was enthusing. 'Better than putting up Nissen huts all day long around Luton – that's how I was serving King and Country until Friday. This is all jolly exciting, by the sound of it.'

Brian poured himself some coffee. 'You could say that, I suppose . . . if you don't mind working in thick mud or sewage at the bottom of a hole.'

'Or bang slap next to a burning building and having to be hosed down while you work,' Alan chipped in. 'That was Brian's last little experience.'

'I say,' marvelled Machin.

'Funny time to join a unit, surely?' asked Brian, more out of polite conversation than any great interest. 'I mean, breakfast time. And from Luton, too.'

'Ah, I didn't come direct, you see. The wife's got a flat in Chelsea. Spent the weekend there.'

'I see.' Brian turned to the Company's Intelligence Officer. 'Any excitements whilst I've been away? Any developments?'

'Not really. Only one thing – the boffins think they've got the clockwork fuse beaten.'

'The Type-17? That's good news.' It had been the most feared of the German fuses, because it could be set for a delay time of anything up to three days, and no sign of when it was on the point of going off.

'Apparently it's an enormous magnet that goes round the bomb and stops the clock so you can defuse the thing more or less at leisure.'

'Does it work – that's the big question.'

'So they tell me.'

'The sooner we get one the better, in that case.'

Captain Francis paused at their table and looked down his long nose at Brian. 'Good morning, Ash – nice to have you back.' The emphasis he put on 'nice' managed to inject a note of sarcasm.

'Bastard,' Brian muttered to himself as the 2-i/c went on his way. Then, 'Any jobs lined up for 347 Section, Alan?'

'A superfluous question. I'll get the list to you inside the hour.'

'Right. Soon as I've finished, we'll go down to the Section, Ken, and get you working.'

'Ready whenever you are, squire.' You would have thought they were off for a game of tennis.

Brian's first job in the Section's billet was to send for Mulley for a private talk. The young Scot, more pale faced than ever, stood rigidly before him, eyes front, fearing the worst.

'I dare say you know why I've sent for you,' Brian opened up.

'Yes, sir.'

There was a pause. Brian, in his first experience of this kind of thing, was almost as uncomfortable as Mulley. He relented slightly. 'All right, relax and sit down.'

'Thank you, sir.'

'I quite realize that Miss Baker behaves rather – er – abnormally – sometimes, especially during air raids. Don't think I want to interfere with your private life, Mulley – the way you behave is your own affair. But for heaven's sake keep your own doorstep clean ... that is, if you want to go on being my batman ... I mean, suppose Mrs Baker came back and found you and Norma ... she'd blow the roof off, go potty.'

'Yes, sir. I quite understand.'

'Good. Just so long as you do understand.'

'There is one thing, sir ... I wonder if we could have another key to the house? At the moment I have to ring the door bell, you see ... and often as not Norma ... Miss Baker ... lets me in.'

'Good idea.' Brian threw the key across to him. 'Get it done and let me know how much.'

That was a weight off Mulley's mind. After twice making a fool of himself, the thought of confronting Norma again was too much; at least for the time being.

The list of work arrived from Alan Pringle by dispatch rider soon afterwards. Priority was given to a Category-A incident, a bomb close to a fire station. The entry point was quickly found in the roadway, and Sergeant James carefully put down the metal probe. As he put the probe to his ear his face told the story.

'Don't tell me,' said Brian glumly.

Sergeant James nodded. 'It's a ticker, sir.'

'Christ, what a welcome back.' He listened too, and reluctantly agreed. 'OK – better get cracking, Sergeant. The sooner we reach it the better. It shouldn't be a long dig in this surface, that's one consolation.'

Back at the safety point, Ken Machin asked, 'What's the technique with a fuse like that, Brian?'

'A Type-17 clockwork? You just hope you're a bit ahead of the clock, that's all . . . Actually, the clock is apt to stop just before it explodes – but then the slightest touch on the bomb sends it up.' He noticed, not without some satisfaction, that some of the enthusiasm had drained from Machin.

The sappers were lucky, and reached the bomb in a little over two hours. It was a 500 kilo, big enough and ugly enough to put the fire station out of action. Approaching the shaft, Brian was relieved to note that he was as cool and collected as ever a man can be under such circumstances. He felt in control, that was the big thing. Obviously his weekend break had done him a lot of good.

Standing isolated at the top of the shaft, Brian told Machin, 'Whatever you do, go carefully down that ladder. I'll lead the way. But for God's sake tread softly. Lesson One is, never leap about near a bomb. OK?'

Machin did it all just right. They crouched by the bomb, and Brian moved a finger gingerly over the fuse boss and read the engraved figures. 'Type-17.' He put his ear against the casing and could still hear the ticking. Then he looked up at Machin. 'Still reckon it's exciting?'

The new man gulped, and almost whispered. 'Can I amend that to – different?'

Brian smiled. Suddenly, he rather liked Ken Machin. 'Right – I'll tell you what I'm going to do.' He ran through the procedure, then added, 'Now, clear out of it. Fast, but carefully. Remember what I said about no leaping around.'

This time everything went according to theory, and quite soon the Section was on its way to Hackney Marshes and the bomb's final demise.

Chapter 4

It continued like that for a whole week – every bomb the Section tackled a textbook case, everything keeping to the theory. In fact the whole Company was having a good run with no casualties for some six weeks. Everyone knew it couldn't last.

Ken Machin was on his last day of watching Brian and was all set to take over a newly formed and badly needed new section when 347 was sent to a Category-A incident only a mile or so from Company HQ. What was obviously a big bomb had landed in a school yard very close to the actual building. From the angle of the entry shaft it had travelled an unknown distance beneath the school. All the sappers could do was to dig and follow the shaft. It might take two or three days, days of mounting tension for everyone during which Brian and Ken could do nothing but watch and wait.

But relief came their way. On the second day a report came in of another bomb. This one was much more straightforward, in the back garden of a house not far from the Bakers'. Taking some of 347's sappers with them, Brian and Ken went off to have a look. Brian put the probe down the hole, listened, and without a word passed it to Ken.

'It's near the surface, at any rate,' he said.

Ken listened, and his face fell. 'Ticking.'

''Fraid so. Corporal Horrocks?'

The big Yorkshireman came to join them. 'Sir?'

'Clockwork fuse, I'm afraid. You know what to do, don't

you? Shouldn't be a long job before you find it. Lieutenant Machin and I are going to fetch the Q-coil.'

'Right, sir. It'll be interesting to see if t'bugger works.'

'It'd better work. Leave you to it, then, Corporal.'

No great problem, given that the coil did what it was supposed to do. The Q was the magnetic clock-stopper that Alan Pringle had mentioned on Brian's first day back off leave. Delivered to 97 Company the day before, no one had had a chance of using it yet. It was a great cumbersome thing, bearing all the signs of a prototype put into hasty production before any refinements could be made, but at least it was a step in the right direction. But nothing was simple when you had to deal with Captain Francis. He demanded chapter and verse on why the Q was needed – where – for how long – who was responsible for it – all the tarradiddle. But at last it was being manhandled on to the truck.

'Any other officers in the whole bloody army,' moaned Brian, 'and there'd've been no question. It's a miracle we didn't have to give Fanny a written application in triplicate, countersigned by the Brigadier.'

The bomb was already part exposed when they got back to the site. Brian decided to wait and deal with it before returning to his chief concern, the incident at the school. Two hours later Corporal Horrocks reported all ready.

'If you're using that thing, sir,' he added, nodding to the Q-coil, 'we've dug it good and wide for you.'

'Thanks. Right, Ken – here we go. And if you value your life, don't drop it.'

Together they began to shift the clock-stopper across the grass. They met the men moving back to the safety point, and Copping said to Brian, 'It's still ticking, sir. Good luck.' The others murmured their agreement.

'They think a lot of you, don't they?' gasped Ken, struggling with his end of the weight.

'My charm.'

'Of course.' And he thought, but did not say, 'The respect you've earned from them, too.'

At the lip of the wide, well-shored shaft, they stopped to get their breath. 'Think we can get it down there without dropping it?' said Brian.

'Got to, haven't we.'

It was an almighty struggle, but they succeeded. 'Lucky this isn't more than a 500 kilo job,' observed Brian. 'I'm told these things aren't so effective against anything bigger. Something to do with magnetic field being weakened by the area of metal.' They struggled again, this time with extreme delicacy and caution, to fit the magnet around the bomb. It was done at last, they switched on, and bang on cue the ticking stopped. The two men grinned at one another and wiped their brows. 'Another triumph for British ingenuity,' commented Ken.

'British muddling through, more like. I mean – look at the thing, will you. Not exactly a streamlined job, is it? Still, it works, that's what matters.'

'Amen to that.'

The words were barely out when they heard an explosion. Not close, but not many miles off, either. Brian looked up sharply, closed his eyes, and breathed, 'Oh no . . . not the school . . .'

Ken looked at him. 'Listen – I know what to do here, now. You get off back there.' Brian hesitated. So he went on, 'That sounded too far off to be your bomb – but even so, that's the big one, isn't it . . . Look chum, I can't spent the whole war crouching in holes watching you work – there's got to be a first one . . .'

'OK. Are you sure?'

'Sure as ever I shall be. Not likely to be any snags on this one now, are there?'

'Not so long as you keep the Q-coil on, until the fuse is out. You're probably right – that might've been too far to be mine going up, but even so . . . Give me three minutes to get clear, then get cracking. Good luck.'

He heaved the canvas bag of tools over, then climbed up the ladder. 'See you later,' he called from the top, and vanished.

Immediately Ken wished he hadn't been so damned brave. It was one thing being down here with a man who'd done it all before, but to be here on your own . . . He felt the well-known urge, stood up, undid his trousers. He could not trust his legs to get him up that ladder so that he could use a convenient tree. Then, unlashing the bag, he began trembling, violently. He stopped work, drew a number of deep, deep breaths. That seemed to help. Slowly, carefully, he withdrew the Crabtree to drain out the juice from the condensers, and began fitting it on the bomb. Afterwards, he had three minutes to wait before he could get to work with the universal key. *No snags*, Brian had said. He kept repeating it to himself to ward off the shakes which kept spurting back into him. *No snags . . . no snags . . .*

Brian drove like a maniac back to the school and let out an audible sigh of relief when he saw the building still as he had left it. He walked as calmly as he could into the safety point. Sergeant James was there, snatching a mug of tea. 'Everything all right, sir?'

'Yes, thanks.' Brian did not mention the explosion they had heard and his thoughts about it. 'Lieutenant Machin is defusing it now.'

'How'd he take it, sir?'

'It was his idea, actually.' The Sergeant nodded his approval.

Wilkins spoke. 'You look like you could do with some char, sir.'

'Thanks, Wilkins. I certainly could. How are the lads doing, Sergeant?'

'Well under the school now. Going to be a real nasty one this. It only needs to be lying awkwardly, and life will be difficult, no mistake.'

Brian thought a second. 'Can we pin-point it, then get at it direct from above . . . from the ground floor of the building?'

'Not happy about that, sir. I wouldn't fancy pick-axing our way through the hardcore and the concrete – might set it off.'

'Just a thought.'

Wilkins handed him the brown tin mug of regulation hot, sweet tea. 'Mind you, sir, if I may say . . . it's my experience that you'll probably find the sodding thing's been bust open. Isn't that right, Sarge – after going down deep as it has?'

Bomb disposal squads were like that. On the job, anyone was by unwritten consent free to chip in ideas. 'True,' Sergeant James agreed. 'Quite possible. In which case, of course, it could turn out quite a—'

He got no further as an explosion roared off, not more than a few streets away. With a sickening certainty, Brian knew where it had come from. He knew that Ken Machin had copped it. 'Oh Jesus Christ . . . no . . .'

The Sergeant spoke quietly. 'Steady, sir. There's nothing you nor anyone else can do . . .'

'That must have been him, mustn't it?'

'Very likely sir, yes. There was no report of any other UXBs in this area. We'll know soon enough. But for now, this is the incident you've got to concentrate on, sir . . . this one here, in this school.'

Wordlessly, Wilkins handed Brian a cigarette and struck a match for him. Brian gratefully drew deep on it, and swallowed more tea. Sergeant James went out of the safety point, as if he was expecting something, or someone. He did not have long to wait. Corporal Horrocks screamed his truck to a standstill, came running and cannoned into him.

'Sarge – did you hear it? Poor bugger – Christ knows what went wrong.' The usually phlegmatic Horrocks was shocked and shaking.

'No other casualties?'

Horrocks shook his head.

Sergeant James gave him a businesslike order. 'All right, Corporal. Get back there, salvage what gear you can, then bring everyone back here. Right?'

'Yeh – yeh – OK.'

It was on the well-tried principle of getting back on the horse that has thrown you.

The Sergeant went back to the safety point. 'I'm afraid you were quite right, sir. No other casualities – only Mr Machin.'

'I shouldn't have left him, should I? By rights, it's me that should be dead, not him.'

'This one was your main priority, sir. You saw him through the worst. You've got nothing to reproach yourself with.'

'He was married, you know.'

'So I understand, sir. Shall we go and see how the tunnel's doing now?' It was the horse thing again. Brian knew it, and smiled up at the burly Sergeant.

'Yep – right,' he said just a little too briskly, swallowed the last of his tea, and went out.

That night Brian, for only the third time in his life, got drunk. Next day there was the Court of Enquiry. Major Luckhurst presided, Captain Francis at his side. Brian, Corporal Horrocks and the rest of the Section who had been at the incident gave evidence. The Court could come to no conclusion, but Major Luckhurst went out of his way to emphasize to Brian that he was in no sense to blame. It was only a small comfort.

The day after, Brian had to go down to Chelsea and tell Ken's wife – widow. He had met her before, when Ken had invited him to dinner with them. She was very young, very blonde, and plainly adored Ken. She was also very brave, taking the news calmly. Brian was shaken to learn that she and Ken had not been married – her parents had put their feet down on that – and that she was expecting a baby. Later he told the Major, who sadly told him that there was nothing in army regulations to cover common-law wives and their children.

'But that's ridiculous, sir.'

'Very possibly – but there's nothing I can do to change it.'

'May I have a collection for her, then?'

'I can see no objection to that,' the Major replied. And immediately tipped in a fiver.

Another twenty-four hours went by before the school bomb was reached. The tunnel Brian crawled along, though a highly professional job with its shoring and roofing, allowed little room for movement. The 500 kilo bomb was resting on an earth platform dug away so that he could get to it more easily. He carried a powerful torch, and saw that the situation was as Sergeant James had reported: the casing had split open with the force of its passage through the asphalt and rocky earth.

That made the job simpler, provided you did not mind slithering around in a scattering of black TNT powder. At least he could get at the fuse with none of that nerve-wracking business of unscrewing the fuse boss. Lying prone, he reached back for the toolbag and up-ended it. He put the torch on the top so that the broad beam fell on to the fuse. It slipped, and he scooped up some earth to bed it down. There was plenty of light, if not much space, and at least it was dry. A good thing he didn't suffer from claustrophobia! Rolling over on his side and drawing his legs up beneath him, he half sat, propping himself against the tunnel wall for support. He wanted both hands free. It was absolutely quiet as he flexed his fingers; he realized for the first time that at least there was no ticking, this was not a clockwork job. Slowly he moved his hands towards the fuse and then stopped, abruptly. Something was funny here. He moved his head slightly, and in the torch-light a glint came from metal where there should have been no metal. He looked more closely, took the torch from its perch and brought it close to the jagged gap in the bomb's casing. He could see a plunger on the end of the fuse. He'd never seen that before. This was something new. He looked at it for several seconds, etching its shape on to his mind. He had been in bomb disposal long enough to know what he had to do – get out of the tunnel and seek advice.

Major Luckhurst listened to Brian's description back in Company HQ. 'A plunger, you say? On the end of the fuse. New one on me.' He rang the Bomb Disposal Directorate, repeated what Brian had told him, gave the address of the school. He was shaking his head as he put the phone down. 'You did quite right to come and report it, Brian. They say it sounds like a ZUS-40 – an anti-withdrawal device. Trouble is, they don't know how to deal with it yet. The backroom people are working on something, apparently, but nothing's been decided.'

Brian whistled. 'So from now on, any bomb we touch . . .'

'Exactly.'

'Do you think that's what got Machin, sir?'

'We'll never know, of course, but yes – you're probably

right. Anyway, they're sending a chap down to confirm. He said he'd be there in half an hour.'

It was a quiet and thoughtful Brian Ash who met the Major from the Directorate. Together they crawled to the bomb, and it needed just one look. 'Yes, that's the 40 all right.'

'So what do we do with it, sir?'

'Nothing. Seal the tunnel up, keep the area evacuated, and leave it.'

They crawled back in silence, and after they had surfaced and were dusting themselves down the Major said, 'You were lucky, there, son. Lucky the bomb had split open.'

'It's a new thing, is it, sir?'

'Don't know how long the Jerries have been using it, of course, but we've known about it for three days, that's all. Suspected it for longer, of course – too many unexplained detonations. You had one yourselves a couple of days ago, did you not?' They were walking across the school yard back to the Major's car. 'One of our chaps found one after a raid on an oil refinery near Swansea. The place was on fire at the time, which I suppose lent a certain urgency to what he did. Anyway he yanked a fuse out, unscrewed the gaine – and then found another gaine among the picrics. How he lived to tell the tale, God knows – must've been a faulty one.'

'How do we treat them?'

'I can only recommend a very long piece of string on every fuse you tackle.'

Brian had been thinking. 'May I ask, sir, why the Directorate didn't warn us?'

Stepping into his car, the Major gave him a level look. Then, 'Morale, son, morale,' he said. 'But don't worry – we're working on it. We'll get it sorted out.'

Brian was left saluting as the car swept off; and fuming at the stupidity of his superiors.

The ways of the upper echelons are mysterious and very self-contained, a fact borne in upon 347 Section nearly a week later. Tension had mounted in the Company over the ZUS. Much string was used, and even the smooth Ivor Rodgers was badly ruffled one day when he reported that a steady tug had resulted immediately in a heavy explosion. Then, as 347 was trundling a defused 250 kilo to its final detonation point on the Marshes, a dispatch rider roared up and handed Brian a signal.

All it said was, '*Proceed with four men, transport* 250 *defused bomb complete with high explosive filling immediately to Bay Tree House, Mickleham, Kent. Contact Dr Gillespie. Rest of Section return to HQ*.' No reason why; no explanation of who Dr Gillespie might be. Just the bald and mysterious order. Still, '*immediately*', it said, and when the army said that it meant not a minute later. The bomb was loaded back on the truck, and they drove as quickly as possible to Company HQ. No one there was any the wiser – they had merely sent the signal on. Maps were dug out, the two thick sandwiches and slice of fruitcake the army was pleased to call haversack rations doled out to each man, and they set off, Wilkins driving, Brian and Sergeant James squeezed alongside him in the cab. Behind in the truck were Copping, Mulley and Powell . . . and the bomb.

Wilkins, from long knowledge, got them out of London. But then their troubles started and there was a great deal of stopping at crossroads and studying of maps. Jolting along the country lanes and marvelling at the sight of trees and open fields and the smell of fresh air, Powell observed, 'Well, I couldn't care less where we're going exactly, but this'll do me. Further out of The Smoke the better, I say.'

'Like – Dundee,' said Mulley.

'Or Melton Mowbray,' added Copping softly. 'That's where my missus is. That's where I want to be.'

Suddenly the three of them were pitched across the truck as it swerved off the road. They had a glimpse of a small white signboard with 'Bay Tree House' in black; then they were rolling up a broad driveway through spacious lawns. Ancient trees dotted the grass, almost bare now with the season. Smoke from a bonfire of leaves curled up from the lawn edge some way off.

'Jesus – will you look at it,' muttered Mulley.

Powell looked hard. 'I don't reckon they blow up bombs, boyo, not here.'

'So much for digging for victory,' intoned Copping.

'Yeh, well, it's one war for the rich and one for us, isn't it?' Powell's tone had an edge to it.

The truck pulled up before the big old house, and Brian jumped down to pull the belltug beside the wide oak door. It was opened by a middle-aged woman in a maid's black dress and spotless apron.

'Good afternoon. I'm Lieutenant Ash – I'm looking for Dr Gillespie. He is expecting me.'

The maid looked at the truck, and did not bat an eyelid. 'I think he's round the back, sir.' Her voice had a soft country burr to it. 'If you go straight round you should find him. By the pigsty, more than likely.'

'Thank you.' Brian returned to the truck and leaned in to the cab. 'He's round by the pigsty, Sergeant.'

Sergeant James, for the moment, did not trust his hearing. 'The pigsty, sir?' he repeated in disbelief.

Brian nodded. 'The pigsty. Hang on here – I'm going to have a look round the back.'

He was halfway along the house frontage, his feet rasping on the neat gravel, when a slim, fair-haired girl in her mid-twenties came round the corner carrying a thick bundle of papers.

'Oh, hello,' she called. 'Thank goodness you've come. My father was getting worried.' She saw the blank look on Brian's face, noted the hesitation in his manner. 'You *are* the bomb disposal people? You *have* brought the bomb?'

'My orders are to report to Dr Gillespie.'

'That's all right. I work for him – I'm his daughter. If you tell your men to drive round into the yard, you'll see the place. My father's there. I'll be back in a bit.' Brian watched her hurry off into the house. Attractive, undeniably, but somehow faintly irritating. Bossy? A touch of the top drawer? He couldn't put his finger on it. With a shrug he waved the truck on and carried on walking.

The yard was large, moss growing between the old flagstones, a shed in one corner. The first thing he saw was an ancient Merryweather boiler outside the shed, a household galvanized tank beside it, and rubber hoses leading from it into the shed. As the truck drew in and switched off, a sound of grinding metal attracted him. He went into the shed, where the noise was coming from, and stopped dead. A tall, very thin man with a mass of greying hair was bent intently over a wooden platform on which was cradled a contraption clamped to a thick metal box. The noise was coming from the contraption, to which led the hoses from the Merryweather outside. The name Heath Robinson sprang to his mind.

The drilling suddenly stopped, and the man muttered, 'Sod.' He turned to go outside, and came face to face with Brian. 'Ah,' he said.

Brian introduced himself, and the man grabbed a rag to clean his hands. 'Marvellous, splendid, glad to see you. I'm David Gillespie.' His handshake was firm and very brisk. 'Hang on – better shut off.'

He dashed out followed by a puzzled Brian, who was just in time to see him closing down the boiler. 'Now . . . may I have a look at it? The bomb. The trouble I've had trying to get hold of a full bomb. Casings, yes – by the hour, day and contract. In the end I threatened to go out and dig up one for myself. That scared them.' He chuckled as he moved through the little group of sappers and heaved himself up to peer over the truck's tailboard.

'Oh yes – excellent. A two-fifty. Just the job. It *is* defused, I take it?'

Sergeant James was the nearest, and replied, 'Yes, sir.'

'Well now – we might be able to get something done, at last.' He jumped down with surprising ease and asked, 'You chaps eaten yet?'

'That's all right, sir. We've got haversack rations.'

'Anyway, let's get the bomb in place first. Is it amatol or TNT filling, do you know, Sergeant?'

For once Sergeant James was at a loss and looked around for Brian who had been inspecting the boiler and was now joining them. Brian had heard the question and came to the rescue. 'I'm sorry – but I honestly don't know. All I've done is to take the fuse out.'

Dr Gillespie dismissed the point. 'Oh well, they're both soluble, aren't they? Right, if you lads can get the bomb into the shed . . .'

Brian nodded to Sergeant James who began organizing the heavy job whilst Brian followed the Doctor into the shed and watched as he began preparing for the new arrival.

Brian was silent for a minute. Then, 'Er . . . you said soluble, sir . . .'

'That's right – I'm going to steam the explosive out. I think that's the only way.' He had a sudden thought. 'Didn't you know the explosive was soluble?'

'Er . . . no, I didn't.'

It was Gillespie's turn for puzzled silence. It lasted just a second or two and then he managed to cover his astonishment. 'Ah.' It was a favoured sound of his.

After a struggle the bomb was nestling on the wooden platform. 'Good – well done,' enthused the Doctor. 'We can have a break now.'

On the nod from Brian, Sergeant James led the men out. Gillespie began examining the bomb, fussing over it.

Brian was uneasy. 'It's a bit near the house, isn't it sir?'

'Hm?'

'If you're going to deal with bombs?'

Nose still close to the casing. '*Defused* bombs.'

'I know that's OK in theory. But we've learned not to trust anything lately.'

'Booby traps, you mean. I'm on the Unexploded Bomb Committee and you're telling me, young man, that I'm an idiot.' Brian stiffened, but Gillespie lifted his face and he was smiling broadly. 'You're quite right, of course. But when we've finished with this one I'm getting a proper place built out in the fields. Very good of your chaps to heave this in for me,' he went off at a tangent. 'Normally I have two men helping me, but the technician's off on a course and the odd-jobber's got 'flu. Do you know, I may be on the Committee but this is the first real live bomb I've seen? With all the red tape that's prevented me seeing one before, I wonder how we're going to win this war, I really do.'

Brian was beginning to like this mildly frantic bundle of energy, and felt he would be quite sorry to leave him. 'Anyway,' he said, 'there it is for you. We'll be on our way.'

Gillespie was suddenly serious and very businesslike. 'Didn't they tell you?'

'Tell us what, sir?'

'To stay. We might have to turn it over . . . all sorts of things. There's a lot of work to be done.'

'I was just detailed to bring the bomb down to you.'

Gillespie threw down the rag he had been rubbing down the casing with. 'Oh, really . . . I told them. I phoned and specifically said . . . Look, can you ring your CO? It'll save me getting on to the Ministry and going through all that palaver.'

'To stay? How long would you want us, sir?'

'Until the job's done, of course. Maybe a day, maybe a couple of days. Who knows?'

Brian was highly doubtful. 'They're so stretched up in London. I really doubt if I'd be allowed to.'

'But the Scientific Research people must have made it clear to your chaps, surely?' Gillespie's tone was one of incredulity and frustration. 'I mean, good God in heaven . . . All right, I admit all I've got is a Merryweather boiler that's long in the tooth. I admit I've got problems with the hoses – but no one else has come up with an answer to the ZUS-40, have they?'

At the name, Brian's attention was doubled. He thought for a second, then said quietly, 'I'll phone my CO, sir.'

Gillespie looked sharply at him. 'You've met it, then.'

'We think it killed one of our men the other day.'

'He wasn't the only one, I'm afraid. You won't have seen one, I take it?'

'No sir.' It was said with the slightest of smiles.

Gillespie moved to a bench and picked up a fuse. 'This is the only known specimen. Someone yanked it out of a bomb down Swansea way – and somehow lived to tell the tale.'

'Yes – I heard about that.'

Quickly Gillespie showed Brian how, by the mere act of

pulling a fuse out, you simply released a spring which shot across and hit a detonator which in turn set off the bomb. 'There are people all over England working on the answer, but it's still a cast-iron killer. As you know only too well.'

Brian studied the fuse. 'Can't you run something down the sides? Glue perhaps? To jam the spring?'

'Trouble is, it's boxed in, usually. I've taken this one to pieces.' He grabbed a pencil and quickly sketched the spring and spring arm with a box around it. 'Believe me, we've tried everything. Susie and I have spent hours filing down bits of metal, but the filings always end up behind the striker, not in front.'

'Some kind of solution that sets after you've poured it in?'

Gillespie smiled, appreciating Brian's mind. 'We tried that too. Take it from me – er – what is your first name?'

'Brian.'

'Take it from me, Brian, we've tried everything. And the only thing that works – in theory, anyway – is what I'm doing. If we can drill through the case, by-passing the fuse, we can steam out the explosive.'

Susan Gillespie hurred into the shed. 'I've just spoken to the factory. They can do another rubber compound, but it'll take a week or two.'

Gillespie groaned. 'Oh, blast. This is Susie, my daughter, by the way.'

Susan nodded the briefest of acknowledgements to Brian. 'We met. What do you want me to do, then, father? Go and see them?'

'No, I'll give them a ring. Susie, be a love and organize something to eat for the army, would you? Perhaps cook can do something?'

'That's all right, sir,' Brian said. 'We've got haversack rations.'

'I know,' smiled Gillespie. 'That's why I thought you'd like something to eat.'

'Very kind of you, sir.' Brian was smiling too as the Doctor led the way out of the shed.

The afternoon sunshine was warm, and the men had sprawled

out on the grass. Powell surveyed the big, mellowed stone house with the ivy heavy around the mullioned windows, and commented, 'Up to our knees in mud we were, this time yesterday.'

Wilkins exhaled loudly and contentedly. 'I could kip 'ere for a hundred bloody years. In fact, when I pack in work I could retire here.'

Copping was staring up at the wash-blue sky, brooding as usual. 'What's the point in fighting a war, anyway?' The peace of their surroundings, broken now only by bouts of cawing from a rookery, made it difficult to believe there was a war on, let alone the nightly mayhem up in London.

'Oh blimey, here we go,' muttered Wilkins.

'I tell you,' persisted Copping. 'They're having us on. For them, it's just a game. Trouble is, once they start a war they don't know how to finish it . . . all they know is winning.'

'You can always lose a war, ye ken,' chipped in Mulley.

'But they'll go on till it's too late, till everyone's dead.'

'Go on, Coppy – tell us about your favourite: life after death.' Wilkins winked vastly at the others.

'You'll find out soon enough,' was all he got in reply.

Mulley whistled. 'Christ – will ye look at this.'

They looked, and watched in awed silence as two white-aproned maids walked towards them from the house. One was grey-haired – the one who had opened the door to Brian's ring – and the other was in her late teens, all life and bright eyes. They carried trays piled high with sandwiches and cakes, and a huge teapot, milk jug, and real cups and saucers.

Dorothy, the grey-haired one, said as she neared them, 'We thought on such a nice day as this a picnic would make a change.'

Amidst general and slightly embarrassed agreement the men took the trays and fell upon the contents.

Dorothy smiled at them then instructed her young help, 'Well . . . come along, Grace.'

Grace had been quite openly giving Mulley the come-on, and withdrew with a final smile to him. Powell caught it. 'Did you see that? You're in there, Gordon boy.'

Mulley said, 'Oh aye,' in flat, disinterested tones. But he found himself comparing Grace to Norma back in London. He hadn't thought of her for a few days. It had seemed to be over, after two fiascos on the trot. She wouldn't want to know him now, bombing or no bombing; so he had resolutely put her out of his mind, letting himself into the house for his batman duties and creeping up to Brian's room as quietly as he could. But suddenly it all came back to him, the shape and feel of her body, how much he fancied her. The others chattered on, but Mulley did not join in.

For Brian, tea was a disturbing time as, with the Doctor returning early to his work, he and Susan sparred. He sensed a certain hostility, and was glad to escape into the shed again. Gillespie was tightening up the clamp holding the drill against the bomb casing, Sergeant James stood watching. The Doctor turned as Brian came in and began speaking as if he had been in full flow, still working. 'The boiler raises the pressure to about twenty-five pounds, you see. There's a small turbine in here that spins round, and through a gear drives this drill.'

Brian took a second or two to adjust his thoughts. 'Then once you've made a hole you can put in the steam pipe.'

'Exactly. Right, Sergeant – the valve, please.'

A hiss of steam filled their ears as Sergeant James turned the valve; but immediately the clamp slipped its way round the bomb.

'Damn and blast,' Gillespie yelled. 'Off, Sergeant. The vibration tends to loosen it – that's a problem I've been meeting consistently.' He caught the look passing between Brian and the Sergeant, and hurried on, 'Oh don't worry – it'll work. I don't think the booby trap will be affected.'

Brian asked quietly, 'Have you been getting many other problems?'

The Doctor was struggling to readjust the clamp. 'Sometimes the drill jams . . . the steam pressure sometimes goes dicky. Teething problems – we'll sort them out, given time . . . Sergeant, I wonder, could you give me a hand here, please?'

Brian was beginning to feel sceptical, and soon asked, 'Do you mind if I make a phone call, sir?'

'No, of course not. Help yourself.'

Deep in thought, Brian made his way back into the house. The phone was in the hallway, and he asked for a London number. Soon he was deep in conversation and did not see Susan coming into the great broad hall from a side room just in time to hear him say, 'It's a bit funny, really sir. There's a mad professor and his daughter . . .' She stopped, frozen, and listened. 'No, I don't see it,' Brian went on. 'It's too big, for a start, and I can't see us shifting it around, not down a shaft. And the thing vibrates and slips around. You'd laugh if you saw it . . . Well that's the point. He wants us to stay here the night . . . Yes. It's Mickleham 405 . . . I'll be here. Thank you, sir. Goodbye.'

He was still replacing the receiver when Susan's voice, cutting and formal, made him start. 'And what was all that about?'

Brian could only grin foolishly.

She came towards him. 'Who's the mad professor, may I ask? And who'd laugh?'

'Look, let me explain . . .'

'If you were talking about my father—'

He was getting impatient. And he was rapidly taking a dislike to this girl. 'I wasn't sent down here just to shift bombs around. I've got very important work in London.'

'Do you know how long my father's been working on that device you find so amusing?' Her eyes were blazing now.

'My job isn't to stand about doing nothing. I have real live bombs to deal with.'

'He's worked on it night and day.'

'I'm sorry if I upset you. Excuse me – we've got to get moving – now.'

'Where are you going?'

'Back to London.'

He admired her spirit, if nothing else. In a funny sort of way, anger rather suited her, too. Suddenly he realized how attractive she was. The donor of the wedding ring she wore was a lucky man. But he went on, 'I've carried out my orders – I've brought the bomb. Now I can go back.'

She moved smoothly and swiftly to the phone and impatiently jiggled the hook. 'The army works for the Government, just remember, Lieutenant Ash. I should hold on, if I were you – that is, if you want to avoid a return journey. Exchange? Get me Whitehall 3434, please.'

She won the point.

Dinner that night – Susan, her father, and Brian – was a difficult meal. There was an atmosphere in the candlelit dining room that even the wine could not dispel. Conversation was jerky, petering out into silences; even Dr Gillespie could not keep it going. To break a pause, he asked Susan, 'Did you ring Stephen today, by the way?'

'No. I spoke to him last night.'

'He must be finding Bletchley pretty bleak. Did he get those socks?'

'I imagine so. He didn't say anything.'

'Hmm. Of course, he'll be home on leave again soon.'

'Yes.' Her tone was just a fraction on the dull side. Brian, assuming it was her husband they were talking about, thought it rather odd.

'What does your husband do?' His question was more to keep the talk going rather than out of any great interest.

'Ministry work. One of the bright boys . . . you know.'

Again the slight lack of enthusiasm. Dr Gillespie looked along the table to her, frowned a little, then took the conversational cue. 'Funny, the way we all end up, isn't it. For instance, what were you doing before you were called up, Brian?'

'I was trying to become a civil engineer – and not getting very far, actually.'

'That's interesting. I worked for a mining company. I patented the pump with them . . . the one that's driven by the Merryweather on this job.' He considered Brian for a moment, then added, 'You know, you're just the sort of chap I need. Someone with practical sense. If I could persuade the Department, how would you feel about working with me?'

Brian could only stare at him, knife and fork suspended.

'I'm serious,' Gillespie continued. 'I think you'd be more valuable to the war effort with me, honestly.'

Susan chipped in, smiling. 'Mr Ash is very busy in London, father.' Brian did not like that, not at all.

'Of course you'd feel it was rather like running away,' Gillespie pressed on. 'But I do assure you it wouldn't be.'

'Would you feel it was like running away?' asked Susan. 'Or would it be missing the excitement that stopped you?'

'I wouldn't say it was exciting,' Brian almost growled.

'But you must get some kind of – what? – thrill? What's it like, working close to a bomb? How do you feel?'

Brian looked her full in the face. 'Tense.'

'Just tense. Isn't it frightening?'

Her father did not care much for her questions. 'Oh, come on, Susie . . .'

'I'm sorry. I just wondered, well, when you tackle your very first bomb for example . . . how do you react?'

Brian gave her a small smile. 'I can tell you that all right. I was sick as a dog.'

Quickly, she lowered her eyes, feeling ashamed of herself.

In the kitchen, the men were finishing supper. Dorothy was heating cocoa, and Mulley was telling the tale of Brian's railway yard bomb.

'. . . so what could he do, but get up there and kick the thing off the wall.'

Young Grace was full of admiration. 'Did he get a medal for it?'

'No, only a burnt uniform.'

When the laughter had died, she added quietly, 'I think he deserved a medal.'

'He'll probably end up with one, love,' Sergeant James assured her, omitting the rider, 'if he survives that long.'

Copping observed, with habitual melancholy, 'He was lucky that time.'

'Take no notice,' Wilkins said, seeing the surprise on the women's faces. 'Old Coppy's a right old Jonah.'

'Jonah sacrificed himself to save people,' Copping quietly corrected him.

'You know your Bible,' Dorothy commented.

'I ought to,' Copping told her, 'I had it for breakfast, dinner and tea.'

Dorothy was reaching up into a cupboard. 'Sergeant – how about a drop of whisky in everyone's cocoa? It wouldn't be breaking any regulations, would it?'

'Well . . . not this once, perhaps. Very kind of you, I'm sure.'

Powell patted his full stomach and watched as the whisky was brought forth. 'Better than being in the army, this, isn't it?'

That night, the quiet kept all the visitors awake for a long time. The bombers droned overhead, but this was not the target area and the guns were all out of earshot up in London. The night sounds consisted instead of an owl screeching, the occasional dog barking in the distance, the passing bombers an almost soothing backdrop. For the men there was the added compensation of beds, and clean white sheets.

Susan Gillespie lay awake in her big double bed for another reason. She felt irritated at herself for being bitchy to Brian Ash, who was after all an inoffensive enough little man doing a tricky and dangerous job; why he should cause this or indeed any other reaction within her she did not know. And she was irritated at Brian for making her feel as she did. Usually she knew just where she stood in life, and she did not like being unsettled. So it was by design that she was late down to breakfast, hoping that Brian would be safely out of the way. The phone rang as she was crossing the hallway, she took the message, and went out into the yard from where she had already heard the Merryweather chuntering away.

In the shed her father and Brian, helped by one of the sappers, were well at work. From an exit hose in the bomb, emulsified TNT was oozing into a puddle on the floor. 'I'm working on an automatic device to keep the pipe up against the filling without the need to hold it as Wilkins is now,' her father was saying.

Brian nodded, intent on the bomb. 'Now all you have to do is keep the cradle from slipping, the drill from jamming . . .'

Gillespie continued for him, grinning. 'And the pipe from

jumping out . . . yes, minor problems. But at least we know it works in principle, don't we? Ugh, this stuff's like rather nasty toffee, isn't it?'

Susan broke in, speaking to Brian. 'There's a Major Luckhurst on the phone. He says it's urgent.'

'That's my Commanding Officer. Excuse me, will you?'

It was still only mid-morning when Brian was standing to attention in Major Luckhurst's office in London. Facing him from behind the desk were a Brigadier and a civilian scientist, asking searching questions on the state of Dr Gillespie's apparatus. Brian answered them truthfully, giving all the snags still to be ironed out. Finally the Brigadier asked him, 'But it does work?'

'Yes sir . . . I suppose you could say it does work – or it could work, given luck.'

'Well, we didn't expect perfection in so short a time.'

The civilian, bulky and untidy, leaned towards the red-tabbed Brigadier, and murmured, 'I think we should give Gillespie another week or two. After all, he himself admits—'

The Brigadier shook his head, crisply. 'No question of that. I have orders from the very top.' He spoke out again, to Brian and to Major Luckhurst, who was standing to one side. 'I'm sure you're both aware of the serious situation in London just now. If we don't find a way round this ZUS-40 booby trap the whole town will grind to a halt and with it a major part of the war effort. The Directorate and the Advisory Council asked myself and Professor Hunter to come and get the facts. We have them now. So which bomb are we going to try first, Major?'

'I think the St Peter's Church one, sir,' answered Major Luckhurst. 'You could call it an A1-plus. It's within thirty yards of the river embankment and the Underground. The trains have stopped of course, and the Tube shelter is closed. It could flood the city, never mind the Tube. And it has two clocks.'

Brian looked sharply across at his unblinking CO. Luckhurst continued, 'Another Section put a clock stopper on the one they found ticking. The other had jammed, probably on impact. Lieutenant Rodgers can't shift the bomb because every time he tries the jammed clock starts ticking.'

The Brigadier had been listening intently, finger on nose. 'Can't be moved . . . can't be blown up on site . . . but got to be dealt with. Dr Gillespie is our only hope, isn't he?' He looked hard at Brian. 'And you, young man, are our sole expert. Don't worry about the apparatus being bulky – we can arrange three-tonner lorries, no problem.'

'Thank you, sir,' gulped Brian, but did not quite know what he was thanking him for.

When put in the mood, even a cumbersome machine like an army can move with alacrity. Soon after lunch an awed Dr Gillespie was standing with Brian and Ivor Rodgers in the debris-strewn crypt of St Peter's, gazing at the huge bomb. Ivor carefully put the brass listening rod against the fuse, the other end to his ear, and nodded in satisfaction.

'She's a bit of a tart, this one. Push her a bit and she'll tick, but leave her alone and she goes all quiet.'

'Not too badly placed to work on, that's something.'

Gillespie spoke for the first time, quietly. 'A pity the stoppers only work on one clock.'

'How long's the other clock been stopped, Ivor?' asked Brian.

'Your guess is as good as mine.'

'But it only ticked a few seconds.'

'Yeh. As far as we know . . .'

'What would you do if it started?' Gillespie asked.

'Run like hell,' replied Rodgers.

They picked their way carefully back out into the open air and walked to the three-ton lorry parked near the safety point.

'I picked this for the safety point because there's three walls between you and the gubbins. Hope that's OK for your stuff?'

'Yes, fine, thanks Ivor.'

Rodgers looked over the tailboard of the lorry at the ancient boiler and the rest of Dr Gillespie's gear. 'If Jerry invades now you can pass yourselves off as roadmenders,' he commented.

'I'll keep your seat warm at the bar. 'Bye, old boy – 'bye, Doctor!'

Gillespie looked nervously at Brian as Rodgers left them. 'For all our sakes, I wish we could have started on something easier, Brian. It's one thing experimenting in my yard . . . something else completely here.'

'Don't worry – we'll make it work.' He damned well *had* to make it work, he knew that. 'Sergeant – get the stuff unloaded. Let's get on with it.' As the men were ordered to work, he turned to Gillespie. 'You realize why you're here, don't you, Doctor? I'm afraid I'm going to need you in there with me, at first, at any rate – to see I get it right.'

'Yes, of course. I wouldn't have it any other way.'

As they moved out of the way they heard Wilkins say, 'Hey, Sarge – Coppy wants to be excused from this job. Says he's not Church of England.'

It was the first time Dr Gillespie had smiled since he had received Brian's phone call in mid-morning telling him he and his machinery were urgently needed.

Unloading the machinery was no easy job and called for a deal of sweat even on a cold late-autumn day, and not a little swearing. But eventually it was done, the lorry driven out of harm's way and the coke boiler lit. Meanwhile Brian, Gillespie and Sergeant James returned to the crypt to clamp the drill on to the bomb casing. Crypts are eerie places at the best of times, but never more so than this one, now, with its debris-littered floor, its 250-kilo parcel of death, and the shadows from the lighting rigged up by Ivor Rodgers. Whilst the Sergeant listened intently for the first renewed ticking from the clock, Brian, with infinite care, fixed the clamp and tightened it. Gillespie checked it, then they went up to the boiler.

'Twenty-four pounds pressure – that's good,' muttered the Doctor. 'I'd say we can make a start now. Brian – can Sergeant James watch the boiler whilst I come down with you?'

'I'd rather you stayed here, Doctor . . . to begin with, anyway.'

Gillespie said quietly, 'I think I should. For your sake.'

Brian admired his guts, but could not take the responsibility.

As tactfully as he could, he replied, 'To be honest, Sergeant James doesn't know much about the boiler, sir. I'd rather you were the one to keep an eye on it.'

He went off with the Sergeant, who stationed himself in the church entrance whilst Brian scrambled gingerly down into the crypt. Alone with the thing, it seemed somehow even more malignant. Brian felt his mouth drying up. He picked up the brass rod and listened for the deadly ticking. Nothing. He hesitated for two, maybe three, seconds; then called out.

'Boiler – switch on!' For all he knew, he might just have pronounced his own death sentence and, as he heard first Sergeant James close at hand and then Corporal Horrocks further away relay the order, he began to feel sick.

He crouched low over the bomb, listening and watching. A rivulet of sweat ran down one temple, another into his eyebrow. The rubber pipe bringing the steam in from the boiler suddenly convulsed and rattled, making him jump. A moment later the crypt was filled with the harsh sound of metal grinding on metal. He listened, ear resting on the bomb, with quick-mounting fever . . . but the bloody drill drowned out everything else. He stood up and pelted across to the crypt doorway.

'Boiler – switch off!'

Again the fading, different-voiced echoes, and after what seemed a lifetime the hellish metallic grinding stopped and the silence of centuries filled the place again. He went back, stooped and listened. Then he sat back on his haunches, closed his eyes and breathed a deep sigh of relief.

He was still sitting when Gillespie hurried down. 'What happened?'

'It's the noise of the drill. I can't tell if the clock's started up or not.'

'If it had jammed on impact you have at least two hours.'

Brian took off his peaked cap, wiped his forehead dry with a sleeve, replaced the cap. 'But we don't know if it did jam on impact, do we. Sometimes they stop only a few seconds before they go off . . . How long do you think this will take?'

'About two hours. I wish we could get some delay.'

'No chance.' He was feeling more sick by the minute. 'Tell

you what, we'll let it drill on its own for ten minutes.'

They went back up just in time to hear Sergeant James arguing with someone. 'I'm sorry,' he was saying, 'but you can't go down there. I don't know who let you through the barrier, but—'

A young woman's voice cut in, equally insistent. 'I've got the cutting bit for my father.'

Gillespie was the first to speak. 'Susie! What on earth are you doing here?'

She held out the cutter. Quite calm, she said, 'You forgot this. The old one's worn out – you'd never've got through with it.'

'Thanks, Susie. Now be a good girl and go back.'

'I'm staying here.'

'Oh no you're not,' said Brian, firmly.

'Who's going to do the notes, then? Time the drilling and the steaming out?'

'This isn't an experiment.'

'The equipment's experimental! If you're going to make regular use of it you'll want to record how it performs, won't you?'

Brian, to himself, conceded that she had a point. Her father compromised. 'Will she be all right behind the safety point, Brian?'

'No idea. I'm not in the insurance business.'

Her tone sweetened. 'That's OK. I don't like insurance.' She smiled at him, and for a second he half smiled back even through his irritation. Then, 'Make sure this lady stays behind the wall, Sergeant. Any trouble, get the police.'

'Sir.'

Brian took the cutting bit from Gillespie. 'Better get this on to the drill, I suppose.' They went back into the crypt.

The cutting bit was changed, and after Susan had counted down the ten minutes drilling Gillespie insisted on going back to check progress. The Doctor's greying hair flopped over his face as he watched Brian apply the listening rod and then say, the relief evident in his voice, 'One thing – if it was ticking it had more than ten seconds to go.'

'So it's likely it jammed on impact.'

'I'd say the odds are favourable. Now – let's see what your drill's done.'

He began to free the clamp, and then Gillespie helped him remove the equipment and peered down on to the casing.

'Oh, Jesus Christ . . .!' It was a groan more than anything.

Brian looked, and saw a shiny ring shape scratched on the bomb's metal casing; but no hole. 'Imperfect steel. We hit a hard bit.'

They sat looking at the marks in despair and did not hear footsteps behind them.

'Dad . . . ?'

Sergeant James hurried down after Susan just as Brian swung round. 'What the bloody hell?'

Gillespie rose and took her arm. 'Susan – come away now.'

Susan, her fair hair tumbling about her face, her slim body taut, was rooted as she stared at the bomb, taking no notice of her father's urging. Then she was aware of Brian glaring at her, and she came to her senses. As Gillespie led her out, Sergeant James explained.

'I'm sorry, sir. She was out of the safety point before I had a chance.'

But Brian wasn't listening. He was staring at the bomb, filled with despair and fear. 'Christ, Sergeant – this is bloody suicidal.'

Sergeant James was kneeling down beside Brian. The two men looked at one another and each knew what the other was thinking . . . two experts who did not need words. They simply exchanged brief nods and looked back again at their enemy.

Gillespie rejoined them. 'I'm so sorry – she doesn't normally behave like that.' No response. 'What will you do now?'

Brian spoke quietly. 'Only one thing we can do. We'll have to shift the bomb over a bit and find a new spot.'

'That means . . . taking off the clock stopper.' Gillespie could feel his throat drying as he spoke.

'Yes.'

'And . . . and how long can you do all that in – before replacing it?'

Brian chose to ignore the question. Instead he said, 'We'll need to dig a shallow trench on the other side of the thing first, Sergeant.'

It was not a job anyone wanted to linger over. In ten minutes the trench was dug and jobs assigned. Brian wedged a crowbar as far as he could under the bomb without disturbing it. Powell and Mulley were drying their hands on the seams of their trousers and crouched ready to shift it. Salt and Sergeant James stood by the huge clockstopper. Everyone was tense and quiet. Brian looked around them all. 'Ready?' Here we go, then. Clockstopper – switch off.'

They could hear Corporal Horrocks shout the order to Copping, and Copping carry it on to Wilkins by the battery switch. At the same time Salt and Sergeant James heaved at the 185-pound stopper, and panted as it came off the casing. Brian shouted, 'Right, you two,' and jammed the crowbar as hard as he could under the bomb. Mulley and Powell shoved with all their strength, boots slipping in the loose debris on the floor, both feeling their muscles straining, both holding their breath with the exertion. 'Come on, you bastard . . .' Brian levered with every ounce of his power. Slowly the great bomb began to move a little bit, then more, until it dropped into the prepared trench having turned ten degrees.

Immediately Sergeant James and Salt lugged the stopper back into place, a split second before Brian had a chance to yell, 'Switch on!' Again the agony of the order going down the line . . . and then, blissfully, a dull clonk as the electrical contact was remade, the job was magnetized again. Brian threw aside the crowbar and picked up the brass listening rod. The others froze as they watched. Slowly Brian relaxed, and the relief from everyone was audible.

They went outside and were met by Gillespie and Susie, questioning looks on their faces. Brian looked as sick as he felt, but conscious of Susie he made an effort to control himself.

'Right,' he said to Sergeant James. 'Now we start over again, from square one.'

Soon the metallic grinding came once again from the crypt as the drill started up. This time everyone stayed in the safety point. Finally Gillespie caught Brian's eye and nodded. 'I think we could have a look now, Brian.'

Susan noted the time, and Brian, her father and Sergeant James went back into the crypt. With the drilling stopped it was absolutely quiet. The Sergeant was the first to reach the brass rod. He grabbed it, put it to the fuse boss as gently as he could within the bounds of speed, and listened.

'OK, sir.'

'That's something, anyway.' Carefully, with no jolting, he began to loosen the bolts on the clamp holding the drill. All the time the Sergeant was listening for the deadly ticking from within the bomb. Then Dr Gillespie helped Brian lift the drill away from the casing . . . and they saw a neat hole glistening against the dull, rough steel. The tall Doctor tossed back his hair and positively beamed at the others.

'Problem number one solved,' commented Brian. 'Let's get the pipe on again.'

Wilkins was beside the boiler shovelling in extra coke, soothed by its gentle hissing, when Corporal Horrocks relayed the order, 'Boiler – switch on!' Sergeant James swiftly turned the valve and did a thumbs-up back to the Corporal.

A few seconds later the pipe into the bomb jerked convulsively as the steam entered it. Brian was kneeling close to it, brass rod to his ear, listening for the clock. After a few seconds the pipe began to rock, steadily at first then more and more quickly.

'Switch off!' Brian's order had an irritated tone in it. Hardly were the words out when the pipe jerked out and sprayed his hand with scalding steam. Brian swore loudly and clutched his hand as the pipe quietened again.

'The bomb, the bloody bomb – keep listening,' Brian gasped. Gillespie grabbed the rod.

'It's all right,' he said. 'Come on – you're getting that hand seen to.' Brian did not protest too much as he was led back to the safety point.

'Tea, sir – hot sweet tea, that's what you need,' diagnosed Wilkins, and poured out a mug. Brian was looking shocked.

'I'll find a chemist,' said Susan and ran to her car.

'Now what the hell do we do?' Brian muttered through the pain.

'We'll manage,' Gillespie reassured him.

'Don't worry about that, sir,' added Sergeant James.

Eventually Susan came panting back. 'Always the way – not a chemist for miles when you need one. Now – let's have a look.'

Gently she began work on Brian's scalded hand. More than once he could not stop himself wincing.

She said, more to keep his mind off the pain than anything else, 'The chemist said not to use tannic acid anymore.'

'Why's that?'

'He said it can cripple the hands and ruin the eyes.'

'We don't want that, do we?'

She looked up at him, and he was smiling at her. She felt embarrassed, and quickly looked down again at her work.

'This is gentian violet and methiolate jelly.'

'Is it, now. You didn't say you were a nurse.'

'I'm not. I just pick things up.'

Silence fell between them. Dr Gillespie came into the safety point. 'Sergeant James has got it to work. He's managed to wedge the steam pipe in.'

Brian snapped, 'What the hell . . . ? He should've waited for me.' Then, more calmly, 'Is it doing all right?'

'As good as ever it will. Stuff's coming out. TNT.'

Sergeant James joined them to be met by Brian saying, 'If you'd killed us all you'd've had me shot.'

A grin spread over the Sergeant's face. 'I took the liberty while you were on sick leave, sir.'

'How long?'

'Steaming out? Twenty minutes, sir.'

'Right.' Brian started to get up.

'Hey – just you wait a minute. I'm not finished yet.' Susan made him sit down again until she had finished and only then allowed him to go back into the crypt.

His bandaged hand resting on his knee, Brian inserted a

stick into the hole in the bomb casing. It touched metal at the far side. 'Well done, sir,' he smiled up at Gillespie.

'Me? Good Lord – it was all you, my boy.' He sniffed at the large puddle of black gooey matter on the floor by the bomb. 'Smells terrible, doesn't it? But by God, the thing works!'

Footsteps coming into the crypt made them look up. Major Luckhurst limped up to them.

'Hello, sir.'

'Good as done, I gather, Brian. Well done – and congratulations, Gillespie. What will you do with this gunge, Brian? Shovel and sandbag it?'

'Yes, sir.'

'Then destroy the case and fuse pockets. I'd better let them know they can start the trains again.'

'What if the fuses should go off, sir? I'm thinking of the Tube trains.'

'Don't worry. It won't do much damage beyond here.' He looked down at the bomb for a minute, hand moving across his mouth. 'That's a hell of a job you've done there, Brian. Believe me, I can appreciate what it must have been like . . . Well, sorry it's such a short visit, but I've got a bomb in Soho to look at. Congratulations again to both of you. And look after that hand, Brian.' He moved towards the crypt entrance, his limping shadow, from the harsh lights, bouncing on the wall. In the doorway he stopped, turned, looked hard at Brian, nodded to himself purposefully as if deciding something, then left.

Gillespie had been watching. 'See that, Brian? It wouldn't surprise me if you get a decoration out of this – I think he just made up his mind.'

'Medal? Me? . . . What about you, then?'

'They don't give civilians medals for bravery.'

'They should. Everyone's involved in this war, aren't they? Not like the last time.'

'Maybe they will, one of these days. Now then – I think our chum here could do with another ten minutes steaming out, don't you?'

'You're the expert.'

Ten minutes it was. Then the piping was finally disconnected and Mulley and Copping began shovelling and sandbagging the gluey mess of TNT off the floor before the fuses were finally extracted. After a few minutes they heard a rumbling from deep below, like the approach of an earthquake, and they both stopped work, listening to it, half afraid. Then Mulley realized. 'It's the Underground, Coppy. No sweat. They've got the trains running again.'

'Oh. I wondered. Had me bothered for a bit.'

'Me too.'

Mulley left, straining with the weight of a filled sandbag. Copping, leaning on his shovel, thought he heard something, and frowned. He looked down at the bomb, knelt and put his ear to it. He was still there when Mulley came back.

'It's ticking,' Copping told him, tension in his voice. Mulley froze in the doorway. 'It is, mate – it's ticking.'

'Come away, then, for God's sake.'

'No – hold on.' Copping picked up the crowbar and wedged it under the bomb.

'What the hell . . . come away, man,' shouted Mulley.

Copping was already heaving on the bar. 'It's all right. If it ticked when it moved, moving it again might stop it.' As he spoke the bomb shifted an inch or two. Quickly he bent down, put his ear to the casing. Mulley had already started up the steps, and he called after him. 'It's OK, Mulley – it's stopped.'

Mulley heard, and cautiously came back. Copping stood looking at him, a shy grin on his face. 'See? It's OK now . . . Funny, I feel good, stopping it. Not scared anymore.' Still smiling, he reached down for the shovel and began work again.

At the safety point, Brian and Sergeant James were having a conference whilst close by Gillespie and Susan were writing up notes. 'We'll have wooden ramps up the steps,' Brian was saying.

'Right, sir. I'll get Powell and Wilkins on that. And shall I get the lorry up to the crypt now?'

'Yes – good idea. We can shift the bomb before they've

finished moving the filling. We can wire round the casing, and if need be the lorry can pull it up the ramp.'

'Very good, sir.' Mulley passed them from behind carrying a filled sandbag to the lorry. 'Get a barrow, can't you, Mulley? Save yourself a lot of sweat.'

'No, there's not enough to bother, Sarge. We'll manage . . . Here, Sarge . . . ?'

'What?'

'Did you hear that train go under, a bit back?'

Gillespie overheard, and looked up from his notes. 'Yes – sounded good, didn't it?'

'Well, Copping said he heard the bomb ticking, then it stopped. After the train.'

Everyone was suddenly alert. 'Did you hear that, sir?' the Sergeant asked of Brian.

'Yes, I did.' Brian was deeply thoughtful, but before he could say anything else he heard – they all heard – the faint growling of another train. The ground at their feet shook a little as Brian, Sergeant James and Gillespie all had the same thought at the same second. Without a word all three began to run as fast as they could towards the church, Brian yelling, 'Copping – get out of there. Copping . . .'

They had not reached halfway when there was an explosion. Instinctively the two soldiers ducked. Dr Gillespie fell with a sharp cry, but Brian took no notice. His attention was on the stairs down into the crypt, and what he would find at the bottom. Slowly, he moved forward, the Sergeant beside him, towards the smoke and thick dust billowing from the doorway.

They choked as they felt their way down the steps and into the crypt, dark now except for the light from the door. They stumbled their way forward. The bomb casing was split wide open now from the force of the detonators going up; lying close to it was the bloody, battered body of Sapper Copping.

It was dusk when Susan saw Brian out to his little MG. He had followed her home, driving painfully with his burnt hand, and she had given him a drink.

'Sorry about your father,' he said.

'Silly when you come to think, isn't it?' she smiled – almost laughed, the first time he had seen her do that. 'All that dangerous work, and he has to break a leg in a fall. Anyway, he'll be home again in a few days.'

'Yes.' He found himself delaying actually getting into the car, reluctant to leave. 'Well . . . perhaps I'll drop in – when he's back.'

'Yes.'

'Good.' He slipped behind the wheel, started the engine. 'And – if ever you're in London, look me up.'

'Yes I will. 'Bye . . .'

She watched him go down the drive. The rooks cawed as they settled in for the night, and the autumn nip made her shiver. She could not work out why, did not particularly want to just now, but she was smiling as she went back into the great old house.

Chapter 5

Salt almost slid into the Section's barrack room. It was a Friday evening, and most of the men were stretched out at ease. For two nights they had been working into the small hours on urgent jobs, and they were glad of the rest. And there was Salt, grinning, trying to hide himself, in his best battledress.

Wilkins spotted him first. 'Bloody hell. Stand to your beds. Room – room – 'shun!'

'Stuff it, will you, Wilkie.'

'Ruddy Guards, now,' Wilkins addressed the room in general. 'Mark my words. Caterham Depot will be like a nursery school.'

The cause of the mickey-taking was the single stripe newly sewn on each of Lance Corporal Salt's arms. Promotion had come out of the blue the previous day and Salt had just been to the Company tailor. 'Thought we might have a jug on it,' he said.

'I'm all for that,' shot back Wilkins, already getting up off his bed. 'Round the Plough?'

'No.' The tone bordered on the scornful. 'Get out of this dump. Up West, where there's a bit of life.'

'Bit o' bombing, an' all,' observed Horrocks in a tone of doom.

It did not deter the hard core, and an hour later Lance Corporal Salt was buying the first round in the warmth and glow of a pub in one of the alleyways connecting St Martin's Lane with Charing Cross Road. Corporal Horrocks had been proved over-gloomy; that night the bombing seemed to be concentrated on the City, to the east. They had hardly settled at the bar before a pair of heavily painted and badly battered pros came up to them.

'Push off, love,' growled Powell amid general assent. He watched them grumble off in further search and added, 'I'd have to be pretty desperate and well tanked before I'd have either of them.'

'If poor old Coppy was here he'd have a fit,' said Mulley. The death of Copping a week ago still bit deep.

Salt finished a long pull at his beer. 'I can just hear him leading off about the evils of the flesh in this corrupt city.'

'He weren't a bad bloke, though,' said Powell.

'Proper moaner,' Wilkins qualified.

Corporal Horrocks blew out a cloud of cigarette smoke. 'He was a bloody good chippy . . . which is more than I could say for some.' It was said straightfaced but he somehow conveyed he was not being entirely serious.

'Thank *you*, Corporal, I'm sure.' The speaker was Sapper Baines, just posted to the Section to replace Copping. He was young, generously built, an outgoing man who had already made his mark.

'Pleasure,' grunted Horrocks.

'Now then, son,' announced Salt. 'I don't know whether they told you, but it's the custom in this unit that the newcomer allus buys second round. Mine's another pint of the best, ta.

Miss – when you're ready.' The last remark was addressed to one of the barmaids, a slim girl with fair hair curling down to her shoulders, mid twenties, an air about her that somehow made her stand out. Salt had been quietly eyeing her since they had come in.

Baines did not quite know whether he was being kidded, but paid up happily enough. The girl flashed a smile at Salt, friendly but with a hint of shyness in it, as she gave him his drink.

'Are we going on, after this?' asked Baines. 'I know a great little pub not far off.'

'You lot can,' announced Salt. 'I like it here.' He was looking at the girl as he spoke.

'Aye, aye . . .' intoned Mulley, following his look.

'Insubordination, that, Mulley. I'll have you,' warned Salt, a flicker of a smile on his face.

'Sorry, Corporal,' grinned the Scots lad.

Horrocks joined in. 'Conduct prejudicial to good order and military discipline, an 'all, Salty.'

'I'd forgotten that one. Ta.'

It was not until two rounds later, with the others talking among themselves or to civvies, that Salt got his chance. The girl had looked across at him several times, but quickly away again as their eyes met. Now she had worked her way down the bar, drying cloth in hand.

Salt nodded towards the pub door as she came opposite him. 'Quiet tonight.'

She smiled, and nodded. 'Makes a change, after some we've had around here.' She put the cloth down, glanced down the bar to check that no one was waiting to be served. 'You boys on your way back to camp, then?'

'Just a welcome night off. We're bomb disposal.'

'Oh 'eck – that's a job and a half, isn't it?'

'It has its moments, aye.'

'You weren't on the job at the Palm Beach across in Soho, were you?'

'No – must've been some other lot. Why – what is it?'

'It was a sort of club – drinks, dancing, floor show. You know. Bit tatty, but not bad, I suppose. They've closed it now, though. Funny that – a bomb doesn't go off, but it can fair wreck a building.'

'Must've been an old one. The building I mean.'

'They all are, around here. I'd worked there for three years, too.'

'Waitress?'

'Dancer.'

'Go on.' There was a slight pause.

'Aye,' she said, more to fill the gap than anything.

'What part of the north are you from, then, love?' The phrases she used, the hint still in her voice, had told him.

She smiled broadly. 'Yorkshire. Bridlington.'

'Manchester, me.'

'Bloody Lancashire.'

'Bloody Yorkshire.'

They grinned at one another across the bar, and suddenly Salt felt happy. He was not a man often given to bursts of happiness.

'What do they call you, love?'

'Michelle. Micky to most folk.'

'What time do you finish here?'

'Closing time – just after.'

'What about a cup o' coffee?'

'Yeh – ta. Meet you outside.'

Next morning, Brian joined Ivor Rodgers and Hamish Leckie at breakfast in the Mess.

Rodgers looked gloomy. 'Sad, sad news, gentlemen!'

Leckie looked up from his *Times*. 'Don't tell us – her husband's coming home on leave.'

'Not as bad as that. But bad enough – it seems the Palm Beach is no more.'

'What was it?' asked Brian.

Ivor shook his head sadly. 'Ah – innocence. A club, old boy – a wicked nightclub, and now felled by that unfeeling monster

A. Hitler Esq. I was nurtured in that hallowed cellar.'

'Did they put up a plaque?' enquired Leckie in the midst of filling in One Down.

Ivor Rodgers ignored it. 'Mona, it was. Took me to her bosom as you might say, gave me my first lessons in the secret arts of the goddess Venus – and taught me more in one single night than I learned in all my years at Cambridge. Dear old Mona. I wonder if she's retired from the fray. She was a bit long in the tooth even in those days.'

'I got my first lesson from a tart in Amiens in 1917,' growled Leckie. 'All I got from it was the clap.'

Rodgers winced. 'Please, Jock . . . your manly but coarse turn of phrase offends me. Pass the marmalade.'

Corporal Mould approached their table with a tray of coffee, eggs and bacon for Brian. There was an envelope on it too, and in best butler fashion he bent down and twisted the tray for Brian to take it before serving him.

'Good morning, sir. A letter for you?'

Brian glanced at the white envelope but did not recognize the writing. The postmark was badly smudged on the stamp. He ripped it open and scanned the brief note. '*Dear Brian – I am coming up to London on Thursday. Any chance of meeting? Daddy sends his regards. Susan* (*Mount*).'

He read it again, and found himself smiling with pleasure. Thursday . . . three days. He ate in thoughtful silence, and when Hamish Leckie left them he cleared his throat. 'Ivor – you know London pretty well, don't you?'

'You might say that . . . some of the more nocturnal aspects, anyway.'

'Only . . . there's a girl, you see. I sort of invited her to look me up if ever she was in London . . . and she is. On Thursday.'

Ivor's eyebrows shot up. 'So . . . you *are* human, and male. Well done, dear boy!'

'One snag – she's married.'

'I should hope so. At your age there's no more dangerous sport than deflowering debutantes. Stick to the married ones. I always do.'

'I thought a show, or something.'

'Well, for a start, they're all shut except for the Windmill, and I wouldn't recommend that. And for a finish, I'd never advise a theatre.'

'No?'

'Think for a minute. If she doesn't go on about Jack Buchanan's figure for the rest of the evening, she may well discuss at length George Bernard Shaw's attitude to middle-class society – and then it's very hard to get her to the boil. How's the overdraft?'

'Not too bad.'

'Then I suggest a champagne cocktail at the Ritz, for a start. Sets the tone nicely, that. She is the sort you can take to the Ritz, I take it?'

Brian did not quite know the sort of girl who got herself taken to the Ritz. 'Er . . . yes. At least I think so.'

Ivor surveyed Brian steadily and lit a cigarette. 'You think so. Perhaps if I knew a little more about her . . . in absolute confidence, of course.'

'She's Dr Gillespie's daughter, actually.'

'Not the bloke who invented that marvellous Heath Robinson contraption?'

'Yes. The Steam Sterilizer.'

'In that case, it's easy. Soften her up at the Ritz, on to dine somewhere – I'll give you a suitable list – then if the omens are good . . .'

'Omens?'

Ivor exhaled deeply. 'Oh brother – problems. Omens – when she's biting . . . laughing, happy, not looking around at other people all the time, not telling that interminable bomb story – then you pick your moment and casually suggest going on somewhere.'

'Yes – but where?'

'A nightclub.'

'Don't you have to be a member?'

'Up to a point.' Ivor was taking his wallet from his pocket and flipping through a wad of membership cards. 'This lot is at your service. Mmmm . . . probably the old Four Hundred's the place. Tell you what – I'll sleep on it and come up with something tomorrow.' He got up to leave.

'Thanks a lot, Ivor. See you.'

Five minutes later Brian was still sitting happily dreaming of Thursday night when Captain Francis passed the table. 'Come along, Mr Ash – there's a war on, you know!'

Brian angrily stubbed out his cigarette as the tall, gaunt figure went out, caught Corporal Mould's eye for a second, and himself went out muttering rude things.

The plan was for the Section to clear a couple of low-category bombs, but that was quickly changed when a Category-A incident was given them. It was in Soho, off their normal track but the unit covering that area was over-burdened. And it proved a nasty one. It had fallen at the tail end of the night's raid into one of the narrow, winding ways that network the area, plumb in the angle of the pavement and the front of a Dickensian silversmith's, and penetrated through the basement flooring. Looking down into the ugly hole with their torches, Sergeant James and Brian quickly saw the reason for its high category: there was a tangle of electric main cables and other public services, very probably a sewer down there somewhere.

'Christ – looks like we've got seven hundred years of London to get through,' muttered Brian.

'And not much space to do it in, either. First thing's to get this place cleared up a bit, I reckon, sir. Few thousand quid's worth lying around, wouldn't you say?'

They swung their torches round the unlit basement. Three big safes were intact but several tall showcases had been knocked over and their contents strewn about. Brian picked up a teapot. 'Yes. Some good stuff here. Get it checked, will you, Sergeant – and all accounted for.' A quick smile passed between them as they both thought of Wilkins but refrained from speaking the name.

The long job of digging began almost immediately, a job complicated now by the maze of cables and pipes. Then, at just after nine o'clock the next morning, Corporal Horrocks and

Tiny Powell suddenly felt their picks meet with none of the usual resistance. A hole some two feet wide opened up beneath their feet. At the same time a thick wave of nauseating gases rushed up to meet them as if released from some confinement.

'Jesus Christ,' swore Horrocks, coughing violently. 'Bloody hell, what a pong.'

Powell, trying not to breathe, shone a torch into the hole. 'Flaming sewer.'

'You can say that again.'

'And there she is – see her?'

A bomb, a big bomb, filled most of the brick-lined sewer and rested in a good six inches of ancient sludge.

Horrocks peered down. 'That's a Hermann, that is. Big bugger, isn't it? Come on, lad – it's officer time!'

Brian and Sergeant James, trying not to retch, carried out their inspection and did not like what they saw. 'We're not going to get it out of there in a hurry, sir.'

'Going to be bloody difficult even reaching it. Sewers . . . Council Surveyor's office, I suppose.'

Sergeant James had a nasty suspicion of what was in Brian's mind. 'Attack it from along the sewer, you mean, sir?'

'I'm afraid it looks like it. Unless you've got any better ideas?'

Two hours later a Council man was opening up a manhole nearly fifty yards from where the bomb lay. 'Don't envy you, guv,' he said gloomily. 'This sewer's not been used for Gawd knows how long.'

'It's either this or letting the thing explode and taking with it about twenty houses, not to mention the main water, gas and electrical supplies for a big slice of central London.'

'I'd let it go up.'

Brian and Sergeant James squeezed down the manhole with torches, fuse mirror and stethoscope. The iron ladder took them down the seventeen feet, and then they were standing in the still, filthy sludge.

'This way,' said Brian, signing with the beam of his torch. His voice echoed along the brick-vaulted tunnel, and they had to stoop slightly as they groped along. Every step seemed to release more stench. They squelched along, rounded a bend, and there it was, seeming bigger than ever in these cramped surroundings.

The good news was that it was not ticking. The bad news was that it was a Type-50 fuse.

'Oh Christ,' breathed Brian as he saw the etched figures.

'I've never seen one of these before, sir.'

'Neither have I. All I know is, don't touch the bomb, not with anything. It can go off with the tap of a pencil. You may be interested to know, by the way, that it's the first fuse the Jerries have designed solely to kill the likes of you and me. At this point we retire and find out how to defuse the sod.'

After Major Luckhurst had spoken to the office of the Divisional Officer, Bomb Disposal, things moved very quickly. By ten the DOBD himself, Captain West, was in the Major's office addressing all the section officers available. He came straight to the point.

'The Type-50 is very much like the other German electrical fuses in design – except that resistances within the interior circuits prevent the current from reaching the condensers until from three to five minutes after the bomb has left the aircraft; sometimes longer. So that wherever it falls it sits there fully armed and very alert. The usual trembler switches are pretty dull by comparison – this one has an extremely sensitive wire-sprung job. The slightest disturbance can activate it.

'The trouble is, it's far too sensitive to be steamed out – and if you try to use the old Crabtree discharger it immediately causes a short circuit and up she goes. I'm sure you all know about some of the casualties we've been having lately. In fact, for a week or two it looked as if the Germans had us over a barrel, but luckily some of the bright boys at the National Physical Laboratory – and Lord Suffolk in particular – have come up with something . . . I believe one of you people has got a Type-50 at the moment?'

He looked around the room and spotted Brian nodding. 'Right – listen carefully, then. This will interest you especially.'

He opened up a neat wooden case and displayed a brass cylinder with a number of rubber pipes. 'This is a liquid discharger. It works on the principle of a salt solution in a mixture of benzole and meths reaching the thing's innards and discharging the condensers.'

Quickly he ran through the method and warned Brian, 'Please be careful. There aren't many of these things in existence, and we lost one in Number Sixteen Company just yesterday.'

Major Luckhurst put it quietly, 'Just the discharger?'

Captain West's voice fell into a mumble, but still everyone caught it. 'Well . . . no . . . not just the discharger. Right,' he added brightly, 'that's it. I'll leave this with you. Thank you, Major.'

He was at the door when Brian managed to grab him. 'Captain West – are you . . . are you not coming . . . to . . .?'

'Sorry, old chap. I've got thirty-five other bombs to look at. Yours seems pretty straightforward from all I've heard.'

With that, he was gone. Ivor Rodgers materialized at Brian's side. 'She'll be proud of you,' he whispered as he went out. Alan Pringle walked out of the room alongside Brian. 'In a sewer, you say?'

'Yes.'

'Mmmm.' He sniffed pointedly. 'Be a good chap, then, and before you rejoin the human race make sure you have a good bath. Lifebuoy soap's the thing, they tell me.' He walked on with a grin.

The Section was not over pleased about being kept on duty. Neither was Brian, particularly, for a tricky job like this one. Fleetingly he had a mental picture of Susan waiting for him tomorrow night in the Ritz bar whilst the Court of Enquiry was busily recording the events leading up to his death; it was a picture he put firmly out of his mind as he spoke in the safety point.

'Two others apart from you and me should be enough, Sergeant.'

'Right, sir. Horrocks and Powell.' They acknowledged their assignment with glum faces and ignored the sympathetic looks from the others.

'We'll need the Merrylees, of course.'

'In the truck, sir.' The Merrylees was the new fuse extractor, descendant of the slightly comic-opera Freddy which Brian had used on his shunting yard incident, by which fuses could be withdrawn from a decent and safe distance.

'Filled sandbags, too. Half a dozen should be enough. And the crowbar – well wrapped in sacking, or something. OK?' He turned to Horrocks and Powell. 'Now – quite apart from anything else, it's very slippery down in the sewer, so be very careful to keep your footing. With this fuse, even the jar of someone falling close to it could set it off.'

'Just one thing, in that case, sir.' Horrocks was frowning.

'Yes, Corporal?'

'If it's as sensitive as that, what do we need the crowbar for?'

Brian put on to his face what he sincerely hoped was a smile. 'Good question. The bomb is so positioned that we're going to have to roll it a bit to get at the fuse.'

'Thank you, sir.' The big Yorkshireman did not quite know what he was saying thank you for; it simply seemed there was nothing else to say. And the way his stomach had suddenly begun churning it would have been well nigh impossible to say much more, anyway.

'Any more questions?' Brian looked at the taut faces. 'Right – let's get going, then.'

'I'll have a mug of char waiting, sir,' Wilkins reassured him.

'Thanks – we'll need it. Be careful about the lights from here, though, Wilkins – ten-to-one the siren will be going soon.'

'Odds on, I'd say, sir.'

The first thing in the sewer was to rig up some lighting. Powell looked at the bomb. It seemed to fill the entire world. 'Jesus – over two thousand pounds, eh . . . ?'

Brian heard him, sensed his mood, and got him working.

'Can you squeeze round it and lay these sandbags to stop it rolling too far?'

'Right.' Powell still had in his mind Brian's warning on how sensitive the fuse was, and tried to make himself as small as possible to avoid touching the bomb.

'Well done, Powell. Right – now to shift it.'

They carefully edged the crowbar beneath it, and eased the pressure on. No jerking, just pound-by-pound increase until all four of them were sweating. After an age, the big Hermann rolled very slightly, not more than a couple of inches but enough to make the fuse boss accessible. The movement was slow, deliberate, like an elephant rolling in the mud.

For a second there was complete silence as they all realized they were still alive. Horrocks coughed. 'Jesus, what a stink around here.'

Then, in the silence, they heard the muffled barking of gunfire from above. Followed immediately by a slower, heavier rumble, and the brick tunnel trembling slightly in the shock wave.

'Siren must've gone whilst we were working, sir.'

'Yes, Sergeant. I was afraid it might. Just have to hope nothing falls close enough to really rock us. Right you two – you can hop off now. Thanks very much.'

'And walk careful,' Sergeant James growled. Horrocks and Powell needed no prompting.

Whilst the Sergeant rigged up the brass cylinder of the liquid discharger from the roof, Brian gingerly fitted a wide rubber tube tightly over the fuse boss and fixed it with a jubilee clip. The tube was connected to the cylinder into which Sergeant James then poured the liquid, and Brian fixed up the bicycle pump which had to serve in the absence of time to design any special tool. He read off the instruction sheet.

'Right. *Pump up the pressure in the container until the liquid rises to the red line on the gauge*. Yes – Captain West warned me about that – for God's sake don't go over the line, he said. Here goes . . .' He pumped away, both men watching the red line.

‘A touch more, sir . . . Whoa! Right on it now.’

‘Good. Where were we . . . oh, yes, paragraph (e). Yes – nothing oozing out anywhere, is there? No leaks? Good. OK – now for it. Turn the tap, will you?’

Sergeant James reached up and turned the tap to ‘On’. For several seconds both men stood tense, not hearing the rumblings from the air raid above them. Then they relaxed.

‘So . . .’ Brian looked back to the duplicated sheet. ‘We now leave it for half an hour, by which time the fuse should be discharged. Good. Time for a cuppa, I reckon.’

‘Motion seconded, sir,’ smiled Sergeant James.

They slithered and lurched their way back down the stinking tunnel, climbed the vertical steel ladder and emerged into a noisy moonlit night. Quite close too was the red glow of a major fire. ‘Oxford Street, I wouldn’t mind betting,’ said Sergeant James.

‘That’s all we need.’

The streets in the cordoned-off area were deserted, but beyond the cordon they could hear footsteps, people calling ‘Goodnight’ as the pubs closed; by now London had grown used to its nightly pounding and at least a vestige of normal life had been resumed as a fatalism spread among the population. *If it’s got my name on it it’ll get me wherever I am* was a much-spoken philosophy.

The urgent bells of a fire engine reached them. ‘Wouldn’t like to be them blokes, hurtling along unlit streets like they do,’ remarked the Sergeant.

Before Brian could reply there came a quick whistling from up above, rapidly growing louder and uglier. Both men dived for the pavement just as the bomb hit and blew up. The ground shook beneath their stomachs; in the sound of the explosion they heard the sharper sounds of breaking glass as the blast rocketed its way around corners, bouncing this way and that. Instinctively both of them listened for a larger, closer explosion from below ground; but nothing came.

‘Hasn’t set ours off, anyway,’ observed Brian, dusting himself down.

'Good night for them, isn't it – moon must be about full, and not a cloud up there. Sitting target.'

As they reached the safety point, Salt was telling the rest of the Section, 'She'll be leaving the pub about now. Got a good mind to nip away and see her home.'

'Smitten, you are, then, Salty,' said Powell.

'What's all that about nipping off, Salt?' Sergeant James demanded. 'You'll do no such thing.'

'Just joking, Sarge.'

'He got this bird, you see,' Baines grinned. 'Works in a pub near here.'

'Never mind that – get the officer and me some tea.'

'All ready,' announced Wilkins, grabbing two big tin mugs.

'Corporals – even Lance Corporals – are supposed to maintain discipline, Salt, not break it,' the Sergeant rubbed in.

Brian could not help himself smiling. Just a few hectic weeks ago he had been on the receiving end of the Sergeant Jameses of this mad world. As the chat ebbed and flowed around the dimly-lit safety point, and the rain boomed and barked outside, he thought about the following night. A thrill of anticipation went through him. He had it all planned, now. Ivor had come up trumps, lent him a card for a nightclub. He and Susan would have a meal, then go on there; afterwards . . . he'd play it by ear. He wondered, was Susan down there in Kent also thinking about tomorrow night?

His thoughts were interrupted by Sergeant James. 'Time, sir?' He was looking at his watch.

'Right.' With a sigh, Brian stood up. Suddenly, with the strain of this one, he felt whacked. The Sergeant noticed the look.

'I'll go, sir. Only a matter of fixing the Merrylees.'

'OK – thanks.' He had an uneasy feeling he should not have said that, but sat down again thankfully. The Sergeant had not been gone thirty seconds when another bomb was heard whistling down nearby. The whistling stopped, there was that split second's silence, then the explosion. The safety point rocked, and they heard the sound of brickwork and masonry collapsing.

'Christ, that was close.' Wilkins dashed out, shouting, 'You OK, Sarge?'

'Yes, I'm all right,' they heard from a short distance.

'Bloody indestructible, that man is,' Powell muttered.

Even so, Sergeant James ran on to the manhole, eager for at least the psychological comfort of a bit of ground above him. At the bomb, he lashed a cord on to the fuse, checked that it was safely coiled over the drum, then made his way back paying out the rest of the cord as he went.

Back again at the safety point, he handed the end of the cord to Brian who took it and said, 'Thanks very much. Right – here goes. Hold your hats.'

Standing in the entrance to the safety point, he tugged gently, taking up the slack. Soon it came tight, and he slightly increased the pull. Down by the bomb, the drum was revolving under the pressure and was in turn working a screwed spindle which loosened the fuse. Ten minutes later he was being watched by Sergeant James as he very, very gently removed the fuse and unscrewed the gaine. The operation, delicate at the best of times, was more so with this Type-50. And their breaths of relief became louder as it was completed and the bomb became an inert lump of metal.

'That's enough for one night,' smiled Brian. 'We'll shift the bomb another time.'

Only later, after he had had a long bath and was in bed trying to sleep through the blitz, did he begin to shake uncontrollably at the memory of Captain West saying how sensitive the Type-50 was, and then him having to roll the bomb.

The air raid sirens were wailing again as Gordon Mulley quietly let himself into the Bakers' house the following night. There was a light coming from behind the closed kitchen door and he knew that Norma would be lurking there. On tiptoe he crept up the stairs and into Brian's room and began checking dressing table drawers to see that the clothing was in order. Then he opened the wardrobe, took the working uniform off the hanger, and sat down on one of the beds.

Sewing was not Mulley's strong point, and he began to concentrate intently. It came as a surprise to hear Norma's silky voice. 'Hello, Gordon – found you at last, then.'

She was standing in the doorway, smiling down at him. He became aware for the first time of gun fire and the droning of the bombers overhead.

'Been avoiding me, haven't you?' she went on, cooing in to the room.

'No.' But he felt himself blushing.

'Putting up a good imitation, then. What's up? Gone off me, have you?'

'Been busy. Oh, damn and blast,' he added as the needle stuck into a finger.

She giggled. 'Not very good at that, are you. Come on – give it here.' She took the jacket from him, and began sewing expertly. 'What is it, anyway?'

'Bomb Disposal badge. Designed for us special by Queen Mary.'

She was impressed. 'Oh – that's an honour, isn't it? Just fancy. Like giving you all a medal, isn't it?'

It was on in two minutes, then she said, 'You got one, too?'

' 'Course.'

'Got it with you? I'll put yours on too.'

'No – it's OK, ta.'

'Don't be daft. You want it put on properly, don't you?'

He gave in, brought the badge from his pocket and took off his jacket. Whilst she sewed the badge on to the bottom of the sleeve, he polished Brian's boots. Once again he felt himself becoming conscious of Norma's figure, and of the sight he must be making in the cursed army issue collarless shirt and broad braces. Soon she held the jacket up for his approval.

'That looks very smart, Gordon. You should be proud of that.'

'Yes. Thanks very much.'

She sat back on the bed, supporting herself with her arms stretched behind her. She knew how to make the best of an already pretty sensational figure. 'So – why have you been avoiding me?'

'I told you – I haven't.'

She didn't press the point, but smiled at him. 'I missed you. Honest.'

He had finished the boots, and stood looking down at her. His throat was going dry at the sight. She said, 'Why don't you sit down here and give me a kiss . . . Come on. We won't be interrupted this time. Mum and Dad are in the shelter, and Brian's gone out, hasn't he?'

He sat beside her and they kissed. Then she sighed dreamily and lay across the bed, smiling up at him, a finger tracing around his pale face. 'I really do fancy you, Gordon. Do you know that? Even when there hasn't been a blitz on, I've been thinking about you . . . True . . . I've even been a good girl, for you.' Gently she pulled him down beside her. They kissed again, wildly, and as his hands felt for her he felt hers reaching for him. 'Oh yes, Gordon, love,' she whispered. 'That's it – you fancy me too, don't you. Come on then . . .'

In Soho, soon after eleven that night, Salt was in the tiny kitchen of Michelle's two-roomed flat on the third floor, concocting a fry-up out of not very much. He had been to her pub and she had suggested they came back here.

'Don't you get scared, living here alone? The bombing and that?'

She came in from the sitting/dining room where she had been laying the table. 'Sometimes. I go down to the ground floor front if it gets bad – and if Molly doesn't have a gentleman client . . . Here, that smells good.'

'My trade, isn't it, love . . . I went to sea as a cook when I was fifteen.'

'Get away.'

'South American run. Packed it in when I got married – the missus wasn't having me out of her sight. Gasworks, after that.' He turned to reach for a plate, caught sight of her, and froze for a second. She had changed from her blouse and skirt and was in a green dressing gown, the thin material tied close around her slim waist. She met his look and smiled a little. He smiled back. They understood one another, knew exactly what would happen a little later.

'Married, then,' she said.

'And two kids!'

'Oh.'

He busied himself dishing up. 'They're supposed to be out of harm's way in Cheshire, but she's going on about getting back to Manchester. I keep writing her, the Jerries'll bomb around there sure as eggs are eggs, but she still keeps on. Right – grub up.'

Over the meal they chatted brightly of old times, her hopes of a dancing job at the Windmill, his more comic adventures in the army. He was opening the third bottle of beer when she suddenly said, quite seriously, 'You – you will take care, won't you, Salty? I mean, messing around with bombs like you do. You're a lovely man, you are.'

They smiled at one another, then he reached out for her. 'Come here, then.' She snuggled up to him on the rather tatty little sofa, and he kissed her. She responded, long and furiously. Then they separated and looked at one another, still close; she made no resistance as he began to loosen her dressing gown.

'It'd – it'd be more comfy on the bed, eh?' he said.

'Just what I was thinking.'

Later still, around two o'clock in the morning, Brian Ash and Susan Mount were dancing close on the minuscule floor of the Four Hundred Club. The evening had gone according to plan from the beginning. They had met in the Ritz bar, gone to a quiet place for a meal, and had been here for a couple of hours. It was dimly lit, the tables discreet, the band low. Most men were in officer's uniform – army, one or two RAF fighter pilots with the top buttons of their tunics left undone, Free French, Polish, Czech. Dancing was more a matter of holding close and swaying gently, and Brian had long since discovered that he liked it that way with Susan, cheek to cheek, feeling the curves of her body along his.

The band reached the end of a number, and they walked hand in hand back to their small table with its red-shaded light. He poured another brandy and soda.

'What are you laughing at?' he asked as a wry smile spread over her face.

'I was just thinking what a world we live in. I mean – here you are, scrumping around in a sewer one day, here the next. What did you want to do, before you joined the army?'

'Build a bridge, mostly. And drive a racing car – beat the lap record at Brooklands. Seems a long, long time ago.' They were facing one another across the table, glasses held before them in hands propped on elbows, heads close in a thrilling intimacy. 'You're lucky – you're doing what you want to do, anyway. I mean . . . you got married.'

'Yes.' The flatness in her tone made him look at her.

'He's in a hush-hush job, isn't he?'

Again that tone. 'So hush-hush you can hardly hear it ticking . . . like our marriage.'

'I'm . . . I'm sorry.'

She smiled at him again, stretched out a hand and ran a finger gently back and forth over his fist. 'Would you like to hear about it?'

'Only if you want to tell me.' The band began another tune, couples left the tables around them for the floor, but they were lost in one another.

She nodded. 'It's the old story, I suppose. I was far too young. I still don't know why we did get married. He was nice, and clever, and had blue and purposeful eyes. He was the best of the bunch at Cambridge, or so I thought. It seemed we complemented each other, you know? And the war was obviously coming – *and* my father objected. Not to Stephen – he liked him. But to our youth – and the times. So – for all the best and wrong reasons, I suddenly found myself in an hotel in Venice, on my honeymoon. Disaster. I for one was an innocent, completely at sea. We were absolutely hopeless in bed. God, I'm being rotten to him, aren't I? – it was probably my fault as much as his. But . . . from that first day to this, a pall of doom has hung over us. It's never lifted, not for one single day.' She looked straight into Brian's eyes, smiled, and squeezed his hand. 'And now I'd like to dance again, please . . . with you.'

It was nearly four o'clock when Brian pulled up outside her aunt's flat in Kensington where Susan and her father were staying. 'I hope I can keep awake for this damned UXB Committee tomorrow – or later this morning, I should say,' Susan said as she climbed out of the car.

Brian was already out and holding the door open for her. Then they were in each other's arms, oblivious of the planes throbbing overhead, not even noticing the air raid Warden patrolling past them.

She gave him a final hug and kiss. 'Thanks for a lovely evening, Brian.'

'No – thank *you*. I – I hope you'll come out again.'

'Yes please.'

She ran into the doorway of the flats, and turned to wave as he got back into the car and drove off. She watched the car disappearing, wistful but happy.

Chapter 6

Early the next week Brian was called into Major Luckhurst's office. The CO was smiling through the tiredness in his eyes and face.

'Two things, Brian. Number One – this weekend, your Section is on leave. All right?'

'That's great sir, yes. I was going to ask you about it as a matter of fact. The men are very tired.'

'They've earned it. I'm afraid one of them will have to stay behind to look after the billet, but that's all – he won't be expected to work. I'm sure you can come to some amicable arrangement about that. The other thing is confidential for the moment.'

'Sir?'

'Yes.' He picked up his spectacles from the desk, fiddled with them. 'You'll remember that first steaming-out operation of yours – in the crypt of that church?'

Brian smiled quickly, then as suddenly fell serious. 'I remember that one well enough, sir. We lost Copping on it.'

The Major nodded gravely. 'I've recommended you for a decoration for it, Brian.'

'A medal? Me?'

'An MBE.'

Brian was shaken rigid. 'Well . . . what can I say? Thank you very much, sir.'

Luckhurst waved the thanks away. 'You've done some very good work, Brian – and you were the very first to steam out a bomb. No one knew for certain what would happen. But I ask you to keep it to yourself – if you can' – here he smiled – 'because just now it's only a recommendation. As you know, x-number decorations are allocated per Brigade or whatever, so I wouldn't say it's in the bag. We might be over-subscribed as it were. And it might be a bit awkward if nothing was to come of it, especially for you.'

'I understand, sir.'

'But I wanted to tell you so you wouldn't feel your work has gone unrecognized.'

Brian left the office and was plunged straight into the harsh realities of the times and the job. He managed to scribble a note to Susan that day whilst waiting in a safety point, mentioning only the weekend leave and asking if there was any chance of a meeting; but the rest of the time was so full, day and night, that he hardly gave the possibility of an MBE a single thought. Friday came before he realized that Susan had not replied, and the realization made him think he was in for a pretty gloomy weekend.

So he was not in the happiest of moods when he joined the rest of the Section in the local pub for a celebration drink on Friday evening. The lads were busily working out how long their journeys would allow in bed with their wives (taking into account adequate time off for the consumption of well-loved local ales); Horrocks was going back to Sheffield, the general opinion being that his chief object was not so much to see his mother as to see his pigeons; Baines was looking forward to sitting in again on the drums with the jazz group back in deepest Essex, and trying to make it with his girl friend; Mulley was going all the way up to Dundee, knowing that no sooner there than he would have to start back but at least having a lungful of real Scottish air; Wilkins, his mother and sister safely in Bristol, was staying with a mate in Wapping and hoping to get down to some serious wheeling and dealing.

'What are your plans, sir?' asked Sergeant James.

'Sleep, mostly. Visit my aunt in Surrey, relax – back on Sunday night refreshed. What about you, Sergeant?'

'Like you, sir – quiet. Home to Bedford, bit of mother's home cooking.'

'I always thought you were married.'

'No, sir. I've had my moments, I won't deny, nearly did get married once – no, twice – but well . . . you know how it is.'

Powell passed a fresh pint to Brian. 'You'll pardon the liberty, sir.'

'No liberty, believe me. Very kind – cheers.'

'Cheers, sir.' Brian turned to talk to Baines and a couple of the others, and Powell spoke to Sergeant James. 'It's old Salty I'm sorry for – drawing the short straw and having to stay behind.'

'He'll be all right. Hasn't he got this girl in tow?'

'Oh surely – he'll not be a hermit. But he's a worried man, is Salty.'

'Why?'

'Didn't you know? His wife's taken the kids back to Manchester. Said they couldn't stand the country life any more. He got a letter last Saturday.'

'She needs her head examining.'

As the Sergeant took a deep draught of his bitter the landlord called out, 'Gentlemen – the air raid has just sounded, if any of you wish to get off home.'

Only three people moved to the door – a sparse, grey-haired woman in a years-old heavy coat who had been in for her nightly Guinness, and a middle-aged couple who bumped into Brian as they passed. The contact made him look up from his talk with Baines – and there, just inside the curtained doorway, was Susan.

She was looking anxiously around the crowded bar, and they saw one another at the same second. She flashed a beaming smile at him, her eyes suddenly alive, and waved. Brian excused himself and hurried across.

'Susie! What are you doing here? I'd given up.'

'I'm sorry, Brian. I couldn't answer your letter, and the phone's been off. Only reconnected last night.'

'I tried to phone twice this morning. But I got your father both times, and I rather lost my nerve. Just put the receiver down on him as soon as he answered, I'm afraid. We don't want him to think I'm chasing his married daughter.'

'Well – aren't you?' It was said with an almost purring smile that sent a thrill through him. 'We must work out a code.'

'I'll work on it. Anyway, how did you know where to find me? You didn't come all this way on the off-chance, surely?'

'You said you were off this weekend, so I went to your billet and the landlady said try the Plough.'

'Well, it's marvellous to see you.'

'You too.'

'What shall we do? I have no special plans. Dinner?'

'Lovely.'

'Good. I take it you're staying with that aunt in Kensington?'

There was the shortest pause before she said, 'No, it's locked up. She must be away. I have friends I can stay with, though. I'll find somewhere.'

Possibilities began to dawn upon him. 'When do you have to be back?'

She shrugged, non-committally. 'Monday morning. You?'

'Sunday evening. Oh God, I'm sorry, I haven't even got you a drink.'

'Must we stay here? I can feel the eyes of your entire Section burning into my neck.'

'They're all on orders Monday morning, in that case,' he grinned. 'Hang on – I'd better just say goodbye.'

The first distant gunfire could be heard as they left the pub. 'Up by car, are you?' he asked.

'Yes. Over here.'

She led him to where her car was parked. He was thinking furiously. When they reached it he said, not at all sure of himself, 'It's – it's a bit early for dinner, isn't it? Look, Susie ... about tonight ...'

'Yes?'

'What did you tell your father?'

'I said I was staying with a friend.'

'So he's not worried.'

She smiled quietly at him as she shook her head.

'That's marvellous, then,' he ploughed on, beginning to feel dry in the throat. 'We – er – we might just go off and – find somewhere.'

'Yes. Why not.'

'You ... you know what I mean ...? It's up to you.'

She began to feel a little nervous herself now, and laughed to cover it. 'No – it's up to *you*.'

'In that case – let's do it, then! Only thing is – where?'

'Don't you know anywhere?' There was a hint of mischief in her voice.

'No,' he frowned, and then added hastily, 'Not around here, anyway. I know – follow me back to Company HQ, will you?'

He turned to walk to his own car, and she called out, 'Company HQ? We're not staying *there*, for heaven's sake?'

'Not likely.'

Ivor Rodgers was Orderly Officer, and once again delivered the goods. 'The Gladstone Hotel in Bromley, old lad, Just the place.'

'*Bromley?*'

'What's wrong with Bromley? Very romantic – in its way. And you won't be seeing that much of it, will you?'

Susan lifted her bag into Brian's car, and he announced they were going back to his billet to pick up his sponge bag.

'Oh Brian, really – do you have to? Use mine.' The intimacy of the idea excited him as, in something of a happy daze, they began the blackout drive to Bromley.

The Gladstone Hotel was not inspiring: two Victorian houses knocked into one, broken stone steps up to the forbidding front door, heavy façade and peeling whitish paint; the clientele consisted of harassed commercial travellers in creased suits, anxiously making up their daily reports over the jam tart and custard, and old ladies whiling away their last days with crochet and Sunday visits from middle-aged nephews. A slammed door caused eyebrows to be raised; the thinnest laughter was disapprovingly commented upon. But for all that, when Brian and Susie came up from dinner and nervous lingering over coffee in the lounge, room seven might have been the Ritz.

She stood by the ancient dressing table whilst he closed the door. 'Just think – no one in the whole world knows we're here.'

'Except Ivor Rodgers. Pretty awful room.'

'It's fine.' She stretched out her hands to him. 'Kiss me?'

He did so, gently at first, then with gathering urgency. He began to fumble with the zip of her dress, but she quietly restrained him.

'I'm not used to this.'

'Sorry. Look – I'll push off for a bit, shall I?'

'No – don't go. It's the same for both of us.'

'Well . . . at least let's have some heat, shall we?'

'Yes – it really is cold. Have you any shillings?'

'Er . . . yes. OK. Thanks.' The coin clanked into the meter, he put a match to the elements, they plopped and began to turn red as the flames warmed them. 'That's a bit more like it. And let's turn this ghastly light off. We can see by the fire.'

'And the moon.' She waited until the room was in darkness, then drew back the curtains.

'We should keep those closed, you know.' It was the professional bomb man talking.

'Brian Ash – you have no romance in you.'

'Just wait and see,' he grinned, moving to her side as she looked out over the moonlit suburbia outside.

They stood, his arm around her waist as she looked at the clear sky. The throbbing of German bombers and the far-distant anti aircraft barrage were the only sounds. 'Those poor people in London,' she said softly. 'Just the thought of them makes me feel guilty.'

'Then don't think about them, Sue.' She shook her head, briefly and quickly, as if jettisoning the thought. He went on, more businesslike: 'All we have to worry about is, we might get an odd stray bomb . . . as punishment.'

'Do we deserve it?' she asked quickly.

'No.' His reply was firm. 'Well . . . ready?'

She made a noise of assent.

'Er – which side do you prefer?' he asked.

She pointed to the side of the high double bed nearer to her. 'This – if that's all right with you?'

'Fine.'

Suddenly there was a certain tension in the room. She opened her small suitcase. Brian caught a glimpse of a jumper, skirt, a spongebag. No nightdress. He lay on his side of the bed, watched whilst she began undressing. In her slip she put a foot on a chair and unrolled her stockings. Then she turned shyly as she drew the white slip over her head, and he saw briefly what a beautiful body she had, the slim waist, flat stomach, the exciting set of her legs, the breasts neither too big nor too small. Almost before the slip was on the chair she was into her street coat and moving to the cracked washbasin.

As she cleaned her teeth, he began undressing, la-la-ing an attempt at a tune. Then, still in his vest and underpants, he used her toothbrush, sensing more than hearing her taking off the last of her clothes and slipping into the bed. He turned as he dried his face and saw her sitting up with the blankets pulled up before her. She was watching him, smiling. 'I'm so glad we're here, Brian, I mean it. Come on – hurry up.'

She lay down and opened her arms to him as he slipped in beside her. Their lovemaking was gentle at first and led to a tremendous peak. Afterwards they were still and quiet for a long time in the faint glow of the gas fire. Then she sighed deeply. 'I really, honestly, didn't know it could be like that!' They turned on their sides, and kissed. 'Tell me something – was it the first time?'

'To be honest – no. Not quite. There was a rather big and very strong girl called Ruth – when I was seventeen. In the car park after a golf club dance. We'd both had rather a lot of cider.'

'What did you think the very first time you saw me? Did you love me then?'

'No – I thought you were rather boringly bossy.'

'I loved you.'

'You were decidedly frosty, I remember.'

'Fighting my instincts, probably. I didn't want to cheat on Stephen. Honestly – I'm not that sort of girl.'

'I know you're not, darling!'

Next morning just before lunch they were stretched out resting after a long and joyous walk through the damp and bare-tree'd woods.

'What shall we do after we've eaten?' she asked.

'Give you two guesses.'

'Is it good for you on a full stomach?'

'I'll get some indigestion tablets,' he smiled.

'Oh, Brian – I do love you.'

He propped himself up on one elbow and smiled down at her for a long time. 'Good,' he said, and bent to kiss her.

There was a knock on the door. Instinctively they both shot up off the bed. 'Come in.'

Mrs Dollery, the ancient, aproned lady running the Gladstone whilst her son was in the army, came in. 'Sorry to disturb you, my dears, but there's a Mr Rodgers on the phone asking for Mr Ash. He says it's urgent.'

'Oh hell. Right, Mrs Dollery, thanks. I'll come down and talk to him.' He turned to Susan, but her face was all dismay, anger, fright, and the words froze in his mind. He could only bite his lip and follow the wheezing Mrs Dollery as he negotiated the steep staircase down into the hall.

Ten minutes later he was in his car, the engine ticking over. Susan, coatless in the cold, was bending into the window. 'Let me come with you, Brian,' she pleaded.

'Believe me, I wish you could. But you know, don't you, sweetheart – you know you can't. It's just our bad luck that so many UXBs were dropped last night and so few people to deal with them.'

'When will you be back?'

'Tonight, almost sure. Could even be earlier. The one they've got for us isn't too tricky a job, from what Ivor said.' He refrained from telling her that Ivor had also said there had been two bombs very close; one had just exploded, killing half the Section working on it.

'You will ring me?'

'Promise.'

'Several times?'

'I'll give you a running commentary.'

She smiled at last, faintly, and kissed him through the window. 'Take care, darling.'

As she waved him off down the road her stomach was churning with the fear that something terrible would go wrong and she would not see him again. In that moment, she knew finally and definitely that for the first time she was in love.

Finding his unsignposted way from Bromley in Kent to Braintree in Essex gave Brian something else to think about than the job before him, but he too had a nasty feeling about it. Luck, he knew, had been very much on his side in the two months he had been in bomb disposal.

As he crossed East London he found three diversions: one from bomb damage and two from unexploded bombs. He was actually glad when at last he found the railway level-crossing he was looking for. A keen, damp wind met him when he got out of the car and ground his cigarette into the asphalt as he looked around. Sergeant James came towards him from the scattered and moving crowd of khaki with its occasional blue-clad policeman, and saluted.

Brian returned the salute. 'Good afternoon, Sergeant. So much for everyone else going on leave, eh? How many of our lads did you manage to round up?'

'Everyone but Corporal Horrocks and Corporal Salt, sir.'

'Really? That was a bit of luck.' They were walking towards the incident.

'The fact is, sir, it developed into quite a party after you and the young lady left last night. No one was in a fit state to travel home.'

'I hope they're all right now.'

A smile flitted across the Sergeant's face. 'I can only speak personally, sir, but I've found the keen air clears the head very quickly.'

He brought Brian up to date with the situation as they walked down the track. The OC of the Section originally on the job, Lieutenant Symes, was sitting on the steps of the signal box, his head in his hands. In his thirties, he had a bushy moustache; just now his face was showing all the signs of deep shock. After introductions, Brian said as gently as he could, 'Right – shall we get started?'

Symes looked up at him, still dazed after the loss of half his Section. 'What?'

'My men are waiting.'

Symes seemed to pull himself together, conscious perhaps of the two pips he wore on each shoulder against Brian's one. 'Yes – for my orders. Why did they bother to call you out?'

'It's my section. I'm in charge now.'

'Like hell you are.' He shouted angrily to Sergeant James. 'Sergeant! Get your men down the track and tell them to start digging.'

Sergeant James hesitated, looked at Brian for guidance. Brian, understanding the situation, nodded, and the Sergeant hurried to organize things.

The entry point of the remaining bomb was quite near the crater where the first had been, and the probe showed it to be only four feet down. Wilkins and Powell began digging whilst the two officers went to the safety point for a mug of tea. Conversation was one-sided, Symes not saying very much beyond grunts and one-syllable replies. Eventually he remarked acidly, 'Your men are taking their time.'

Brian ignored him and glanced down at his watch. 'Do you know if there's a phone around here?'

'Down the road. Out of order.'

Lieutenant Symes was chain-smoking, fidgeting, his eyes darting everywhere. Brian said, 'Look, you've had a hell of a day. I can handle this . . .'

Before Symes could reply, Sergeant James was shouting, 'We've found it, sir.'

They quickly went out to the shallow shaft. Sergeant James greeted them with the bad news. 'Two fuses, sir – 17A and a 50.'

Symes knelt down to examine them whilst Brian listened through a stethoscope. 'Ticking.'

Symes looked up sharply at the word, a wild look in his eyes. To Sergeant James he rapped out, 'Get the clockstopper run out.' The Sergeant hesitated, knowing it to be the wrong order, but Symes barked at him, 'Get a bloody move on!'

'And the liquid discharger, Sergeant,' Brian added quietly.

Sergeant James shouted orders whilst Symes said to Brian, 'There's no time for the discharger. We've got to stop the clock.'

'Look – we've got to fix the 50, first.'

'You want us all to be blown to bits, don't you?'

'We will be blown to bits if you put the clockstopper on. Surely to God you know that?'

Symes gritted his teeth. 'Listen, Ash, or whatever your name is. It'll take you half an hour to immunize that 50 – when the 17 could go up at any moment.'

'That's a risk we just have to take, isn't it?'

Symes looked at Brian with something not far off outright hatred. During the pause the gear arrived. 'Sergeant – tell your men to put on the clockstopper or I'll have you put under arrest.'

Brian bit his lip. This was getting ugly. If he bowed to authority and let the shell-shocked Symes have his way, there most certainly would be more casualties. He decided to play it quietly, and waved Sergeant James aside, at the same time speaking to Baines with the discharger. 'Over here, Baines. Help me assemble it, Sergeant.'

Symes finally went over the top. He grabbed Brian by the arm, seething with anger. 'Look – I gave an order . . .'

Brian became angry, and shook him off. 'Get out of the way, will you? Get back to the safety point, you bloody idiot!'

'It's my bomb.'

'And my men's lives at risk. Now bugger off – we're wasting time.'

Symes went white and started trembling. 'I'll have you court martialled – the lot of you.'

Once again Brian ignored him, busying himself with the discharger. 'All right, Sergeant, I can manage now. Get the men back to the safety point. And take Lieutenant Symes with you, please.'

As Brian worked on, Symes could only watch him, barely able to contain himself. He showed no signs of leaving. Sergeant James prompted him. 'This way, sir.' The shocked Lieutenant looked up at him, hesitated, got up and walked away, muttering, 'I'll be reporting the lot of you.'

Knowing only too well that the 17A fuse was still ticking its – and very possibly his – life away, Brian set up the liquid discharger as fast as he could. Not that he could do that very quickly, for the 50 fuse was ultra-sensitive and the slightest knock against the bomb could set it off. It was the kind of situation you never got used to. You knew that, if the worst happened, one second you would be a living, breathing thing, the next there would be no single trace of you. No pain, no warning, just instant oblivion. Something deep inside the human soul, some instinct for survival perhaps, or a terror of death no matter how easily it came, made every bomb disposal man sweat at moments like these. Brian was no exception: he knew as sure as night follows day that afterwards – if there was to be an afterwards – he would be sick as a dog.

Luck was still with him – so far, at least. The liquid was

safely pumped in and he retired for the half-hour wait whilst it did its job. Symes pointedly ignored him at the safety point, just sat there quietly smouldering. Brian wondered what Susan was doing. For sure she would be worried sick that he had not rung. That was no fault of his, but the last thing he wanted was to worry her. The thought made him realize something, and the realization made him smile and shake his head. Wilkins, at that moment refilling his mug, caught the smile and gave him a puzzled look. He could not know that Brian had just thought to himself, 'Ash, you are thinking like a man in love . . . and by Christ, that's exactly what you are.'

He checked his watch, saw the thirty minutes was up. 'OK, Sergeant?' he asked. He pulled gently on the cord of the Merrylees extractor until the Sergeant said, 'Feels about right, sir.' Then the two of them went back to the bomb and Brian carefully withdrew the fuse, unscrewed the gaine. 'Right – clockstopper now.'

At last they could work quickly. The heavy gear was hauled into position and Sergeant James shouted the switch-on order. The familiar and comforting clunk came as the magnet came into operation, and Brian put the stethoscope to the bomb casing. Silence. Blissful silence. He breathed a deep sigh of relief. Luck was still with him! 'OK – get the discharger off. But keep the stopper on.'

Sergeant James yelled orders back to the safety point, and Brian walked back already feeling sick. He was just in time to see Lieutenant Symes walking away to his car, and a stranger with a Major's crown on his shoulders coming towards him.

'Lieutenant Ash? Major Pullar – Roger's Company Commander. All clear now?'

Brian saluted. 'Yes sir.'

'Good. The railway people were asking how long it would be. Er . . . look . . . I don't quite know what passed between both of you, but Roger Symes seemed a bit het up . . .'

'I think I would have been the same, if I'd just lost half my Section, sir.'

Men were milling round them, so the Major led the way to a

quieter corner. 'Quite. Just as I thought. And you've done the job, that's the main thing. Whatever the argument was . . . I wouldn't put it in writing. Only leads to a fuss. And Roger'll be right as rain in a day or two.'

'That's fine by me, sir.'

'Good.' The Major nodded vigorously. 'Convey my thanks to your chaps, will you? As I will personally to Major Luckhurst.'

He strode off, and Brian just made it to a fencing post before he was sick. Before he could drive back to Bromley there was the loading of the bomb to be supervised, the journey to the Hackney Marsh 'graveyard', the final blowing up. It was a frustrating, irritating aftermath, but it had to be done; and the result was that it was after six o'clock before he set course again for Bromley. He stopped at the first telephone box and, using his cigarette lighter for illumination, dialled the Gladstone Hotel.

After an age, an uncertain voice answered. 'Hello – Gladstone Hotel.'

Brian recognized the voice. 'Mrs Dollery – Brian Ash here. Could I speak to – to Mrs Ash, please.' He cursed himself for hesitating, probably giving the game away.

'Oh the young lady left, my pet. Good hour ago. Paid the bill and left, she did. Yes, a good hour since – maybe more.'

Brian managed to keep his curses to himself. 'Did she say where to? Did she leave any message?'

'No – no message.'

'All right. Thanks, Mrs Dollery.'

Elation to desolation in two seconds. Now what? He didn't want to ring her at home, he might so easily get her father again and then *he* would suspect. Feeling miserable, he drove to Company HQ, hoping at least to see her car still parked; but it too had gone. The billet? Maybe she was back there, sitting in his room or in the kitchen with the Bakers, waiting for him. He drove straight out of the school, making for the Bakers' house. It was in darkness, with the quiet of utterly unoccupied houses. But he dashed up the stairs, still hoping. Nothing. Dark and empty as the rest of the house. He flung himself on to the bed, and despite everything fell asleep. It was nine o'clock when voices from down below woke him. He recognized Mulley's soft Scots, and Norma's bright London – laughing, enjoying themselves. He needed company, a drink. So what if he got himself loaded, he was officially on leave, it was no concern of the army's, not until Sunday evening, and that was still twenty-four hours away.

He slipped out of the house and drove off to nowhere in particular. For once there was no blitz; *poor devils up north probably copping it for a change*. He drove for half an hour before he realized that without knowing it he had automatically pointed the car in the general direction of Kent. He found a decent-looking pub on the outskirts of London and was glad when someone asked him about the badge sewn on his sleeve and started a conversation.

Meanwhile Norma, amidst great hilarity, was teaching Gordon Mulley to dance. He had at least two left feet, but that made no difference. After a while they stopped for a cup of tea.

'Know what the trouble is,' announced Norma as she put the kettle on. 'You're used to all those flings and reels they dance up in Scotland.'

'I canna dance them either,' mourned Mulley.

'Pity. I was hoping you'd teach me.'

'Ever been to Scotland, have you?'

'No. What's it like?'

'Grand.'

'I'd like to go there, some day.'

'There's a lot I could show you, yon.'

'That would be nice,' she said quietly. She sat at the table opposite him, reached out for his hand. 'When you said this morning you'd been called out to a bomb, I was so worried for you, Gordon. I mean, glad you weren't going away, but so worried something would happen, and . . . you know . . .'

He smiled at her. 'I'll make sure it doesn't. Come here.'

She came round the table and obediently sat on his knee. They kissed, hard and long. 'My,' she said as they broke, 'you are losing your shyness, aren't you.'

'You'd like Dundee, Norma. It's a grand wee town – fresh air, folk who'll stop and talk to ye . . . aye, you'd like it.'

'Gordon Mulley – are you proposing to me?'

'No,' he said hastily, then 'At least . . .'

She smiled at him, smoothing his fair hair. 'Never mind, there's time.' She kissed him again, and she felt his hands on her breasts. 'There's time for that, too, love. In a bit.' She got up and made the tea.

He went quiet and shy again as they drank. Finally, he said, 'Ye ken, Norma, I thought of you at first as a girl wi' a smashin' figure, someone I'd like to get to bed with. Not much else. But . . . well . . . I mean, I've messed around before now, back home, but . . . well, you're somehow – different.'

Norma leaned across and kissed him just once on his cheek. 'I'm glad, Gordon. I really am.'

Closing time came too quickly for Brian, and all too soon he was out in the pub car park not quite knowing what to do. He finished up by simply driving, rather too fast, in the direction from which he had come. He drove most of the night, aimlessly, until shortly before dawn he found himself outside the driveway gates to Dr Gillespie's house. He parked a little way down the road, and settled down to wait. Despite the cold creeping into his bones he managed to doze off, until a dog barking right beside the car roused him. It was nine-thirty. He yawned, stretched, and lit a cigarette.

Ten minutes later he was ringing the bell by the great front door of the old house. The old maid, Dorothy, opened it, and recognized him.

'Yes of course,' she beamed. 'He's at breakfast, but I'm sure the Doctor will be glad to see you, Mr Ash. This way.'

She led him through the wide hallway and into the breakfast room. 'Mr Ash is here, Doctor,' she announced.

Brian went in. Susan was there, a look of shock on her beautifully proportioned face, and another man.

'My dear chap – what an unexpected pleasure!' Gillespie said, obviously pleased to see him. 'What on earth are you doing in these parts? You look as if you've had rather a time of it.'

Suddenly Brian felt uncomfortable and a little foolish. 'I'm sorry to burst in. I've been up all night with a bomb,' he lied, and added by way of a measure of truth, 'on a railway line.'

'Round here?' beamed Gillespie. 'Bit off your beaten track, isn't it?'

'We're getting pushed all over the place at the moment. I was helping out – it was my weekend off, actually.' At last he dared to look at Susan. 'Hello, there,' he said.

'Hello, Brian.' There was just a touch of anger in her voice.

Dr Gillespie waved a hand towards the other man at the table. 'Ah – I don't believe you've met. Brian Ash – Stephen Mount . . . Susan's husband, you know.'

It took a second or two for the enormity to sink in, but as they shook hands it slowly did so. A numbness spread through Brian. The thought struck him that perhaps he should have reeled back, at least done a double-take or been struck speechless. Heavens above, only yesterday he had been in bed with this man's wife and now was in love with her. Instead he found himself giving Stephen a quick appraisal. In civvies – a reserved occupation, he presumed, like so many boffins – medium height and inclined already towards the plump, drawn face, the hollow eyes of extreme tiredness. Even allowing for that, there was something about him that made Brian put him down as a dull man.

Susan broke into his thoughts, still not quite managing to hide her anger. 'What can we do for you?'

'Well, I came really to beg a bath before going back to town. Which is very presumptuous of me.'

'Nonsense, my dear fellow,' Gillespie said. 'I'm sure we can accommodate. You could probably use a razor too, couldn't you? Organize things with Dorothy, would you, Susie?'

'Thank you so much. I really do apologize for butting in. I'll see you later, then.'

'No, no – have something to eat whilst you're waiting.'

Susan left to see Dorothy and managed to throw Brian a hostile look as she did so.

Forty-five minutes later Brian, freshly shaved, was basking in a deliciously hot bath. It was a luxury, but he was wishing he had behaved less like a lovesick schoolboy and had not come. Suddenly there was an urgent knocking on the door.

'Who is it?'

'Me. Let me in,' Susan whispered urgently.

He got out of the bath and grabbed a towel. Steam billowed through the door as he opened it, and a none-too-friendly Susan came in, locking the door behind her.

'You're taking a risk, aren't you?' he said.

'They're in the garden – father's very proud of his garden. But Brian, how could you?'

He was getting back into the bath. 'How could I what?'

'Turn up here? Are you mad?'

'I didn't know your husband would be here, did I? All I know is, I wasn't free until nearly seven and you'd left the hotel. Left me high and dry.'

'I left *you* high and dry?' She sat on the cork-topped bathroom stool, distraught.

'Anyway, I just had to see you, Susie. It's our weekend.'

'It was! I couldn't have stayed in that hotel a minute longer, not on my own. You might at least have kept your promise and phoned me.'

'Hardly my fault if all the lines were down, was it? And that's the truth.' He was getting angry himself, now. 'So you ran back home... and was he here? Or did he arrive this morning?'

'He was here.' There was a pause whilst they looked at one another. 'Apparently they spent most of the day phoning the girlfriend I'd told father I was staying with. Thank God she was away.'

'So you spent the night with him.' He said it quietly, almost accusingly. 'You know what I mean. Did you?'

She flared up again. 'Yes, yes! I couldn't lock him in the spare room, could I? Don't talk about it.'

'I see!'

'Oh God, don't get jealous. That's all I need.' She tossed the towel to him and he climbed out, began drying himself.

'Of course I'm bloody jealous. What else do you expect,

the way I feel about you? Why in hell's name did he have to choose this weekend?'

She seemed to have no answer, just sat there wringing her hands. 'Oh God . . . Look, if father asks you to stay for lunch—'

'It's all right,' he cut in. 'I'll make myself scarce.'

Not too far from tears, she gave an agonized look and then abruptly left. He took his time getting dressed and tidying up, giving himself a chance to simmer down, to get his emotions under control.

Late morning drinks was worse. They were all in the big sitting room with its low ceiling, beams and comfortable chairs. Stephen said not very much for a long time and then, out of the blue, brought the talk from gardens, rationing, and such mundane matters back to reality. 'You chaps in bomb disposal . . . must say I admire you tremendously. Must be terrifying, what you're doing every day of the week.'

Brian was embarrassed. 'You get used to it. It's a job, like any other.'

Susan put a cigarette between her lips and he reached for his own lighter but Stephen beat him to it. Brian watched with a shot of jealousy going through him. She said, 'You have an equally important job, darling.'

'If you like . . . but it hardly compares, does it?' Stephen muttered.

'What is it, exactly?' asked Brian, trying to ignore that 'darling'.

'He can't say,' Susan jumped in. 'Top secret.'

Stephen shrugged, 'In a word – decoding.' He obviously wanted to talk about it. 'We're shut up twenty-four hours a day. No outlet, that's the big problem. Cooped up a million miles from the war. Games, formulae . . . like crossword puzzles. That's all it is, when you get down to it – a gigantic, never-ending crossword puzzle. Not the real thing at all. Not like you.'

Stephen was actually trembling, turning his glass round and round in tightly-gripping hands. Everyone noticed; it was Dr Gillespie who filled the awkward moment.

'I believe the sterilizer's on issue now, Brian?'

'Yes. Not many so far, but we've got one. Just now the fifties seem to be all the rage with the Jerries, and of course they're too sensitive.'

'But you have the liquid discharger.'

'And marvellous it is too. I believe you had a hand in that too, sir.'

'Yes, I did.'

'Goodness knows how many lives you've saved in the last few weeks through it. I do hope you realize how grateful everyone is to you.'

He meant every word of it, and Gillespie was visibly touched. 'Well . . . thank you, Brian. It's nice to think one has done something.'

Stephen gave a nervous laugh. 'You see? You can talk about your job.'

'We're not supposed to,' Gillespie told him.

'But it must help.' It was almost a cry from the heart.

Susan changed the subject. 'Would anyone like another drink?'

'Not for me,' Stephen said hastily. 'One's enough.'

'Your glass is empty, Brian,' said Gillespie.

Brian glanced at Susan at the drinks cupboard. 'I'd love to – but I really ought to think about getting back. I'm on duty this afternoon,' he lied, standing up.

'No time for lunch with us?' Gillespie sounded genuinely disappointed.

'I'm afraid not. Thanks for the bath and everything, though. I'll see myself out.' Suddenly he could not get out of the house quickly enough.

Susan did not move, did not even smile. 'Goodbye,' she said.

Before dinner in the Mess, Brian was drowning his sorrows in a stiff Scotch. Ivor Rodgers was sympathetic, but rather enjoying his tale of woe.

'The whole escapade was a disaster,' moaned Brian. 'I can't see anything developing, not now.'

'Hotel was all right, though?'

'Oh yes. That side of it – great.'

'I'm only sorry I had to flush you out. The Old Man was tearing his hair because you hadn't let the Orderly Sergeant know where you were. In a spot of bother there, I reckon – apologies due.'

'Yes, I've realized that.'

Major Luckhurst came into the Mess. 'He's here now, old sport. I'll line up a stiff one for you.' Tactfully he slid out of the line of fire.

The Major, looking every inch the schoolmaster, made straight for Brian. 'Ah – Brian . . .'

'I know what you're going to say, sir,' said Brian, all contrition, 'I'm very sorry. It completely slipped my mind.'

'We were lucky Ivor knew where to find you. Don't let it happen again, will you.'

'It certainly won't, sir.'

Corporal Mould turned up bang on cue in that reliable, old-retainer way of his. 'Excuse me, sir, telephone for you,' he murmured to Brian.

Luckhurst turned to go. 'Right, Brian – off you go. We'll have a drink later, for the damn good job Major Pullar says you did.'

'Thank you, sir.' From that minute, Brian would have jumped off Tower Bridge if Major Luckhurst had told him to.

The corridor was busy with officers coming in to dinner, and Brian was bothered by the lack of privacy. He had a feeling this was the final, and not very fond, farewell.

'Brian . . . darling?' Susan, miraculously, was not angry. He swallowed hard. 'I'm sorry about today!'

'It was all such a shock, what with Stephen, and you turning up looking like an escaped convict.'

'At least no one could suspect us – could they?'

'No. I don't think so. Look, I can't stay long—'

'Is he still there?' Brian cut in.

'No.' There was the slightest pause. 'Thank you for Bromley!'

'Thank *you*. I mean it.'

'I love you.'

'Yes – it's rather public here.'

'I love you and I want to be with you this minute. In bed with you. Fix another Bromley soon, please?'

'Soon as we can, I promise. Look—' But there was a click, and the phone went dead. He was smiling again as he went back into the Mess to rejoin Ivor with the promised drink.

'Your married lady?' asked Ivor. 'And all well, by the smug look on that chubby face. Now – your Uncle Ivor wants to hear all about it, step by faltering step . . .'

Brian took a deep drink, put the glass down and smiled at Ivor. 'Mind your own business,' he said.

Chapter 7

'May I remind you, sir – your Section's returns for this month . . .?' The Orderly Sergeant was an understanding man, and phrased the question as gently as he could.

Brian was in the Company Orderly Room on routine business – a week after the so-called forty-eight-hour leave. He sighed: 'Sergeant, you're a lovely man, but do you know the earliest I've packed up work this week? Two o'clock in the morning. This morning it was four.'

'I fully appreciate the problems, Mr Ash – but the OC gets his behind kicked if they're not sent in, and he passes it on to the Adjutant—'

'—who passes it down. I know. Well, never let it be said that a humble Section Commander, RE, cocked up the war effort because he didn't fill in a form. Let's have it – I'll try and get it done today. OK?'

'Very kind of you, sir.' He passed the imposing double-sided form over. 'There's some mail here for 347 too, if you wouldn't mind.'

'No – give it here.' Automatically Brian flipped through the dozen or so envelopes, but there was none for him. Leaving the office, he was accosted by Hamish Leckie and Alan Pringle.

'Well now, here's a stranger,' Leckie greeted him. 'I was beginning to think you'd deserted, or something.'

The three of them walked down the corridor. 'I'm not far off it,' Brian admitted. 'Anything for a quiet life.'

'I'm afraid you've been pushed a bit, recently,' Alan Pringle said.

'Night work, is it?' asked Lieutenant Leckie sympathetically.

'And then some. That's why I haven't been in for dinner. Too bloody late, not to mention shagged out.'

'That's the way of it, laddie.' They had reached the main entrance to the school, and in the doorway Leckie drew close and dropped his voice to a conspiratorial whisper. 'Eh, have you heard the buzz, either of ye?'

'What buzz?'

'The Old Man being posted.'

'What?'

'That's what I've just heard – from usually well-informed circles, as they say. Leaving us early next month.'

'That's bad.'

Leckie looked hard at the silent Pringle. 'Come on now, Alan . . . you're supposed to be the Intelligence Officer around here. Cough up.'

'News to me, Jock. Truly. Are you sure?'

'My sources are usually highly reliable. We'll just have to await events,' Leckie pronounced, and waved a farewell as he sauntered off to his waiting truck.

'I hope it is only a rumour,' Alan said, frowning.

Brian nodded. 'Me too. The idea of Fanny Francis as OC really does make me feel like deserting!'

The day turned out like any other – nothing straightforward, everything Category-A, every bomb deep and awkwardly placed, which meant hour after hour of digging and shoring.

The Section was beginning to grumble under the strain and lack of rest; at mealbreaks the usual joking and banter was being replaced by mutterings. Today was no exception.

'If we don't get a night off soon,' Wilkins grumbled, 'I'll have someone's guts for garters. I was just getting a nice bit of business lined up – and what happens? Haven't seen the bloke for a week, have I. Haven't had the chance. He'll have gone cold on me by the time I do.'

Sergeant James looked up from his corned-beef hash. 'You're not in the army to do business, Wilkins. There's more important things.'

'On my pay, Sarge? A man's got to live. Anyway, I've an old mother to keep in gin, and a sister to keep off the streets.' The others laughed, but it was not entirely a joke.

'All of us have problems.' It was the privilege of rank to have the last word, and Wilkins was left muttering into his mess can. All during the break, Sergeant James had been watching Salt sitting away from the rest, gloomy, reading and re-reading a letter he had received that morning. The Sergeant took his tea mug and moved down the safety point to sit beside him. 'Nice for some of us, getting mail. I haven't had any for bloody weeks.'

'Know something, Sarge?' called out Baines from nearby. 'The way he's carrying on, I reckon it's from his girlfriend – I reckon he's got her in the club.'

Salt glowered. 'Just shut your mouth, cheeky sod – unless you want me to shut it for you.' Salt was not given to talking like that. Baines got the message, and shut up. Sergeant James said quietly to Salt, 'Come outside for a bit.'

The cold air made them shiver after the snugness of the safety point. Sergeant James gave Salt a cigarette and they paced up and down in silence. 'Something on your mind, mate?'

Salt glanced at the Sergeant. It wasn't often a three-striper called a one-striper mate, and it struck a chord. 'It's the wife, Sarge.'

'Oh Christ, don't tell me she's . . . ?'

'No, nowt like that. It's this living in the country thing. She's gone back to Manchester, you see.'

'Yes, I'd heard.'

'And they'll be giving the place a plastering any night now, the Jerries will. I know it. They've been to Liverpool already. It's not right to take the kids back into all that. Not when she's got a safe place to be. I keep telling her, but all she writes back is what a grand time they're all having, the kids love being back with their Nan, going to the pictures and the fish and chip shops, all that. Never answers what *I* say. Never once.'

'I can see your point, Salty. Must be worrying. But on the other hand – how many people are there in Manchester?'

'I dunno. Three quarters of a million, I suppose.'

'And how many people get hurt in a raid? The odds are pretty good, you know.'

'That's as maybe – but the risk's still there.'

'Very true – but that's war, mate. And you're not the only one, either. Look at Horrocks. He's got his mum in Sheffield, and they've caught it twice.'

'Horrocks is Horrocks. But I'm me. I can't help how I feel. Besides, he's got no kids.'

'All I'm saying is, Salty – get it into proportion. For your own sake, and for the sake of your mates in the Section. In this job, we all depend on one another, whoever we are.'

Salt took a long last pull at his cigarette, inhaled deeply, and ground out the butt with his heel. 'Aye. OK, Sarge – thanks.'

Two days later the situation had become such that Brian asked to see Major Luckhurst.

'I'm sorry to burden you, sir,' he said, 'but the Section has averaged four hours sleep a night for the last ten days. They're very, very tired – little squabbles keep springing up. And any time now, someone – possibly me – will be getting careless, with the usual results.'

The Major took off his glasses. 'Yes, I know. You have been pushed hard recently.' He considered. 'The best I can do is a twenty-four-hour break as from 1600 hours Saturday. Not much, but better than nothing.'

'Anything will be welcome. Is that official, then, sir?'

'Yes. You can take it as that.'

'Thank you very much, sir.'

'Possibly my final act of kindness.' The Major smiled, rather sadly. 'I dare say you've heard . . .?'

'Yes, there have been rumours. We're all very sorry, sir.'

'Most kind. They call it promotion – I call it more being put out to pasture. So, as from seventh December, Captain Francis will be your Commanding Officer.'

'Oh.' Brian could not keep his feelings out of his voice.

Major Luckhurst contented himself with a knowing smile. 'Which reminds me – I must chase up about your MBE.'

'Good Lord – I'd forgotten all about that.'

'I'd like it to be confirmed if possible before I go. Anyway – Sunday off for you. And Brian, if you do go away for the day, *do* tell the Orderly Sergeant where we can find you. Just in case.'

Brian exchanged smiles with him. 'I'll remember, sir. Thank you.'

Watching Brian leave his office, Major Luckhurst reflected briefly on the cruelties of war. A few short weeks before Brian Ash had walked into this office, knowing very little about life. The same Brian Ash now was a man, his face lined with the strain of his work, sure of himself, on daily nodding terms with death. In that short time he had seen more and experienced more than any human being can reasonably expect to see and know in a lifetime. It was only to be hoped that the Brian Ashes of this world, the ones that were left, were not too deeply scarred and hardened by it all.

Four o'clock Saturday was a long time coming, but it came at last. Brian had arranged to meet Susan at the Gladstone Hotel again; the rest of the Section were planning to catch up on sleep. But first there was paperwork to clear up, and Sergeant James was helping him in the Section office when there was a knock on the door and a serious and worried Lance Corporal Salt marched in.

'Sorry to bother you, sir,' he said, snapping down from a salute.

'What's the matter?' Brian asked.

'I've – I've been listening to the news, sir. On the radio. They were bombing the north again last night.'

'Manchester?'

'No, sir. But close. Merseyside again.'

Sergeant James stood by Brian's chair; he asked, 'When did you last hear from your wife?'

'Yesterday, Sergeant.'

Brian did not quite follow. 'Wasn't she evacuated?'

Salt swallowed. 'She went back, sir. Her and the kids. Sir, all I need is forty-eight hours, just to talk to her face-to-face. I could get her back to Cheshire, I know it. What with the trains, twenty-four hours isn't enough, sir, not to get there and back.'

Brian was already sadly shaking his head. 'You know as well as I do, Corporal . . .'

With added urgency, Salt almost pleaded, 'Compassionate grounds, sir.'

'Leave's hard to come by even when it's your turn,' Sergeant James chipped in. 'Now you want to jump the queue.'

'A thirty-six,' burst out Salt. 'That'd give me just about enough time to get up there and put them on a train out of it. I can persuade her, sir, I know I can.'

'Asking Captain Francis to bend the rules is a waste of time, you know that as well as I do,' Brian said as kindly as he could. 'I'm sorry, I really am.'

For a long moment, Salt stood there, his face working. Then, 'Thank you, sir. Sorry to have bothered you,' he said, saluted, and marched out.

He went up to the barrack room, where most of the Section were already stretched out exhausted. He sat on his bunk for a long time, his head in his hands. From below he heard Sergeant James wishing Lieutenant Ash a good leave, and the Lieutenant closing first the office door, then the street door. Ten more minutes he sat, not knowing what to do, only that he had to do *something*, anything. Then he snatched up his forage cap and clumped noisily out of the room, down the stairs, out of the house. He didn't know where he was going. All he wanted was oblivion. From there, the train of thought led on: oblivion meant booze, and booze meant pubs, which meant Michelle, and Michelle meant . . .

Her eyes lit up at the sight of him, and then quickly darkened with concern as she caught his mood. 'Salty, love – what's up? What's happened?'

'Nothing.' He strode past her up the narrow staircase to her flat and flung himself into a battered easy-chair.

'I wish you'd tell me – something's wrong, isn't it?' she prompted.

'I don't want to talk about it.'

'Fair enough. You're here, that's the main thing. Like a cup of tea?'

'Please.' As they drank, she chattered about what she'd been doing, how she'd missed him. Then he said, 'I've got twenty-four hours. You doing anything?'

'Only work at the pub. Are you planning to – like – stay, then?'

'Yeh. Starting now. Come here, gorgeous.'

They made love, violently and repeatedly, until he hurt her. But she did not complain; she only knew that for some reason he needed her this way and, Salty being Salty, she was happy enough. That was how his twenty-four hours went. Love-making, boozing, more lovemaking. Oblivion.

Brian drove into the Gladstone's car park, locked the car and ran into the hotel's empty hallway. Mrs Dollery shuffled out in answer to his ring and beamed. 'Hello, dear. The same room . . . She's up there waiting.'

Susan was in her dressing gown painting her nails when he burst in. They gazed at one another for a second, then he said 'Hi.'

'Hi.'

There was no tension this time. He moved easily to her, kissed her gently and lovingly. 'I'm glad we've got the same room.'

'Mrs Dollery's an old love. She said people like us made it all worthwhile.'

'Made all what worthwhile?' He was unpacking his small overnight bag.

'I'm not quite sure. The war, I think.'

'As long as someone thinks good of it. Here . . .' He produced a box of chocolates and handed them to her.

'Feasts in the dormitory.' He took her in his arms and they just looked at one another. 'Oh darling, darling, darling – I love you.' They kissed hard, hugging tight, and then collapsed across the bed and lay flat on their backs, hands touching.

'What's new?' she asked quietly.

'Nothing much. Working too hard. The OC's being posted, which is bad news. Oh, and I forgot to tell you before – I've been put up for a medal.'

'Darling, that's wonderful. Congratulations.' She was all life and animation now, propped on an elbow, beaming down at him. 'You deserve it, God knows. What will it be?'

'MBE, I'm told. If it happens. It was for the steaming-out job at that church – so your father deserves half of it at least.'

'He doesn't do half what you do. I'm very, very proud of you, my darling.' She kissed him, then settled down again beside him. 'What else?'

He considered a while. 'I've fallen in love again.'

'You're a fickle man.'

'Aren't I, just.'

There was another pause, not an uncomfortable pause but the quiet between lovers who do not need words. Then she said, very quietly, 'Brian – I'm frightened.'

'Why?'

'All this – us – it's too good to be true.'

'But it is true.'

'It's never happened to me before, you see.'

'Not even with Stephen? Not for just a little while?'

'No.'

Brian squeezed her hand. 'Do you think he – you know – suspects anything?'

'Not the least. Positive.'

'And your father?' She could only shrug. 'What did you say to him, about today?'

'He's gone to Cambridge.'

'Dorothy?'

'She's all right. She never liked Stephen, anyway.' She turned her head and smiled at him. 'Oh, what does it matter? It's none of their business. This is our little heaven.'

He was serious as he turned to look at her. 'But it will be their business one day, sweetheart. One day, and soon, we'll have to face all sorts of fireworks.'

'But not just now – not today. That's probably the one good thing about a war, isn't it? There's no use planning for tomorrow – it's today that matters. All that's real is this one small room in Bromley, and you and I in it!'

They kissed, long and deeply. And the future was not mentioned again.

Sunday evening and the end of the rest period came all too soon, followed by the realities of Monday. Salt was last out of bed, groaning and holding his head.

'Don't look to me for sympathy,' Horrocks told him. 'My, but you were in a state last night.'

Salt tried valiantly to stand up. 'Was I? I've got a mouth like a vulture's crutch, and bloody hell, there's steel hammers going like the clappers in my head.'

'Think yourself lucky the Sergeant wasn't here to see you. Remember getting home, do you?'

'Tell me.'

'Poured out of a taxi, you were. Took three of us to get you up here.'

'Taxi? Me? How did I pay for it?'

'Lucky again. Your girlfriend had given the bloke the money. Here's the change.' He handed over three shillings and sixpence, and Salt looked at it blankly.

'Girlfriend . . . ? Oh aye . . . yes. Ta.'

Salt's world slowly if painfully came into focus, and by the time 347 Section's truck was jolting and jarring its way to the day's first job, he was conscious of what was going on. He was conscious too of something else, a sense of something not very far from shame. He loved his wife Betty, thought the world of her and the kids, and the thought of how he had been behaving with Michelle sent shivers down his spine. All in all, he was not the happiest of men.

The incident was down by the river. Snug beside a gas holder lay a 250-kg bomb. It had skidded along, and lay on the surface. Brian and Sergeant James were shown the marks by the policeman. They did not even have to move it to check the fuse boss: a Type-50. 'Get a couple of the men to clear round it,' Brian told the Sergeant, 'but see they don't touch it whatever they do. And we'll need the liquid discharger, of course.'

They walked back to the safety point, huddled against the bitter wind sweeping around the wide open spaces straight off the river. Wilkins and Baines were sent with shovels to clear the rubble away from the bomb; the rest unloaded the truck, Salt wincing with every move, much to the delight of the others. Finally it was done, and Brian went with Sergeant James to set up the discharger. Salt, feeling like death and sick of the crude jokes at his expense, walked down the concrete roadway of the dockside, hands in pockets, deep in misery. He had wandered over a hundred yards when a voice called him.

'Hey!'

He looked up and saw a man with a mongrel dog beckoning at him.

' 'op it,' Salt snarled. 'No civilians allowed.'

'You one of the bomb lot? 'Cause I've found one.'

'We've got it in hand. Now scarper.'

'Not this one you haven't.'

Salt looked at him sharply. 'Where?'

The man pointed behind him. 'Back there. Saw 'em both coming down, you see, and I reckoned one of 'em would hit the offices back there. And I was right.' The man chuckled with self-satisfaction.

'Show me.'

They came to a badly battered single-storey building, one wall completely caved in. Salt looked along the tarmac roadway and saw a long, deep groove heading straight for the office building.

'What's that?' asked the man eagerly. The dog was sniffing around it, tail wagging.

'Where it bounced. Right – like I said – 'op it.'

'It's my bomb. I found it. I should get some credit.'

'You'll get yourself blown sky high if you're not careful. Whatever is in there is most likely going tick-tock, tick-tock . . .'

Suddenly the man took fright, called his dog, and vanished at speed. Salt peered in through the great, ragged gap in the building wall. The office was smashed, papers and files everywhere, desks pulped, phone wires tangled. Carefully he picked his way into the wreckage and saw the tail fin of the bomb. He recognized it as another 250-kg, and quickly began to thread his way out again to fetch help. But three careful steps out he stopped dead. He could have sworn he had heard a voice from among the wreckage; a weak cry, a woman's.

'Hello?' he called. 'Anyone there? . . . Where are you . . . ?'

Very weak, it came again. 'Help me . . . please, help me.'

'Where are you . . . ? Keep talking so I can find you . . .'

Salt thrust his way through the wreckage, guided by a small voice, shoving masonry and ruined filing cabinets aside. He found a young girl, not more than twenty, face uppermost under a mass of crossed beams and wooden pieces from the collapsed roof and piles of brickwork. He knelt as close beside her as he could.

'I – I can't move . . .' she whimpered.

'Lie still, lass. We'll soon have you out.'

'Beryl,' the girl whispered. 'Where's Beryl?'

'Who?'

The girl wildly turned her head this way and that, then saw Beryl – lying face down, very still, six feet away, her dark hair spread wide. 'Oh my God no! Beryl love, Beryl . . .'

Salt edged across to Beryl, knelt and felt her neck, reached for her pulse. The trapped girl watched him, saw his grave face, then began to scream hysterically, struggling against the weight across her, disturbing it, making things worse for herself. Salt moved quickly to her, took a handful of her fair hair and yanked her head sharply round. The pain stopped her instantly.

Very soothingly and softly, Salt said, 'Sorry, love. Had to do something.'

The girl whimpered again. At least it was better than the hysterics. 'She didn't want to go to the shelters. I said I'd stay with her . . .'

'Listen,' Salt said. 'Listen to me. Can you move your fingers and toes, and your back?' She made the effort, nodded. 'Great.'

'But there's something heavy across my middle.'

It might have been worse. A huge wooden beam, its end propped on a toppled metal office chair, was keeping a ton of rubble off her. And the bomb was just behind her head, mercifully just out of her sight.

'Don't move,' he said, urgently. 'Don't try to shift. Just lie still.'

He stood up, carefully selected a piece of wreckage and tried to heave it up. All that happened was that plaster and pieces of the ceiling sprinkled over them – and on the bomb. He knew that if he carried on he'd bring the lot down, burying the girl completely and most likely setting off the bomb. Panting, he knelt down again.

'What's your name, love?'

'Jean.'

'Mine's Jack. Listen, Jean. I'm going to bring some of the lads to give me a hand. All right?'

'I just remember the crashing noise,' she said.

He lied blatantly. 'A bomb went off by the river. You caught the blast. Hasn't half made a mess of your filing!' She smiled for the first time. 'Did anyone else stay behind?'

'No. Beryl couldn't stand being cooped up in the Underground, so I stayed with her.'

She turned to look at Beryl again and began crying. 'Here – look at me, Jean. Look at me. Just keep looking this way. There's nowt you can do for her, I'm afraid, but there's a hell of a lot you can do for yourself. You've had all the luck so far. Don't spoil it, love.'

'OK.'

He took off his jacket, folded it, and slipped it beneath her head. 'Good girl. I'll be back in a jiff with my mates. Don't wriggle about! And don't go away.'

He edged his way past the bomb and out into the bitter wind. He shivered as it pierced his shirt. Without stopping he ran back to the safety point. Brian and Sergeant James were still dealing with their bomb. Horrocks stood by the Merrylees extractor; the others were standing around.

'There's another one, in a wrecked office,' Salt panted. 'A 250, same as this; but there's a girl trapped right next to it.'

'Oh Christ,' Corporal Horrocks said.

'We got to get her out,' Salt panted.

Everyone moved in, ready to help. 'We can't all go,' Horrocks said hastily.

But Salt took command. 'Right. Wilkins and Baines stay here. You, me, Tiny Powell and Mulley – come on, she could snuff it any second!'

The cautious Horrocks, still unhappy, looked back to where Brian and Sergeant James were working. 'All right,' he conceded. 'Wilkins, cop hold of the Merrylees – they'll be needing it soon.'

'And bring the block and tackle,' Salt ordered. Powell and Mulley picked it up and followed the others.

They reached the ruined office, went in through the gap and edged their way around the bomb. Mulley kicked a beam and a shower of rubble fell on it.

Horrocks said through gritted teeth, 'For Christ's sake mind the—'

He got no further as Salt's great hand clamped itself across his mouth. 'There is no bomb, right?' whispered Salt. He pointed to where Jean was lying, and the rest of them nodded and understood. Salt crawled down beside the girl.

'Still here then, love? I brought some muscle to give us a hand, like I said.' He waved to the others who came and grinned sheepishly down at her. 'Thick as two planks the lot of them, but strong as oxes. Right – we're going to get you out of it now, love. OK?'

The men scrambled back behind her and held a whispered conference. Then they carefully picked the beams and bits of rubble that could be taken off without disturbing the rest; but it wasn't easy. Showers of stuff fell upon them and the bomb. Then the bomb itself shifted, just an inch, and they looked at it in horror. There seemed no way of moving the beams without setting the bomb off. They retired a short distance for a quiet conference.

'Look,' said Horrocks, 'I want her out as much as you do, but if we move any of them beams we'll all be blown to Kingdom come.'

Salt bit his lip, looked around him seeking ideas. Up in the roof a strong beam was still in place six feet above the bomb. 'Reckon that beam would take the block and tackle?' he whispered.

'It might,' said Horrocks, doubtfully.

'You mean raise the beam that's on her?' queried Powell. 'Everything else would come and crush her to pulp, man.'

'I don't mean the beam,' whispered Salt. 'I mean the bloody bomb.'

'We can't touch the bomb. Only an officer can do that.' Horrocks was wide-eyed in alarm.

Jean suddenly called out. 'Jack – Jack, are you there?'

Salt scrambled into her line of sight and knelt beside her. 'I'm here.'

'What's all the whispering about?'

'Got to be careful, that's all. Anyone shouts in here and the roof'll cave in.'

'It's starting to hurt.'

'You're doing fine, Jean love. Just keep smiling.'

'You've got a nice face, haven't you?'

'I bet you say that to all the lads.' She smiled, and he grinned happily. 'You see, you can smile if you try. Now just keep it there – won't be long now.'

He patted her cheek and rejoined the others.

'Look—' started Horrocks.

'I know the rules,' cut in Salt. 'I know only officers can touch them. But we haven't time, not with her. We can't move the beam, so we move the bomb – unless you've got any other ideas?'

Without waiting for an answer, he climbed carefully across to the bomb, looked for the fuse, read it, rejoined the anxious group.

'It's got a seventeen,' he reported.

'Clockwork,' Mulley breathed.

Horrocks grabbed a piece of tubing from among the wreckage and put an end on the bomb casing. He listened intently, then shook his head. At least the thing was not ticking – yet.

The block and tackle was quickly slung from the surviving roof beam and placed above the bomb. Powell was helping Salt fix the chains around the casing when Jean called out, 'What are you doing?' She had been able to see the tackle being fixed, but couldn't understand why.

'Clearing a way to get to you, Jean. You OK?'

'I'm all right.'

Mulley had found a docker's trolley and was dragging it along the tarmac towards the wrecked building. He rejoined the others as they were preparing to haul on the rope. At first nothing happened. They pulled harder, straining every muscle, then slowly, very slowly the bomb began to come free, creating little avalanches of loose rubble. The beam above them creaked from the strain, began to bend. Inch by inch the great beast came up until it was swinging free and they had a struggle to steady it.

'Trolley,' ordered Salt through gritted teeth. Mulley let go his hold on the rope and the other three strained more. Desperately he wheeled the trolley as close as possible under the bomb. Half inch by half inch, they began to lower it. Suddenly the beam above them cracked, and Jean let out a cry of alarm. Unable to do anything but hope it would last out, they could only carry on. With another six inches to go, the beam cracked again. Finally the bomb was on the trolley; and at that same second the beam collapsed. Salt looked up just in time to see the block and tackle falling off it straight on to the bomb, and just had to stand there and let it happen. With a great clank it hit the metal casing and bounced off. Salt quickly put an ear to the bomb, and his face told the others all they wanted to know. The clock had been started. Without a word they began the job of hauling the trolley away towards the river, at the same time clutching the bomb to prevent it rolling off. They sweated and strained, moving as fast as they could over the pitted, rubble-strewn roadways, their one object to get to the river and dump the bomb before it got them.

It was at this time that Captain Francis chose to visit the site. Brian was dismantling the discharger on the original bomb and took the news passed on by Sergeant James with a calm amounting almost to indifference. Without hurry he finished the job and then walked slowly back to the safety point. They arrived there at the same time as Captain Francis.

'How are you doing?' asked the gaunt Captain.

'All right,' Brian replied, without saluting. It was not a calculated insult, it just never occurred to him. 'That one's defused.'

'What was it?'

'A fifty.'

'Good. Mr Ash – where is the rest of your Section?'

Brian looked around. There were only Wilkins and Baines, starting to clear up. 'Wilkins – where are the others?'

'Er . . . sir . . . I, er, I don't know.'

Captain Francis exploded. 'Then find them. They're supposed to be here, at the point!'

No one had time to move before a great roaring explosion made them duck. They looked up in time to see a massive plume of water hanging in mid air, seemingly still for seconds before it fell in on itself.

'That wasn't ours,' said Brian.

'In the river, sir,' added Sergeant James.

They began walking quickly in the direction of the explosion, Captain Francis forgotten. But the Company's 2-i/c, although he had taken a little longer to recover, soon caught them up. Halfway down the road they met Mulley running towards them.

Sergeant James stopped him. 'Mulley – where the hell are you going?'

Breathless, Mulley told him. 'To get the truck, Sarge. There's a girl badly hurt.'

Sergeant James let him go, and they walked more quickly on to the wrecked building. They could see Salt and Powell dismantling the block and tackle, and the girl lying in the roadway on their outstretched jackets.

'Corporal Horrocks,' bellowed the Sergeant. 'What's happening here?'

Horrocks, weary and still panting, waited for the Sergeant to come to him. 'There was a girl trapped, Sergeant. We've been getting her out.'

Captain Francis demanded, 'Was that bomb that exploded anything to do with it?'

Horrocks was unhappy and dumb. Salt said simply, 'Yes, sir.'

'What bomb, Corporal?' Brian asked quietly.

'Never mind the questions now,' Captain Francis snapped. 'I want a full report on precisely what happened here this morning.' He walked briskly away.

In the silence that followed, Salt edged up to Brian and spoke quietly, not wanting Jean to overhear from where she was lying. 'I found her, sir. There was no way of getting her out without moving the bomb, and you were busy. It started ticking, and we just made it to the river before it went up. That's all, sir.'

The truck came up and they gently lifted Jean into it. Settled on the floor, she called 'Jack.'

'Yeh?' Salt bent over her.

'Are you married?'

'Yeh.'

'Pity. She won't mind, though, will she?' She took hold of

his shirt with a shaky hand, pulled his face down, and kissed him softly. Salt looked embarrassed, jumped down from the truck.

'OK, Gordon – away you go, and take it easy,' he called to Mulley, the unofficial driver.

Brian looked from Salt to Horrocks and back again. 'Sounds to me,' he said, 'as if you did well. But you heard what Captain Francis said – I have to give him a report.'

The document was in Captain Francis's hands the next morning. Major Luckhurst was away for three days and the 2-i/c lost no time in getting behind his desk. Brian stood at attention before the desk as he read the report.

The Captain put the document aside, ran a long finger down one side of his sour, humourless face. 'Corporal Horrocks and Corporal Salt will remain confined to barracks when not on duty until Major Luckhurst comes back and can deal with them.'

'Is that absolutely essential?'

'These men deliberately broke the rules, Mr Ash. Salt is obviously the ringleader and neither he nor Horrocks is trained to deal with UXBs but they did so deliberately and recklessly, thereby placing the lives of other men at risk.' In his style, he was talking like a training manual.

'He also saved a girl's life.'

'Perhaps you would like him to be mentioned in despatches.'

'No, but—'

'These men must learn that to ignore or disobey the rules in BD is virtually guaranteeing somebody's death.'

Brian could have added that Salt and Horrocks had learned more about bomb disposal – and learned it the hard way – than Captain Francis would ever know, but there would have been no point. At least they would get a fair and sympathetic hearing from the Major.

That night Salt was a long time getting off to sleep. He could not stop himself thinking about Jean, lying helpless with that mass of rubble over her, trapped, unable to move. He had forgotten to ask how long she had been there – all night, probably. With a bomb just behind her, and a building likely to collapse on her at any minute. Cold, miserable, alone, terrified. It could just as easily have been his own wife Betty. All through the night he kept putting Betty's face in place of Jean's, and the thought pounded through him like a sledge-hammer.

Brian was at his desk in the Section billet the next morning. Sergeant James came in, saluted.

'Good morning, Sergeant.'

'Morning sir. I have to tell you Corporal Salt's gone missing, sir.'

'He's what?' Brian sat back with a start.

'Skipped off, sir. Gone AWOL.'

'How long?'

'During the night, it seems.'

'The bloody fool.'

'Some of the lads are saying he ought to get a medal, not CB, sir.'

'I'm quite aware of what's being said, Sergeant. But the hard fact is, he broke regulations. Sorry, but he'll have to go on report. And the Red Caps will have to be alerted, I suppose.'

'Right away, sir.' The Sergeant saluted again and went off into his own office. The idea of Salt being hunted down by the Military Police did nothing for Brian's morale; but facts were facts, and as OC he had his duty.

Not that Salty cared a monkey's about the Red Caps, not just now, anyhow. He was sitting in a Manchester Corporation bus, going down the familiar streets, growing increasingly worried as he spotted patches of bomb damage. Nothing bad so far, but enough to show the dangers of living in the city. He had left the billet about four that morning, creeping out as quietly as he could. He thumbed a lift to the station, caught the first train up.

He left the bus, huddled deeper into his greatcoat, and set off into the maze of cobbled streets with their little back-to-back houses. This was home. On Mondays the streets were festooned with washing blowing on lines stretched from one side to the other, at weekends and holidays they were packed with laughing, running kids, the old folk sitting in doorways chatting. It was quiet now, only a few folk about, hurrying off to the shops mostly. No kids.

At his front door, he hammered the knocker. After a bit, his wife opened it, frowning at first at the unexpected visitor. 'Hello, Bet . . .'

Her harassed face, growing rounder now with the years, was a study. 'Jack!'

He grinned. 'Are you going to let me into my own house, then?'

He went in and she closed the door after him, still speechless. There was no hallway; the street door led straight into the front room. It was a neat room, a little on the dark side, but comfortable. He kissed her and they embraced for a moment.

'What are you doing here, Jack?'

'I wangled a forty-eight. Where are the kids?'

'Round at mam's.'

'OK, are they?'

'They're grand. Jack, you don't just get a forty-eight-hour leave without warning. Why didn't you write and tell me you were coming?'

He still had his greatcoat on. He moved to the window, looked out on the familiar street. 'What's the point of writing?'

'*What's the point?*'

He turned and looked seriously at her. 'I've written and written you about getting out of here. You never answered.'

'I've answered all your letters.'

'The bits you wanted to! How the kids loved the shelters, and not going to school, all that stuff.' They weren't having a row. They didn't live like that. Just . . . talking things over.

'There hasn't been much bombing, not much at all.'

'There's been some though, hasn't there? I saw the damage, coming on the bus.'

'Why did you come here? You haven't gone absent, have you?'

'I'm taking you back down to our Eileen's.'

'Like heck you are.'

'I'm taking the kids, at least. If you want to stay . . .'

'You're not taking them anywhere.'

'I am, Bet.' He was quiet, but firm.

'We've got shelters – right there at the end of the street. Anyway, there's nowt the Germans would bomb.'

He showed a flash of anger. '*You're* telling *me* what they bomb? I've lived among it for weeks, remember. I've seen houses, and ships and hospitals and churches – flattened. Just the other night they killed a girl on an empty dockside.'

As usual she responded to his rare flashes of anger with a flash of her own. 'I'm not going, and that's flat. I'm not leaving this house. All my friends are here . . . It's all right for you, off boozing with your mates every night. But what about me? Stuck out in the country with nowt but that snotty sister of yours and her dreary husband for company – what do you know about it?'

He hated to see her upset, and immediately took her into his arms. 'Bet love . . . Don't you see – you can't stay here. This war isn't going to be over for a long, long time, and there's going to be a hell of a lot more bombing before we're done.'

The strain of it all, of knowing what he was doing in London, of expecting a War Office telegram every day that passed, showed itself and she wept quietly on his shoulder. 'Oh, Jack . . .'

He let her weep for a few moments, gently stroking her hair. He noticed a few more streaks of grey in it. Then, 'Get the suitcases, love . . .'

'I don't want to go to your sister . . .'

'All right, love, all right. We'll find somewhere else. But it's wrong to stay here, wrong for the children, wrong for you. I won't make you go anywhere you don't want to. We'll find somewhere. Just to let me sleep at nights, Bet!'

'You think *I* sleep, worrying about you all the time? I'd rather have you fighting than with all them bombs.'

'I know.'

She shook her head, still leaning against him. 'To you, I'm the one being selfish, I'm the one risking the lives of the children. You don't have to do this bomb work, Jack. Maybe you ought to think a bit more of your family now and then . . . The kids'll be back soon. I'll go and pack.'

They hugged again, tenderly. Then she moved to the door, but she got no further. Suddenly there was a deafening explosion and the whole house rocked. There was the sound of windows breaking, and broken plaster filled the air. Salt had a split second to register the roar of a plane low overhead, then everything went blank.

He came to a little later. At first he did not know where he was, what was going on. He was on a stretcher, blankets over him. He could see air raid Wardens and ambulance men; there seemed to be a great amount of dust everywhere and it made him cough. An ARP man, tin hat askew, heard him and came to kneel by him.

'All right, lad, you're all right. Take it easy.'

Salt looked around him wildly. 'Bet . . .'

'Your house, then, was it?'

'Where's Betty . . .?' He tried to sit up but the ARP man gently held him down.

'We'll soon have you comfortable. Just waiting for an ambulance. Don't move for a bit, lad.'

'What happened?'

'Sneak attack. No warning. One bomb a couple of streets away, one here. Can you tell me, was there anyone else in the house?'

'No, just the wife and me. Where is she . . .?

'Don't you worry. Just lie there – just a bit longer.' The ARP man walked off behind Salt and spoke quietly to some men digging in the ruins of the little house. 'All right, leave it. There was only the two of them.'

Coming away from the wreckage, the rescue team had to skirt round another stretcher, upon which lay the blanket-wrapped body of Betty Salt.

It was two weeks before Salt rejoined 347 Section, and even then one hand was still bandaged and a plaster was on his forehead. The next day he stood outside Major Luckhurst's office, an escort on either side of him; the Company Sergeant Major called, 'Prisoner, hat off – prisoner and escort, quick march, left, right, left, right!' in the machine-gun style used on such occasions. Salt, stiffly to attention, vaguely heard Major Luckhurst intoning the charge.

'. . . being absent without leave from . . . apprehended in Manchester . . . anything to say?'

Salt forced his attention to the desk before him. 'No, sir.'

'You can elect to appear before a higher authority, or you can accept my punishment. Which do you choose?'

'I'll accept your punishment, sir.'

The Major leaned back, touched the peak of his cap, clearly finding all this not to his taste. 'Mr Ash?'

A blur of Brian, something about Salt being an exemplary soldier, no previous record; Captain Francis, after the slightest pause, having nothing to add; then the Major addressed him.

'. . . blotted an otherwise unblemished copybook . . . reprehensible offence . . . considerable domestic pressure, and I know of your tragic bereavement . . . must act on the letter of the law and the gravity of the charge . . . reduced to rank of Sapper and lose one week's pay.'

Cap on, about turn, quick march, left, right, left, right . . .

As the door closed, Luckhurst took off his cap and threw it down on the desk. 'If I were that man I would feel hard done-by. He saves a girl's life, loses his wife and I punish him for trying to save his children.'

Captain Francis sniffed slightly. 'That's not quite true, sir. He went absent quite deliberately, when he was confined to barracks.'

'Unofficially confined to barracks,' the Major corrected him. 'What would you have done in my place?'

'No question. It was a court-martial offence. If I may quote the *Manual of Military Law . . .*'

'Please don't, Michael.' The Major was lighting his pipe, waving away the cloud of smoke. 'Things aren't quite what they were in peacetime, you know. This bomb disposal business is hard on everyone. There had to be discipline, I quite agree. But not the old sort, out of the book.'

Brian began to feel uncomfortable. 'If you don't need me, sir . . .'

Plainly he had been forgotten. 'Ah – no, Brian, that's all, thank you very much.'

When they were alone, Captain Francis pursued his point. 'Even though there is a war on, sir, I don't see how we can throw away the rule book. Salt set an appalling example as an NCO.'

'And would sending him to the glasshouses do anyone any good? The man's badly hurt enough as it is. Tolerance, old son, learn a bit of tolerance. Everyone should be perfect, I know, but no one is. These chaps didn't volunteer for bomb disposal but they're stuck with it and they're doing one hell of a good job. They're a special breed and they need careful handling. I hope, Michael, you will remember that when you're in this chair.'

Brian went quietly into the Section barrack room and, as he expected, found Salt alone, sitting on his bed. Salt got up, but Brian waved for him to sit down and sat on the next bed. The stripe was already off Salt's arm.

'Still on the sick list, I believe.'

'Yes, sir. Couple more days and I'll be OK.'

'Good. What about a week's leave after that . . . go up to your sister's place and see the kids.'

'No thank you, sir. Not just yet.'

'I was talking to Sergeant James, and we were wondering... would you like a transfer to another Company – even another branch of the Sappers?'

Salt raised a smile. 'Get shot of the troublemaker, sir?'

'Christ no. Nothing like that. As a matter of fact, you'll make a damned good Sergeant yourself one of these days. We just thought . . . a new start, you know . . .'

'Kind of you, sir, but no thanks. I'd rather . . . see it through

. . . do what I can to get back at the bloody Jerries.'

Brian stood up. 'Good man. Get yourself fit soon.'

As he turned to go, he noticed that Salt was fighting back the tears. He left him alone to his thoughts.

Chapter 8

The departure of Major Luckhurst developed into that rare army event, a display of affection. Much booze flowed in the Officers' Mess the night before he left; there was much abandoned singing of dubious songs, and many a thick head in the morning. But there was a certain sadness behind it all. The Major had commanded with understanding and indulgence, appreciating the risks his officers took every day of their lives and the tensions they lived with, and had earned their respect and devotion in return. Now they waited to see how Fanny Francis would govern, fearing the worst.

Their misgivings were soon confirmed. In no time at all there followed a regime of kit inspections, of charge sheets flying like confetti in the wake of petty offences, with extra duties for many officers for alleged slackness; of everything being done strictly by the book. All this, under the banner of 'tightening up the discipline', and coming on top of the workaday tensions and dangers, soon brought its own result. Discontent grew. There were mutterings in both Mess and barrack room, and morale collapsed. Fanny Francis soldiered on, apparently oblivious. For some reason he especially had it in for 347 Section and Brian Ash.

Just a fortnight after taking over, the new CO called a Section Officers meeting. Shortly before the appointed hour he called Ivor Rodgers, now a Captain and the 2-i/c, into his office, and indicated a pile of thick books.

'Make sure everyone gets a copy,' he said.

'Sir. They're assembling in the Mess now.'

Francis nodded and dismissed Ivor, who staggered, laden, out of the room. Presently there was a knock on the door and Hamish Leckie came in. Leckie disliked the room now. Under Luckhurst it had had an amiable feel about it, a sort of ordered disorder; it had been a human kind of room. Now everything had its place and was firmly in it; there were maps on the walls with coloured pins marching across them; obligatory returns demanded by Brigade were dealt with on the dot and not a minute later; all was austere and cold. What was more, Leckie was in it all too often, for Francis had appointed him Welfare Officer and had evidently come to regard him as something of a confidant. It was Francis' nearest approach to a friendship.

'Ah, Hamish. Finished in good time.' Leckie had been holding interviews under his Welfare hat.

'Not too much this morning, sir.' The old Scot, never at ease, couldn't decide whether to sit unbidden or remain at some cross between stood-at-ease and attention. 'Only two, as a matter o' fact. Mulley wanting to go on an engineering course, and Salt putting in for an advance on his pay.'

Francis, the Major's crown still bright and new on his shoulders, put his pen down and – for him – relaxed. 'Another quiet night last night. Good to get some undisturbed rest.'

'Aye. It must be ten days since we had a raid now. I wonder how long it will last.'

'Hull got it last night, I understand. At least it gives us a chance to make a start clearing up all the low-category bombs we've had to leave.'

'I just wonder how the BD lads in all these places are coping.'

'Pretty well, I imagine. After all, they've got our experience to draw on.'

Leckie liked that 'our'. Francis would run a mile if someone gave him a bomb to defuse; probably wouldn't know where to begin anyway. There was an awkward pause before Major Francis unfolded himself from behind the desk and began gently to pace up and down.

'Mulley and Salt, you said. Ash's section, aren't they?'

'Yes, sir.'

'Again.' He shook his head more in anger than sorrow. 'Slack leadership, that's all it is. With a firmer hand there wouldn't be all this trouble . . .' Leckie failed to see how welfare matters came under the heading of trouble, but let it pass. He had to admit that trouble there had been. The CO went on pacing, his voice taking on a slight edge. 'I blame Luckhurst. Far too free and easy.'

Leckie felt it incumbent upon himself to agree. 'Oh, yes.'

'Always on about it being "a family show", and all that. The trouble with families, Hamish, is that they have arguments. We're not having that in *my* company. Look at Ash – Luckhurst's blue-eyed boy. Could have been a very good officer, but he was spoiled.' He suddenly stopped and gazed pensively at his highly polished boots. 'He and Ivor Rodgers are as thick as thieves, you know.'

'You don't have to tell me.' Leckie seized the chance to raise a subject that had been bothering him. 'Can I ask, sir – why was Ivor made 2-i/c over me? I had seniority.'

'Brigade, Hamish – Brigade. Not my doing . . . Things can change, though.' Francis sat down behind the desk, fidgeting with neat sheaves of papers, rearranging files. 'Keep a weather eye open for me, will you? I'd be obliged. You know – things said in the Mess. Ivor's a little too matey for my liking. Yes. I'm going to shake a few things up, Hamish, make one or two examples – Ash being one. I get more trouble from his Section than any of the others.'

'People like Salt, you mean . . . the "drunk" charge he was on.'

'Exactly. A damned slack officer – should never have allowed things to get so much out of hand. Never.'

For a fleeting second Leckie considered pointing out that the restrictions imposed by Major Francis himself were at least part of the cause. He contented himself with, 'Salt came to me this morning for a sub. For his children. Bit of a sob story.'

Major Francis was not interested. He suddenly shot out, 'Ash has a got a woman, hasn't he?' He might have been accusing him of having smelly feet.

Leckie was taken by surprise. 'He's got a girl, aye. Most of 'em have.'

'I said a woman.'

'Well, a woman, then.'

'Know who she is?'

'No. He doesn't exactly confide in me. I think he's had the same girl most of the winter, though.'

'*Had.* You mean he sleeps with her.'

Leckie became cautious. 'I gather from what I've heard some of the others say he goes off and meets this wee girl at some hotel or other, so I presume . . .'

'Married?' Francis cut in.

'Who?'

'Is she married? This woman.'

'Aye – I think mebbe she is. I heard Ivor ribbing Brian about it one evening.' He was beginning to feel distinctly uncomfortable. 'Look – I'm not one to be telling the tales out of school.'

'I don't look favourably on that sort of thing, Hamish.'

'I don't really think it does much harm. Just a bit of fun. They're all under a strain.' Privately, he envied his juniors their 'bits of fun'. His wife Sally had died four years before in 1937. They had had no children, he still missed her more than he cared to admit, and at his age 'bits of fun' were hard to come by.

He noticed that Major Francis was clenching his hands furiously. 'It does harm. I happen to know. I – I have a similar problem myself. My wife . . . home in Devon . . . my wife and a serving officer . . . It's been going on for months. And I don't know what the hell to do about it. He's a – a Second Lieutenant.' There was an awkward silence. Leckie did not know where to look. Francis broke it. 'However – that's neither here nor there. I know you will respect a confidence, Hamish. I'm glad we've had this talk – it's confirmed one thing for me: we've got to get rid of Ash. He's a thoroughly bad influence, he's the cause of most of the trouble in this Company; quite apart from this – this *woman* – he's insubordinate, slack, pleased with himself. He's simply got to go.'

'That would be a bit difficult, sir. He's an experienced bomb disposer, and a successful one – and a bit young to be booted upwards.'

'Oh no, not promotion, not on any account. I wouldn't have that, not even to get rid of him. Why shouldn't I get him posted?'

'Where to?'

'Brigade? Another Company, perhaps.'

'You'd have to give your reasons, sir – and then it might look just a wee bit personal.'

'It's not for me. It's for the Company.' Francis drummed the fingers of his right hand for a few moments on the desk top, then reached down and pulled a large buff envelope from a side drawer. 'One thing I can do, however . . . and I'm going to do it now. Luckhurst left me a report he'd drafted about Ash for the Brigadier. He asked me to implement it. Well, I haven't. I've waited.' He had taken out the long, typewritten document and was scanning it. 'Mostly about that church bomb, the one where they tried out the steam extractor. Saying what a marvellous job Ash had done.'

'Well, he did, didn't he.'

'The plain truth, Hamish, is that his Sergeant did the whole thing. Ash made some excuse about scalding his hand. And because of his slackness – and, I might add, I strongly suspect his sheer funk – one of his men was killed, if you remember. There's a fulsome letter too from that old fool of a boffin . . . Gillespie, that's him. Would you believe, the whole thing recommends Ash for an MBE. *Ash*, mind you. Well – there's only one place for all that lot . . .'

Leckie could only stare as Major Francis tore the report into shreds and tossed it into the wastepaper basket. This was all something new in his military experience; it needed thinking about.

Francis stood up, put on his cap, and picked up a copy of the book that Rodgers had earlier been sent off to distribute. 'Now, Hamish – now we really begin to pull this Company together.'

The two men went through into the Mess; Ivor Rodgers brought the Section Officers to attention and reported all present. Francis stood for a second behind the table that had been prepared for him, smiled what was for him a warm smile. 'Very good, gentlemen – you may sit down.' He did likewise, cleared his throat and picked up the bulky volume he had brought with him. 'You all have one, I take it?' Murmurs of assent. 'The new *Manual of Bomb Disposal.* It's your bible, gentlemen. But before we come to that, a few words about your other new acquisitions. I refer to the new Austin Utility vehicles now at your individual disposal. Please remember that each of you has a driver. No officer will drive his Utility, and no civilian will be carried at any time. Mr Ash, I believe I saw you driving your Utility yesterday evening . . .?'

Brian felt himself colouring slightly under the schoolmaster look. 'Yes, sir.'

'Why? Was your driver not available?'

'No, sir . . . I mean . . . we . . . er, I mean usually it is we who drive . . .'

'We don't, Mr Ash. It is laid down that you don't, if you took the trouble to read the regulations; indeed, the reason that you are provided with a driver is that he shall drive you. Be kind enough to remember that, will you, Mr Ash?' He turned to the room in general. 'Another thing. Work tickets will be checked daily and handed in each night to the M/T Corporal. This Company, I need hardly remind you, has lost three officers and sixteen men in six months. Some of those deaths were caused by mock heroics. There will be no more individual heroics, gentlemen. Do I make myself clear? From now on *everything* will be done by the book. From now on you are academics.' He was glancing back and forth from Brian to the room. 'Discipline starts with the morning work parade

– not the shambles I sometimes see. And not with men going down the street to the Mess hall in braces. I hope I have already established the last point.' This was a reference to the fact that three of Brian's Section were on 'jankers' for just that crime, despite the fact that they had returned late off a job with no time to dress if they were to get anything to eat that evening.

Francis continued. 'I have already made a start on kit inspections, and from now on we will have smart work parades, too. Further, I personally shall be down at the garage every night to check your Utility vehicles, gentlemen – and I shall want to see them clean.' He paused. 'While on the subject of parades, I think we should start a Mess dinner once a month. We seem to have lost the regimental feeling – if indeed we ever had it. I suggest a start this Thursday.'

The glum faces in front of him worried him not at all. On the contrary, they only confirmed that he had been right, this Company did need pulling together. 'Now,' he droned on, 'let's look at the *Manual* in detail . . .'

It went on for three solid hours. Afterwards, over tea and sandwiches, Brian moaned, 'What I want to know is, what have I done to deserve special attention?'

'Didn't you know – you're the mock hero he was on about,' grinned Alan Pringle. Brian looked puzzled.

'Rule One: BD officers will not, repeat not, play football with 50-kilo bombs.'

'Oh, that.' Brian fell in.

'Don't worry,' Alan cheerfully reassured him. 'He descended on my work parade yesterday like a demented dervish. Flattened everybody.'

Gresham, a recently joined Second Lieutenant of gloomy look and habit, chipped in. 'He stuck my driver on a fizzer last night because he had a dirty mudguard.'

A voice in the background murmured, 'Come home, Luckhurst, all is forgiven!'

Alan Pringle stirred his tea thoughtfully. 'He's windy, of course. And if he's picking on you, Brian, it fits.'

'How?'

'He's jealous of you. All this bull about theory. He's never been up against a bomb perched on a burning wall. He's never been up to his waist in freezing water at the bottom of a shaft. So this is what he does. He's jealous – and bitter.'

'You mean he'd rather be out defusing bombs?' Brian was puzzled.

'Good God no,' Alan said. 'I think the truth is he's windy as a coot. Simple as that. What's more – he knows we know he's windy.' Food for thought.

Two days later 347 Section was given food for thought, too. They had been due for a kit inspection, which pressure of work seemed sufficient to excuse. Not to Major Francis, however; Francis merely postponed it to nine o'clock the same evening. As if that was not bad enough, the inspection itself was a disaster. Four men had their names taken, which meant charges. It was as if Francis really expected them to do a mucky job, digging in wet soil, scrabbling about with tackle and bombs, and emerge spotless. Afterwards he told Brian curtly: 'Frankly, this Section needs shaking up. They'll do two extra parades under the CSM, and be confined to barracks next weekend.'

The news, relayed in the barrack room by Sergeant James, was not well received. 'This isn't war – it's bloody prison,' exploded Powell after the Sergeant had left them.

Wilkins snarled, 'Bloody Francis . . . he needs sorting out, that bastard,' and he meant every syllable of it. 'Booked me for a dirty pack – look, Salty – can you see any muck there?'

Salt examined it, and shook his head. 'I tell you one thing – we're being buggered about.'

'Something else too,' moaned Baines. 'I reckon Ash is in on it, an' all. You can't tell me he couldn't stop all this lark. All it needs is for him to go Francis and tell him: *look mate, knock it off, the lads are working too bloody hard for all this caper*. That's what he needs to tell him.'

There was general assent. Mulley said, 'So what can we do about it?'

'Sweet f.a., that's what,' growled Salt.

'Refuse to work?' suggested Powell.

'Refuse what you like,' Salt growled. 'But count me out – I'm in too much clack as it is.'

'Maybe if we went to Ash . . .? Mulley suggested.

'Wastin' your breath, mate,' Wilkins growled. 'I thought he was all right, but he's an arse-crawler, that's all he is.'

Brian, meanwhile, was in the Section office catching up on paperwork and feeling less than happy with life. He heard a truck draw up outside, and Alan Pringle walked in.

'Hello, Brian. How did it go?'

'Bloody awful. He tore the Section to shreds – but that was the object of the exercise, I suppose. We only got back after tea. Honest, Alan, I'd like to blow that bastard Fanny to smithereens.'

'There's no justice, though. I reckon, if the entire German air force dropped their whole stockload of bombs in this square mile, Fanny would be the sole survivor.'

'He'd make bloody sure he was, don't worry.'

'Never mind, chum – here's a nice friendly Category-B to keep you happy tomorrow. Meanwhile, why don't you chuck all that bumph out of the window and come and have a drink.' Brian needed no second invitation.

The bomb was not as straightforward as it might have been. A 50-kilo, it had skidded along solid concrete and come to rest with the fuse pocket very nearly detached and clearly visible through the split in the casing. Brian took one look and called up the Divisional Officer, Bomb Disposal. Captain West came promptly, shivering in the damp cold from the reservoir.

'That's about the loosest fuse pocket I ever saw,' he remarked, crouching low over it. 'There can't be more than a quarter of an inch holding it. And you aim to yank it free, do you?'

'I thought, if we tied some cord to it and gave it a good pull

. . . I know the book says we should use the liquid discharger, but with it being so loose . . .'

'Yes, there's not much to cling on to, as the actress said. It's not boobytrapped, that's one good thing.' The short, stocky Captain West stood up, looked again at the bleak expanse of water and the surroundings, and shivered again. 'You've had a recce around this God-forsaken spot, of course?'

Brian nodded, huddling too into his greatcoat. 'I had a Water Authority bloke along with me. There's no buildings, and no people about, so he's quite happy.'

'What about the concrete?'

'It would only do superficial damage.'

Captain West thought for a brief few seconds. 'OK, fair enough.'

Horrocks, Salt and Powell built a sandbag wall around the bomb, and were sent back to the safety point. Then Captain West expertly made a loop in some fisherman's line and very, very gently slipped it over the fuse in the bomb. He carefully tightened it, and then with Brian walked back to the safety point paying out the yarn behind them.

There, he gently pulled on the line, taking up the slack. When he felt it become taught, he looked round. 'Who's the strong man? Want a go?'

He had spoken to Powell, who gulped and retorted, 'Any extra pay, sir?'

Everyone grinned, including Captain West, and Brian said, 'No, but you can tell your grandchildren you defused a bomb singlehanded.'

Powell took over the line. Captain West said quietly to Brian, 'It's your bomb. Over to you.'

'Thanks. Just remember one thing, Powell – duck down as you pull.'

Powell nodded, and gazed at the line in his hand with immense concentration. Then he took a breath, jerked hard and dived. Silence.

Brian and the Divisional Officer left the safety point and found the fuse pocket lying a few yards from the bomb. Brian gingerly picked it up, unscrewed the gaine and threw it into the water.

Half an hour later Brian and Sergeant James were overseeing the loading of the bomb into the lorry, along with all the gear, when Major Francis's Utility drew up a little distance ahead. Brian threw a despairing look at the Sergeant, then walked briskly up to meet the OC and salute him. 'Sir.'

Francis said nothing, but looked carefully at Brian as he returned the salute, as if inspecting him. Then he walked past him to the lorry. Everyone stopped work.

'We detached the fuse, sir,' Brian said. 'Now we're taking the bomb off to the cemetery.' Francis looked sharply at him, turned on his heel, marched back to his wagon and rummaged inside. He returned leafing through the bomb disposal manual.

'You detached the fuse? How exactly did you detach the fuse?'

'Well, sir, as you see the casing had split open and the fuse pocket was too loose, so we tied a cord to it and pulled it.'

'You . . . *pulled it.*'

'Yes, sir.' Brian could feel his hackles rising, conscious that the men were all within earshot. Major Francis now realized that, too.

'A word, Mr Ash.' He led the way for a few paces, then turned to face Brian, his eyes blazing. 'Are you deliberately trying to be stupid? It clearly says here . . . Why do you think these things are written? Read it. Aloud.' He thrust the manual into Brian's hand. For a moment Brian considered refusing, aware of his men watching intently.

Instead, he lowered his head and quietly read the words: '*When bombs are broken up on impact every effort must be made not to remove loose fuses when—*'

'There you are,' Francis cut in.

Brian calmly read on. '*—when attempting to identify them.*' Suddenly he felt he had the situation under control. 'I was not trying to identify it, sir. It was clearly marked – a fifty-kilo with a type-fifteen direct short-delay impact fuse.'

'You moved a loose fuse.'

'If I'd used the liquid discharger the risk might have been greater.'

'That's your opinion. The book clearly states—'

'There was no risk to us,' Brian interrupted, tight lipped. 'Nor to the reservoir.'

'That is not the point. You have deliberately broken the regulations again, Ash. You should know – if you are in any doubt you must consult a senior officer, the DOBD.'

Brian looked steadily at his CO and said quietly, 'He was here. He gave me permission to do it my way.'

Major Francis glared at Brian with something very close to hatred. His breathing became heavy. Then he snatched the manual. 'You think you're very clever, don't you? Always got the answer, haven't you?'

He marched back to his Utility, the driver put in the gear and drove off rapidly. The watching Section exchanged grins.

'Right – get moving, you lot,' bellowed Sergeant James, and they went to work, happy in the knowledge that Brian Ash was on their side after all.

Later that afternoon Gordon Mulley reported the confrontation with all his dour Scottish glee to Norma Baker. 'Aye, it was grand to see. We misjudged Mr Ash, no doubt about it.'

Norma was preparing herself a beans-on-toast tea. 'Well I must say it's nice to see you more cheerful, Gordon. Come to that, it's nice to see you.'

He smiled. 'You don't know what it's been like, lass. All the bull, an' the extra duties an' that, not to mention the work. We're all of us just about flat. Much more of it and I'll be glad to be out of it for good.'

She looked up sharply from the cooker. 'Get away? You're not leaving, are you?'

'Didn't I tell you? I've put in for an engineering course.'

'Oh.' The disappointment was clear in her voice.

He grinned. 'Knowing my luck, nothing'll come of it. But if I do go, it won't mak' any difference, will it? To us, I mean.'

She turned to him and smiled. 'I hope not, love.'

The front door opened and closed, and Mrs Baker came bustling into the kitchen. 'Ah, you're getting your own tea, are you, Norma? Good. That Mrs Jordan does go on so – I couldn't get away. Her Geoff's been made a Petty Officer, just fancy. Hello, Gordon – haven't seen you for a bit, have we?'

'Working hard, Mrs Baker.'

'You're safe and sound, that's a lot to be thankful for. Is Dad in yet, Norma?'

'Not yet.'

'Funny – I wonder what kept him. I'll just go and pop the heater on in the shelter, then I'll see about his meal.'

She hurried out into the garden. Gordon said, 'Don't tell me they still sleep down there? We haven't had a raid for some time?'

'Force of habit. I think they'll quite miss it when the war's over.'

He moved to her side, sliding an arm round her waist. 'How about you? Still sleeping in the house?'

'What did you have in mind?'

'No prizes offered.'

'You don't have to be back early, do you? They go down about nine – in time to hear the news on the wireless.'

'I'll be here.'

They kissed, breaking apart as her mother's footsteps came up the garden path. Norma said, 'Meanwhile, have a cup of tea.'

In Bromley Brian drove his MG to the Gladstone Hotel and ran up to the usual room. Susan had phoned him two nights before, suggesting Thursday for them to meet. He had no chance to tell her of the Mess dinner complication. She was reading, and after a long kiss he flung himself on the familiar bed.

'Sorry I've been so elusive lately – but what with work, and all the bother with Fanny Francis, life's rather painful at the moment.'

'The dinner you mentioned – is that part of it?'

'Yes.' He yawned, rubbed his tired eyes. 'We all have to dress up, best bib and tucker. You'd never know there was a war on.'

'What time do you have to be back?'

'Oh, about seven. Lots of time.'

She moved to the dressing table, taking off her earings, and began to unbutton her blouse.

'I wish . . .'

His sleepy voice came from the bed. 'What do you wish?'

'I wish we could see each other all the time.'

'How can we?'

'If it wasn't all so . . . so sneaky.'

She was nearly undressed now. 'Supposing we faced up to it, Brian; supposing we were absolutely honest and told everyone. Not all at once, perhaps . . . but I love you; no one else. I don't care what happens, as far as I'm concerned.'

She turned, naked now, towards the bed. Brian was asleep. Her surge of disappointment gave way to a wave of pity. Very gently she lay down beside him, content to hold his unresponsive hand and listen to his deep, regular breathing.

Retribution came the following morning when Brian was called into the CO's office immediately after breakfast. He stood before the desk feeling like a fourth-former. 'I'm very sorry about last night, sir . . .'

'We looked everywhere, even sent round to your billet.'

'I went up to town to see a friend, and . . . well, I'm afraid I fell asleep.'

Major Francis put on his most piercing look. 'This friend – was it the woman you're seeing?' He stared at Brian's astonished face. 'You don't think I have the right to ask that question? You didn't think I *knew*?'

'I . . .'

'I have a perfect right to ask since it's quite plain your work is suffering as a result of this . . . this friendship. You only have to look at your Section. And you, Ash – you're not quite a model of discipline, are you?'

Brian began to grow angry. 'Sir, I told you, I was exhausted. I just—'

'Let me tell you, Ash,' Francis cut in, 'that last night was a parade like any other. Mess dinners are as compulsory for officers as drill parades for the men. And if an immoral liaison is causing you to fall down, then I have the right to tell you so.'

'*Immoral?*'

'Yes, immoral. A married woman, isn't it? And what about her husband, a serving officer. How is it going to affect his work?'

'Who said he was a serving officer?' Brian retorted angrily.

Major Francis was triumphant. 'Then you admit it.'

'No I don't.'

'You won't take the responsibility for anything, will you, not even for that,' Francis snarled at him. 'That is typical of you, Ash, just typical.'

'I've apologized for my absence from dinner last night. May I go now, sir?'

'Yes, you can go. And you can do a week's extra orderly officer, starting from tomorrow.'

The CO's hands were shaking as they rested on the desk. Brian saluted and marched out. After lunch the talk in the Mess was about nothing else.

'Mind you,' Carter-Brown told Brian, 'you didn't miss much.' Carter-Brown was a new officer, slim and earnest. 'One of the most macabre evenings I've ever spent. Come the cheese and biscuits, and I was pinching myself to remind me there was a war on.'

Gresham chimed in: 'The King's health was bad enough – nothing disloyal, you understand, but you know what I mean – but the "Gentlemen, you may smoke" bit . . . well I mean, Jesus Christ . . . Oh, and did you know – 347 Section's on CB now, for a dirty wagon.'

'And did you know something else,' added Carter-Brown in conspiratorial tones. 'He's got Part Two Orders out saying there's to be a morning work parade even if you've been out on an all-nighter. He's off his chump.'

'That's nothing,' Alan Pringle moaned. 'Ivor's just told me that if we want to speak to Francis we have to book an appointment. Isn't that right, Ivor?'

The new 2-i/c joined them. 'Afraid so. But don't worry – I'll pencil you in if I possibly can. No – seriously – it's all getting beyond a joke. I'm going up to see a mate of mine in Group ... have a go at getting him moved.'

Hamish Leckie had been observing the scene from up at the bar, watching the heads bent close around the table, noting the earnest and whispered talk. For some time now, since Francis had more or less adopted him, he had increasingly felt an outsider in the Mess. There was a limit to that sort of loyalty, however. He, too, had had enough.

He picked up his Scotch and went over to the table. The talk died down as he approached. He cleared his throat, conscious of a measure of animosity. 'Fairly obvious what – or rather, who – you're talking about, but may I join you? I have something that could be of interest.' He pulled a chair into the gap they shuffled for him, and looked at their expectant faces. 'I know you all think I've been sucking up to Francis, but believe me I've been as troubled as you. I've been in a very difficult position, don't you see. As a matter of fact, it is my opinion that if he hadn't had me to talk to, he would have gone round the twist long ago. But that's beside the point. The thing is, I think I know what's up with him.' Everyone looked at him with renewed interest; old Hamish played to them, like an old actor timing his lines. 'You see – his wife back home, she's being serviced by another man. What makes it worse is, he's an officer. Worse still, he's only a Second Lieutenant.'

'Good Lord,' breathed Ivor.

Brian was frowning. 'So that's it ...'

'Yes, Brian,' said Hamish, 'that's it. What we do about it, of course – short of mutiny – is another question. But that is, as you say, it.'

December dragged on, and Major Francis ruled remorselessly. The London nights were peaceful, with one exception. One night close to Christmas the Luftwaffe made a determined effort to set fire to the entire City square mile and very nearly succeeded. For something like four hours incendiary bombs poured down. High explosive ruptured nearly all the water mains; and with the Thames a mere trickle at its lowest ebb for years, and the fire services stretched to breaking, they had the place at their mercy. Then, just after 11 p.m. and as suddenly as they had come, they stopped. By that time a host of offices and business premises, some of Wren's finest churches, and much else besides were gone. St Paul's itself was lapped by the flames on all sides to make a picture that for the rest of the war was a symbol of defiance, the great dome outlined intact against the fires. Newspaper headlines could be read in the glare eight and more miles away in the suburbs, and the ruins were still being dampened down by exhausted firemen four days later.

Once again the bomb disposal units were working flat out, and it was not until just after the New Year that Brian was able to meet Susan again at the Gladstone Hotel. By then Francis had driven him near to breaking point.

He sat, head in his hands, pouring it all out to her. 'He's jealous – frantically jealous. He's even jealous of us.'

'How does he know about us?'

'Well, not you – he doesn't know who you are. But you know what a Mess is when it comes to gossip – a regular snake pit. It doesn't matter, really, I suppose.'

'I'm sorry, darling. I think it does matter.'

Brian could only shake his head with a gesture of despair. 'The man's quite bonkers, he really is.'

She was sitting at his feet, her hands clasped on his knee. 'Surely you can do something, send in a secret report or something.'

He shook his head. 'Any getting rid of has to come from above. Ivor checked.'

'So why doesn't the next man up do it?'

'That's the Brigadier – and he's got other things on his plate.' He let out a long sigh. 'I'd ask for a posting if I thought it would help.'

'You mustn't do that, Brian. It would be giving in to him.'

'All I know is, it can't go on. Not for much longer. The

latest thing – it'd be almost funny if it wasn't so bloody pathetic. Hamish Leckie told me, a couple of days back. Luckhurst left a report about the church bomb – the one you came to, remember? – and a letter from your father. It was a recommendation for my MBE, really. And know what? Francis tore it all up. I mean, what do you do with a man like that?'

'So bang goes your medal.'

'That doesn't worry me. It's the—'

He stopped. He had never seen her so angry.

She said: 'Leave it to me, darling. I think I've got an idea.'

She was as good as her word. Next morning she was in the sitting room at home typing a report for her father. The door opened and Dr Gillespie hurried in with some notes.

'Darling,' he announced, 'some notes on the new bomb locator – rather important if you'd be awfully kind and type them up. We've got a meeting of the Unexploded Bomb Committee tomorrow and I want to give them a nasty shock.'

'You mean it doesn't work.'

'Shall we say, it might come in useful if you were in the scrap metal business. Any trouble with my writing, just shout.'

'As I usually do,' she smiled.

He grinned back and moved to put a log on the fire.

Susan swallowed. 'Father . . .'

'Mmmm?'

'I wondered if you knew . . . I mean . . . did you know, I've been seeing quite a bit of Brian Ash.'

Dr Gillespie suddenly stood up from the fire and turned to look at her. He picked his words with some care. 'Yes – I had realized. You'd have to be blind and deaf to live in this house and not know.'

'Oh. I'd hoped we'd been rather, well, discreet.'

'All those telephone calls? All those sudden visits to – I presume – imaginary girlfriends?' He was smiling again. 'Quite apart from the fact that you're different.'

'I'm happy, that's why. But anyway, the thing is—'

Her father interrupted gently: 'Seeing that you've brought the matter up . . . it's your life, Susie, and I try not to interfere with it. I know it's tough for you, with Stephen cooped up at Bletchley, and everyone has to, well, to let off steam from time to time . . . but don't make a fool of yourself, sweetie. These things can get terribly messy.'

'That wasn't actually what I wanted to talk about.'

Dr Gillespie laughed, throwing his head back. 'Oh dear – that's put me in my place, hasn't it.'

'The thing is, Brian's got a new Commanding Officer who's absolutely bloody – the whole Company's on the verge of mutiny. I'm not exaggerating. And he's especially bloody to Brian.'

'Oh dear. But what's this got to do with me?'

'It so happens that Brian's Brigadier is on your committee . . .' She said it with the most winning smile she could muster.

'My dear child – I can't start interfering with the army. It's simply nothing to do with me, not to say it would be completely unethical.'

'Funnily enough, father, it is something to do with you.'

'Oh?'

'You wrote a letter about Brian – a very nice one – after the steam extractor business in the church and your broken leg. And Major Luckhurst drafted a report.'

'Yes, I do remember that. He was very keen that Brian should get some sort of recognition. Rightly so.'

'Major Francis, the new CO, has destroyed both the letter and the report.'

'Has he just? That's naughty. Very naughty. But honestly, darling, I don't think I can remember all the details . . . so much happens so fast, these days.'

'Oh, don't worry – Luckhurst sent us a copy of his report and I kept a carbon of your letter.' Gravely, she produced the manilla file.

'Well now, great heavens, there's a thing, isn't it?' He was smiling broadly as he took the file, opened it and began to read.

*

The power of Brigadiers verges on the awesome; and after a private conference with Dr Gillespie before the next day's meeting, this one demonstrated the fact in full measure. Just one week later the news of Major Francis's posting came through; he was to report immediately to a General Construction Company in Scotland.

It was a bewildered Francis who broke the news to Hamish Leckie. Seated dejectedly at his desk, his hands twisting together, he could only repeat, 'What did I do, Hamish? Where did I go wrong? All I did was to try to save men's lives . . . what did I do?' Hamish could not find it in him to explain.

There was no party on the eve of Francis's departure. The Mess was very much business-as-usual, with the one notable absentee. No one saw Major Francis until the next morning when, looking neither to right nor left, he walked stiff-backed to his vehicle and was driven away from Company HQ and out of their lives.

It was later that afternoon that Ivor Rodgers, Acting CO, met Brian as he came in with some completed paperwork. 'Here,' he said, 'I've just had the most embarrassing phone call from the Brigadier. I've been told to draft a citation for gallantry – for an immoral, slack little brute name of Brian Ash.' The mask slipped, and he grinned as he shook Brian's hand. 'Well done, chum – always knew you'd make good. Eventually.'

The Investiture was at the beginning of April. Susan went to Buckingham Palace with him, Aunt Do-Do made one of her rare forays from deepest Surrey. Afterwards he took them both to tea at Fortnum and Mason's. As they were putting Aunt Do-Do into a cab for Waterloo she whispered to him, 'Super girl, Brian. Marry her, if you can – and count on me for any help.' She was still waving as the cab turned down St James's.

It was a warm afternoon of soft spring sunshine. Susan linked her arm in his, 'Well, Brian Ash, MBE, shall we walk in the park?'

They went down St James's, Brian rather self-consciously returning the salute of the sentries outside the Tudor Palace at the bottom, and crossed the Mall into the quiet park with its fresh green leaves and illusion of peace. Susan sighed. 'Sometimes I think, the sooner we lose this bloody war the better.'

'Come off it – who said we're going to lose it?'

'Whatever happens, I wish it were all over. Eighteen months, and it seems like eighteen years. I'm beginning to feel like an old, old woman.'

'You don't look like one. Anyway – I love you.'

They sat down on a bench, facing the regal and unblinking façade of Buckingham Palace through the trees. Susan sighed a second time. 'Oh Brian, darling, I just wish we could stop running.'

'What do you mean, running?'

'We *are* running, all the time. The hotel in Bromley, all those dreary little tea shops and suburban pubs . . . everywhere, meeting in secret. They're bolt-holes. What was once so marvellous has all become sort of sneaky hole-in-the-corner. Oh, I don't know.'

This was frightening him. 'I thought that was how you wanted it.'

'I suppose it was . . . but not now.'

'What do you want to do, then? Drop it all?' He spoke very quietly, terrified of her answer.

'No – *no*.'

He smiled with relief, and they sat in silence for a while. Then, quite suddenly, he said, 'I could ask you to marry me.'

'Could you?'

'I could, but I haven't.'

'Because you don't really love me enough.'

'Oh, darling, don't be daft. I love you plenty enough – I think about you every moment of the day and night. But how the hell can I ask any girl to marry me? I've no money and no prospects – not even sure of living very long.'

'That's just silly.'

'The thing is – I would very much like to marry you.'

She gave a little squeal. 'Oh darling – you are accepted as

soon as asked.' There and then, in broad daylight and in front of passersby, she kissed him. 'When?'

He laughed. 'There are a few things to sort out, first.'

'Yes, that's true. But I'm not a bit scared about getting divorced, you know.'

'Apart from that. There's your father, for one.'

'I'll tell him this evening. Oh darling, I'm so very, very happy.'

'Me, too.' This time it was he who kissed her.

That night at home, Dr Gillespie was full of a new job he had been given, his own staff and laboratory in Cambridge. He enthused about it, full of plans for closing the house up, plans for this and that. Susan listened less than enthusiastically, and finally screwed her courage up to tell him. 'Father,' she said in a fleeting pause in his talk, 'Brian asked me to marry him today.'

He gaped at her. 'And – what did you say?'

'I said I'd like to marry him, if and when I could. Could I have a drink, do you think, please?'

'I'll join you.' In silence he poured two brandies, handed her glass over, then said heavily, 'I had rather thought . . .'

'It was all over? Or did you mean *hoping* it was all over?'

'That's a bit unfair. But you haven't seemed all that happy the last few months.'

'No. What you've never realized and what it's awfully hard to explain to you, father, is that my marriage to Stephen has been a disaster from start to finish. That's the truth.'

'I knew it wasn't going terribly well, but . . .'

'Oh, we've always put on a pretty good act, even in front of you, the good old British stiff-upper-lip stuff.'

He put his glass down, leaned towards her from his chair opposite hers, took her hand in his. 'Susan, believe me, I've got nothing against Brian, absolutely nothing. But it's you I'm worrying about, darling. You're the most valuable and important thing I've got on this earth. All I want is for you to be happy . . . I thought – I think – that you and Stephen never really had a chance. The second you get married the war comes, he's rushed off to a hush-hush job . . .'

She was oddly moved, and could only say, quietly, 'Is it really as hush-hush as all that? Isn't all that stuff just an excuse?'

'No. I can't possibly tell you what it is, nor can anyone. Only that it's one of the toughest and hardest and most important jobs in the war. But the war won't go on forever, Susan. You'll both be different people afterwards. Give it a chance. Quite apart from what it will do to Stephen, if you rush off and marry Brian, how do you know it will work?'

She took a sip of brandy, looked him straight in the eye. 'To be crude, father, I know damn well it does work.'

'What about after the war? His prospects of survival aren't that good . . . you'd be left a widow, possibly with a child.'

Susan smiled. 'Oh come on, father. You should be writing romantic novels – have 'em all in tears. Anyway – you don't approve.'

'You asked me what I thought. And, after all, you are over twenty-one.'

'Yes, I am, aren't I?' She stood up. 'Let's eat, shall we?' They went in to dinner.

It was the next evening, after a long phone call to Brian, that she counted three, touched wood, and dialled the Bletchley number. Her father was out and she was glad of it; telling your husband that you no longer love him, that you want your freedom to marry another man, is never easy – and still less so with other ears to hear it. But the Bletchley switchboard could not find Stephen. And, on the point of leaving a message with the Duty Officer for Stephen to ring her, she was cut off.

Whilst she was jiggling the receiver Dr Gillespie came in.

'Ah – there you are. Been in long?'

'Half an hour. I've been trying to get Stephen. God, they're inefficient in that place. First they can't find him, then they have trouble tracing the Duty Officer. And then everything went dead.'

'It is nine o'clock. Our local exchange closes down then, remember?'

'Oh, bloody hell . . .' Her impatience was born of stress more than anything.

'I've just been down to the Newtons, talking about the move to Cambridge. There – there was a message for you whilst you were out.'

She looked up quickly, and he saw with a touch of sadness the sudden excitement in her eyes. He shook his head. 'No – from Stephen's boss. He wants you to go over and see him tomorrow at Bletchley.'

She frowned. 'This isn't some kind of plot, is it?'

'Not on my part.'

'Don't see why I should go.'

'They're sending a car specially. I think you should.'

The car was at the house early the next morning. It was a warm day but with a fine, misty rain which did not improve the long journey. Eventually, close to noon, the car turned off a narrow country lane and entered a long drive with broad parkland stretching on either side. They drove for nearly two miles before the mansion came into view. Her own house was grand enough, but nothing compared with this. She recognized it from Stephen's description. They pulled up at the overwhelming front entrance, where an armed sentry checked her papers, ticked her name off a list and called for a Private to take her to the office of someone whose name she did not catch.

It was an utterly characterless room, furnished as spartanly as only the services could furnish a room. She sat for what seemed half a lifetime on a hard chair until at last a middle-aged Flight Lieutenant hurried in, his Air Force blue uniform rumpled and rather faded. His effusion was natural and not nervous.

'Mrs Mount?'

His hand shot out and as she took it she noticed how red the skin was, red as a beer drinker's face.

'I'm puzzled as to why—' she began, but got no farther as he butted in.

'My name's Fenwick. I'm chief security officer in this madhouse. I know your husband Stephen well . . . plays a marvellous game of bridge. I'm an absolute duffer, I confess. Do you smoke?'

'Thank you.'

He offered his packet of cork tips, swiftly followed by a box of matches. As she drew on the cigarette, he said, 'You have a spotless record, Mrs Mount.'

His own cigarette was alight now and he moved back behind the desk. The desk was quite bare, and she realized this was some sort of spare office.

'After all,' he said, his eyes boring into her, 'you are Stephen Mount's wife and Dr Gillespie's daughter. A rather important person, dear lady.'

'Is Stephen all right?'

'Oh yes.' It was casual, almost offhand, as the fingers of his right hand smoothed the desk top. Then, 'Have you any idea what his job is here?'

She chose her words carefully. 'Not really. He's not allowed to tell anyone, is he? Something to do with ciphers, isn't it?'

'Quite right,' he said, delighted. 'Couldn't have put it better myself. I'm afraid he's not awfully well.'

The sudden switch to the last statement took her by surprise. 'What's the matter?'

'Put simply, he's had a fairly nasty breakdown. A nervous breakdown, you understand.'

'Can I see him?'

He began to talk very rapidly so that she had no chance to put questions. All the time his cigarette was twisting in his fingers. 'Of course. He's in Oxford. Under fairly heavy sedation. There's a marvellous chap at the hospital – best man in the business for this sort of thing, they say. In confidence, I want to tell you this, Mrs Mount – this "something to do with cipher" business is hellish hard work, and just now there are developments coming up in the war that I'm sure you'll appreciate I can't mention, but which make the pressures worse. The boys here really are having a tough time, too much for several of them, including Stephen. Overwork, that's all it is. He's doing a vital job, Mrs Mount, a marvellous job – quite priceless to the war effort. You understand.'

'Yes.'

'That's why we need your help so badly.'

'My . . . help?'

'As I say, he is a sick man just now, very sick, but he'll be over the worst in a week or so. Then, we want you to take him away, down to Exmoor. I've booked you into a little hotel miles from nowhere – we'll be keeping an eye on you both but you won't realize it. Look after him, Mrs Mount . . . cherish him . . . good food . . . rest . . . lots of exercise . . . sort of honeymoon. Got the idea?'

In a few moments Susan's world had crashed about her. As Fenwick was speaking, pictures flashed across her mind. *Brian coming from the church crypt, his hand so badly scalded, on that day she first felt really attracted to him. The room at the Gladstone in Bromley the first time they made love. Brian turning up so distraught the next day at home, Stephen there, his glass being almost crushed in his tense hands. Brian at Buckingham Palace with the insignia of his MBE, his proposal in St James's Park later.*

'For . . . for how long?' she asked.

'Six weeks – two months – as long as it takes. Then bring him back to us good as new.'

'I see.'

'Just enjoy yourselves,' Fenwick added cheerfully. 'All on the house, won't cost you a penny. That's how much we value him, you see. Now – I've got a car waiting – shall we nip over to Oxford and give the old boy a nice surprise?'

Still stunned, she walked through the door held open by Fenwick with an old-world courtesy. He took her set face, her silence, for shock at the news of her husband's condition, and wished he had been more the type to break these things more gently. She did not say a word in the car, but sat watching with unseeing eyes the damp countryside, and then the streets of Oxford.

The sight of Stephen did shock her. He lay in a private room and hardly recognized her. His face had fallen in; there were black rings around his eyes. Yet drugged though he was, his eyes lit up at sight of her, and his hand moved weakly to hold hers. There were tears in her own eyes at that moment. She felt no overwhelming love, but a tremendous pity. The tears were for herself, and for Brian; for she knew she did not have the heart to abandon Stephen now. And she was realist enough to know what that meant.

Away from him, in the car being driven back to Kent, she was still not certain. By the time the army driver left her unlocking the front door, she still had not decided. All she knew was that she had to write to Brian, and she went straight up to her room, sat down with the notepaper on the dressing table before her. She wrote without thinking, relying on instinct to guide her.

A day later in the billet of 347 Section, Brian was gazing out of the office window. Sergeant James came briskly in.

'Section ready for your inspection, sir.' He saluted, and as Brian turned gave him a hard look.

'Thank you, Sergeant.'

He picked up his cap, settled it. He had had a letter in the morning post, with a Kent postmark. As they walked to the barrack room, then went through the motions of kit inspection, Susan's voice filled his mind as if she was reading it to him. '*. . . Darling, I love you and I always shall . . . Oh my darling, I wish I didn't have to hurt you so badly . . . it's the very last thing I would ever want to do . . .*'

Corporal Horrocks, Mulley, Salt, Baines, Powell, Wilkins and the rest, coming to attention as he reached their beds, reported their name and number, the state of their kit. '*Some terrible hand of fate is against us. For your sake I wish we had never met . . . the fun and the happiness we have had together is the best thing I shall ever know in my life. Thank you for them, darling. . .*'

The end of the line of beds. 'Carry on, Sergeant.' Salutes exchanged. '*Please don't try to find me or see me or write to me or telephone. Please. This war is so awful and so mean to play these tricks. I know I am right. I wish, I wish, it was otherwise. Oh, God, isn't this war so* mean *to play these tricks.*'

Back into the Section office, footsteps following, Sergeant James's voice: 'We've got that Category-C in Eltham to deal with, sir.'

'Yes. Get the men into the trucks. I'll be out in a minute.'

'Sir.' Alone again, orders barked about the house, boots clumping. And Susan's voice: '*God keep you and look after you and may He help you to forget me. Goodbye. Susie.*'

He covered his face with his hands. The action caused his forearm to press against his breast pocket and he heard and felt the letter crumple within. The war was indeed a bastard. How the hell was he going to face whatever life was left to him, after this? How the hell could he defuse the bomb waiting for him? '*Goodbye. Susie.*'

He took three deep breaths and walked outside to his waiting Section. 'OK, Sergeant – let's get going.'